PARENT AND CHILD IN FICTION

PARENT AND CHILD IN FICTION

Edited by

Robert D. Strom

ARIZONA STATE UNIVERSITY

BROOKS/COLE PUBLISHING COMPANY
MONTEREY, CALIFORNIA
A Division of Wadsworth Publishing Company, Inc.

Printed in the United States of America

10   9   8   7   6   5   4   3   2   1

Library of Congress Cataloging in Publication Data

Main entry under title:
Parent and child in fiction.

   CONTENTS: Peers and belonging: Saroyan, W. The first day of school. Suckow, R. The big kids and the little kids. Suckow, R. The valentine box. Crane, S. Showin' off.—Play and creative behavior: Baldwin, F. The gossamer world. Munro, H. H. The toys of peace. Bradbury, R. The Veldt. Lavin, M. The sand castle. [etc.]
   1. Parent and child—Fiction.   2. Short stories, American.   3. Short stories, English.   I. Strom, Robert D.
PZ1.P212 [PS648.P33]   823'.01   77-24920
ISBN 0-8185-0246-0

Production Editor: *John Bergez*
Interior Design: *Jamie S. Brooks*
Cover Design: *Katherine Minerva*

To Shirley,
Our Parents, Our Grandparents,
and Our Children

PREFACE

One way to get in touch with the problems of families is through fiction. By using stories, we can trigger the sharing of related events and circumstances that have actually happened to us. The tales presented here have been chosen for their value as discussion sources for people learning about child development, family relations, and parent education. They are grouped into six divisions that correspond to goals common to parents and children of each generation. These goals are: achieving acceptance by peers, learning to enjoy life, coping with fears and anxieties, finding a model for success, achieving a favorable view of self, and choosing a worthwhile set of values.

At the end of each story, there are questions designed to invite a comparison between the fictional situation and your personal experience. In order to present my own viewpoint about the concerns illustrated by these stories, I have written a companion volume to accompany this book. *Growing Together: Parent and Child Development* is an informal blend of research and practical advice. Each of the 23 stories in *Parent and Child in Fiction* corresponds to a chapter in *Growing Together*. Although either book can be helpful if read independently, they offer greater benefit when considered in combination.

All of us who learn from *Parent and Child in Fiction* owe thanks to the participating authors for allowing their work to be reprinted here. In addition, I want to acknowledge the following reviewers for their helpful comments on the manuscript: Carol Copple, Institute for Research and Human Development,

Educational Testing Service (Princeton, New Jersey); Cheryl Goeree, Carmel High School; Freda Rebelsky, Boston University; and Elaine Smith, North Seattle Community College. Various members of the Brooks/Cole staff, especially John Bergez, Andrea Guillobel, Jamie Brooks, and Todd Lueders, have provided much assistance in this collaborative effort. I also appreciate the ideas and encouragement offered by Shirley, my wife and valued partner.

Robert D. Strom

CONTENTS

1 PEERS AND BELONGING   1

   1 William Saroyan: The First Day of School   3
      Children's expectations of school

   2 Ruth Suckow: The Big Kids and the Little Kids   9
      The appeal of older peers and their potential influence

   3 Ruth Suckow: The Valentine Box   23
      Effects of mobility on school adjustment

   4 Stephen Crane: Showin' Off   37
      The need to sense power through territoriality

2 PLAY AND CREATIVE BEHAVIOR   45

   5 Faith Baldwin: The Gossamer World   47
      The merits of solitary play

   6 H. H. Munro: The Toys of Peace   62
      Toy selection and weapon play

   7 Ray Bradbury: The Veldt   68
      The future of play

8   Mary Lavin: The Sand Castle   84
Peer play as a means of learning

3   **FEARS AND ANXIETIES**   **97**

9   Robert Lowry: Be Nice to Mr. Campbell   99
The divorced parent and child rearing

10   Richard Wright: Black Boy   114
Mistreatment of children by peers

11   Alan Sillitoe: The Night Enoch Slept Downstairs by the Fire   119
Child abuse and neglect

12   R. V. Cassill: The First Day of School   130
Racial prejudice and fear of rejection

4   **MODELS AND OBSERVERS**   **137**

13   Robert M. Coates: A Different World   139
Children and parental conflict

14   John De Meyer: Boys Are Afraid of Girls   146
Adolescents and the opposite sex

15   Helen Laurie Welch: A Time for Waiting   160
Parental trust of teenagers

16   Bernard Malamud: In Retirement   165
The changing role of the elderly

5   **IDENTITY AND SELF-CONCEPT**   **177**

17   Frank O'Connor: The Cissy   179
Sex-role expectations

18   Susan Kuehn: The Hunt   193
     Family guilt about a retarded son

19   Dale Eunson: The Hero's Son   208
     Father/son conflict over ideals

20   Gilbert Rogin: The Regulars   222
     Parental boredom in a leisure society

6   **BELIEF AND MORAL DEVELOPMENT**   231

21   William Saroyan: The Sunday Zeppelin   233
     Learning to express differences with adults

22   Philip Roth: The Conversion of the Jews   249
     Accepting doubt without coercion

23   Shirley Jackson: Charles   266
     Understanding the young pretender

PARENT AND CHILD IN FICTION

1

PEERS
AND
BELONGING

1

THE FIRST DAY OF SCHOOL

William Saroyan

He was a little boy named Jim, the first and only child of Dr. Louis Davy, 717 Mattei Building, and it was his first day at school. His father was French, a small heavy-set man of forty whose boyhood had been full of poverty and unhappiness and ambition. His mother was dead: she died when Jim was born, and the only woman he knew intimately was Amy, the Swedish housekeeper.

It was Amy who dressed him in his Sunday clothes and took him to school. Jim liked Amy, but he didn't like her for taking him to school. He told her so. All the way to school he told her so.

I don't like you, he said. I don't like you any more.

I like *you*, the housekeeper said.

Then why are you taking me to school? he said.

He had taken walks with Amy before, once all the way to the Court House Park for the Sunday afternoon band concert, but this walk to school was different.

What for? he said.

Everybody must go to school, the housekeeper said.

Did you go to school? he said.

No, said Amy.

Then why do I have to go? he said.

You will like it, said the housekeeper.

He walked on with her in silence, holding her hand. I don't like you, he said. I don't like you any more.

I like you, said Amy.

Then why are you taking me to school? he said again. Why?

The housekeeper knew how frightened a little boy could be about going to school.

You will like it, she said. I think you will sing songs and play games.

I don't want to, he said.

I will come and get you every afternoon, she said.

I don't like you, he told her again.

She felt very unhappy about the little boy going to school, but she knew that he would have to go.

The school building was very ugly to her and to the boy. She didn't like the way it made her feel, and going up the steps with him she wished he didn't have to go to school. The halls and rooms scared her, and him, and the smell of the place too. And he didn't like Mr. Barber, the principal.

Amy despised Mr. Barber.

What is the name of your son? Mr. Barber said.

This is Dr. Louis Davy's son, said Amy. His name is Jim. I am Dr. Davy's housekeeper.

James? said Mr. Barber.

Not James, said Amy, just Jim.

All right, said Mr. Barber. Any middle name?

No, said Amy. He is too small for a middle name. Just Jim Davy.

All right, said Mr. Barber. We'll try him out in the first grade. If he doesn't get along all right we'll try him out in kindergarten.

Dr. Davy said to start him in the first grade, said Amy. Not kindergarten.

All right, said Mr. Barber.

The housekeeper knew how frightened the little boy was,

sitting on the chair, and she tried to let him know how much she loved him and how sorry she was about everything. She wanted to say something fine to him about everything, but she couldn't say anything, and she was very proud of the nice way he got down from the chair and stood beside Mr. Barber, waiting to go with him to a classroom.

On the way home she was so proud of him she began to cry.

Miss Binney, the teacher of the first grade, was an old lady who was all dried out. The room was full of little boys and girls. School smelled strange and sad. He sat at a desk and listened carefully.

He heard some of the names: *Charles, Ernest, Alvin, Norman, Betty, Hannah, Juliet, Viola, Polly.*

He listened carefully and heard Miss Binney say, Hannah Winter, what *are* you chewing? And he saw Hannah Winter blush. He liked Hannah Winter right from the beginning.

Gum, said Hannah.

Put it in the waste-basket, said Miss Binney.

He saw the little girl walk to the front of the class, take the gum from her mouth, and drop it into the waste-basket.

And he heard Miss Binney say, Ernest Gaskin, what are *you* chewing?

Gum, said Ernest.

And he liked Ernest Gaskin too.

They met in the schoolyard, and Ernest taught him a few jokes.

Amy was in the hall when school ended. She was sullen and angry at everybody until she saw the little boy. She was amazed that he wasn't changed, that he wasn't hurt, or perhaps utterly unalive, murdered. The school and everything about it frightened her very much. She took his hand and walked out of the building with him, feeling angry and proud.

Jim said, What comes after twenty-nine?

Thirty, said Amy.

Your face is dirty, he said.

His father was very quiet at the supper table.

What comes after twenty-nine? the boy said.

Thirty, said his father.

Your face is dirty, he said.

In the morning he asked his father for a nickel.

What do you want a nickel for? his father said.

Gum, he said.

His father gave him a nickel and on the way to school he stopped at Mrs. Riley's store and bought a package of Spearmint.

Do you want a piece? he asked Amy.

Do you want to give me a piece? the housekeeper said.

Jim thought about it a moment, and then he said, Yes.

Do you like me? said the housekeeper.

I like you, said Jim. Do you like me?

Yes, said the housekeeper.

Do you like school?

Jim didn't know for sure, but he knew he liked the part about gum. And Hannah Winter. And Ernest Gaskin.

I don't know, he said.

Do you sing? asked the housekeeper.

No, we don't sing, he said.

Do you play games? she said.

Not in the school, he said. In the yard we do.

He liked the part about gum very much.

Miss Binney said, Jim Davy, what are you *chewing?*

Ha ha ha, he thought.

Gum, he said.

He walked to the waste-paper basket and back to his seat, and Hannah Winter saw him, and Ernest Gaskin too. That was the best part of school.

It began to grow too.

Ernest Gaskin, he shouted in the schoolyard, *what* are you *chewing?*

Raw elephant meat, said Ernest Gaskin. Jim Davy, what are *you* chewing?

Jim tried to think of something very funny to be chewing, but he couldn't.

Gum, he said, and Ernest Gaskin laughed louder than Jim laughed when Ernest Gaskin said raw elephant meat.

It was funny no matter what you said.

Going back to the classroom Jim saw Hannah Winter in the hall.

Hannah Winter, he said, *what in the world* are you *chewing?*

The little girl was startled. She wanted to say something nice that would honestly show how nice she felt about having Jim say her name and ask her the funny question, making fun of school, but she couldn't think of anything that nice to say because they were almost in the room and there wasn't time enough.

Tutti-frutti, she said with desperate haste.

It seemed to Jim he had never before heard such a glorious word, and he kept repeating the word to himself all day.

Tutti-frutti, he said to Amy on the way home.

Amy Larson, he said, *what, are, you, chewing?*

He told his father all about it at the supper table.

He said, Once there was a hill. On the hill there was a mill. Under the mill there was a walk. Under the walk there was a key. What is it?

I don't know, his father said. What is it?

Milwaukee, said the boy.

The housekeeper was delighted.

Mill. Walk. Key, Jim said.

Tutti-frutti.

What's that? said his father.

Gum, he said. The kind Hannah Winter chews.

Who's Hannah Winter? said his father.

She's in my room, he said.

Oh, said his father.

After supper he sat on the floor with the small red and blue and yellow top that hummed while it spinned. It was all right, he guessed. It was still very sad, but the gum part of it was very funny and the Hannah Winter part very nice. Raw elephant meat, he thought with great inward delight.

Raw elephant meat, he said aloud to his father who was reading the evening paper. His father folded the paper and sat on the floor beside him. The housekeeper saw them together on the floor and for some reason tears came to her eyes.

SHARING YOUR IMPRESSIONS

1. Try to remember your first days in school, and tell something about your experience.

2. How do you suppose being in the first grade is different now from the way it was when you were there?
3. What do you think the success or failure of a child's beginning days at school should be based upon?
4. Identify the conditions that would enable most children to enjoy life at school.
5. What advice can you offer parents and teachers for improving the experience of beginning students?
6. Comment on the importance of the nonacademic aspects of primary school.
7. What kind of a person should parents consider when choosing someone to care for their preschooler?

2

THE BIG KIDS
AND THE LITTLE KIDS

Ruth Suckow

Mr. and Mrs. Thompson had gone to call on Grandma
Brewer this beautiful summer evening, too beautiful for any one
to stay in the house. They had left the girls washing dishes in the
kitchen. Jessie washed, since she was the older one, and Doris
wiped. Jessie was in a hurry to get through, but Doris wanted to
make it take as long as it could. Dish-washing was the best time
for playing their special games which they couldn't play with any
one but each other. It was the time when the little sister could
have the big sister's attention all to herself.

"Sister, listen, you've got to tell me! If you could have
twenty-five children—"

"I never would have, you little idiot!"

"Well, some of them adopted. Twenty-five girls and twenty
boys. What names would you choose to call them? What name
would you choose for the first girl and the first boy, and then the
next-oldest girl and boy, and then the other ones?"

Sister always knew such wonderful names, that actresses
and countesses might have, so much finer and fancier than Doris
could think of for herself.

"Oh, I'd start at the first of the alphabet and go along."

"Tell me some of them. Please, Sister. I want to hear what you say."

"Well, then—Angelica, Barbara, Cynthia—Diantha—"

"That isn't twenty-five!"

"Oh, Dorrie, it takes too long. When I get the names said, then you'll want me to tell you how they're going to be dressed and all the rest of it. We've done all that so often. I don't want to play that tonight."

"Why not, Sister?"

Jessie kept glancing toward the screen door. Outside it was clear and cool and dusky, with just an exciting thrill of autumn in the air. Vacation was almost over. School would begin next week. Doris was away down in the lower grades, but Jessie was going into high-school. Somebody whistled out there. Jessie tried to look careless, as if she hadn't noticed it. But Doris was suspicious at once. More whistling—sweetly shrill, enticing through the dusk—and then above it sounded the long-drawn-out, piercingly hideous call of the crowd, Sister's crowd, the big kids. . . .

"PHEE-EE-ee-bit!"

Jessie wrung out the dish mop and hastily washed her hands. She had finished, but there was a whole stack of plates still to be wiped.

Doris was wild. "You're going to play outside tonight. The big kids are."

Jessie would not answer.

"Wait for me, Sister. Wait! You know I'm not through. I can't do it as fast as you can. Don't go off without me!"

"That wasn't for you."

"I don't care, I'm coming along!"

In wild haste she put away the plates still wet, although she knew her mother would scold when she found them all sticking together in the morning. She flew out of the house, let the screen door bang, jumped down the steps onto the cement walk that sent a jar all through her teeth and joggled the loose ones. Mabel and Bee had come past for Jessie. They were all three almost to the corner now. Doris went running down the walk after them, stopping once to hold her side, sobbing and frantically calling:

"Sister! You've got to wait. You can't go off and leave me at home all alone. Wai-ait!"

The three big girls turned. Doris had nearly caught up with

them now, and they saw her straining eyes and woe-begone, tear-stained face.

"You go back!"

"I won't do it."

"I'm not going to look after you."

"I don't have to be looked after."

"Oh, well, I suppose we'll have to let her tag along."

They were going to play in the vacant lot. The little kids had that all to themselves in the daytime, but when the big kids wanted it in the evening, the little ones had to skedaddle. Some of the little kids were there now, playing pom-pom-pullaway. It was still light outside, and until it began to get dark, the real big kids, like Red Bishop, scorned playing. But they were beginning to gather. The little kids didn't have much time left. Even if the big kids had been willing to let them stay, the mothers would be out calling them.

"Why don't you play with those kids?" Jessie asked.

"I don't want to."

"Well, you needn't think you can be in our game. You'll just have to sit here and watch. You won't like that."

Doris didn't answer.

The three big girls were walking about now, Jessie in the middle with her arms around the waists of the other two. The boys were watching them, and they knew it. A subtle, new delight had crept into their old wild enjoyment of the games this summer, making it more thrilling than ever before to play out on the vacant lot in the evening. But the games were not quite the same.

Doris kept by herself at the edge of the walk. She liked pom-pom-pullaway. She had been caught only twice this summer, and both times by Robert Nichols, who was such a fast runner it didn't count to be caught by him. But pom-pom-pullaway was so tame compared to the big kids' games, the kind you could play only at night, in the darkness or by moonlight. She didn't want those little kids to get hold of her.

The three big girls came back on their promenade.

"They're calling you, Dorrie," Mabel said. "They won't like you if you don't play with them."

"You could have so much more fun," Bee coaxed her. "You

could keep up with them. You can't run fast enough to play with us. You'll be left 'way, 'way behind, and just think how lonesome you'll be!"

"Oh, let her alone," Jessie said severely. "She'll have to find out."

It was dark now in the street under the shady trees, but the vacant lot still lay in a clear twilight. The dresses of the little girls flashed white as they ran. "Pom-pom-PULLaway!" But there was a minor tone now to the cry—the players were dropping out—the game was ending.

They were trying to keep on, but a long call sounded from across the street through the evening air—"El-see-EEE!"—and one of the big kids said, "Your mother's calling you." A woman came picking her way through the dewy grass to get her two, and one of them went scampering ahead of her, while the other pulled back and was wailing.

Jessie said to Doris, "If mamma knew you were here, that's what would happen to you!"

Word had been sent from one of the big kids to the other, "Going to play outdoors tonight!" They were gathering now from all sides, running and flocking.

"Why don't we begin?" some one asked impatiently. "Make those little kids stop playing."

"We can't begin until Red gets here."

He was coming down the street now. His carroty hair flamed even in the dusk, and they could see his white shirt and recognize the masterful ease of his swinging stride. He was the fastest runner and the biggest boy. The crowd never did anything without him.

"Hey, Red!"

"Hey!" He leaped the ditch and came over to the crowd. "Looks like the gang's all here, huh? Hey, kids, you beat it. We want this place."

The little kids tried to act as if they didn't hear him—except Bennie Salter, who was always obedient and scary, and who scampered at once. Billy Godolphin smartly stuck out his tongue. But there was a scared bravado in his smartness. He ran around a circle all by himself on the playground, after the others had scattered, but in a few minutes he had faded out like the rest of them.

"What are we going to play?"

The big kids were crowding around Red. Pete had come, too, another big boy, and some of the bunch were ready to listen to him. Some of them wanted Beckon. But the word had already gone around that Red said it was to be Run-Sheep-Run tonight. Such a night couldn't be wasted on any other game. Besides, it might be the last good chance they'd have. School began next week. Somebody might have put up a house on the vacant lot by next summer.

"Who says Beckon?"

Two hands went up—found themselves the only ones—wavered . . .

"How many vote for Run-Sheep-Run?"

"AYE!" came in a great roar.

"Run-Sheep-Run has it."

Red and Pete were to be the leaders. That might make a few others jealous, but the leadership belonged to them. Pete was a great big fellow. He weighed a little more than Red. But all of them—the girls especially—wanted to be chosen on Red's side. They were pretending to be airily unconscious, but the watchful, hopeful glint of their eyes gave them away. Only Jessie Thompson, to the secret envy of the others, could be really unconcerned. She was sure of being chosen. She was the fastest runner of the girls, the prettiest and most popular. Already there was a young-lady look about the little swish of her skirts as she went down the street. Mabel and Bee were chattering with great animation. They didn't seem to notice that sides were about to be chosen now. But there was a breathlessness in Mabel's shrill laughter.

"Who's going to play? Everybody here? Now get out, you little kids."

The few little ones who remained—those Whaley kids, whose mother didn't care how long they stayed out—had withdrawn into a watching, respectful row at the edge of the lot. The big kids were too much absorbed to notice Doris. She stood on the rim of the crowd, her eyes dark and bright, praying that somehow she would be chosen.

"Let me be chosen—oh, please, please, please, dear God and Jesus!" she prayed.

She kept her eyes shut tight, feeling that if she couldn't see she might not be seen. She was in the bunch, anyway. They were wrangling over the sides.

"Who has first turn?"

"Pete. Red chose last time."

"Aw, get out!"

"That's the truth!"

"But Pete has to hide first. Don't you remember?"

"Well, don't you know—?"

"Aw, go ahead. Somebody choose! Let's get going."

Every one knew it was because Red and Pete both wanted Jessie Thompson. That made some of the boys tired. Jessie could run fast enough for a girl, but not as fast as lots of the fellows. When that kind of business got into it, games were spoiled. Jessie thrust out one foot, pointed as if for dancing, and fastened back a curl with a tiny hairpin. She was afraid the hairpins would all fall out when she ran tonight. Pete was the one who got her this time. Jessie gave Red a long, sidelong look as she stepped daintily over to Pete's side. Red chose Bee then, just to show her. When Doris finished her prayer and opened her eyes, most of the crowd were on one side or the other. They were getting down to the undesirables. Robert Nichols was such a fast runner that they had let him stay; and now with proud nonchalance, superior to his short trousers, he swaggered over to stand beside Pete. Mabel had not been taken. She was too fat to run. She was pretending not to be aware of her unhappy isolation, but when Red glanced toward her, she made little conscious movements.

"Well, I guess I choose Mabel," Red drawled.

She proudly joined his flock, with a triumphant glance at Jessie. At least she was on Red's side. She knew that was where Jessie would rather be.

"Are we through now? Everybody chosen?"

Only Doris was left, desolate and small.

"Who's that kid?"

"Oh, it's just Dorrie!" Jessie said that with disdain. "She tagged along. She doesn't need to play. Don't bother about her."

But somebody else was coming—Chink Watson, and a good runner, too! "Hey, folks, hold on!"

They had to wait for Chink.

Then that left one too few on Red's side. It wouldn't be fair.

"Why not take Jessie's kid sister?"

"She's too little. She couldn't run fast enough."

Her heart, so aching and forlorn a moment ago, now was beating fast. And Robert Nichols, her old enemy, was standing up for her.

"She's a fast runner. Honest. I can hardly catch her sometimes."

"Aw," said Pete, disgusted, "we don't want any of those little kids."

Oh, how she hated Pete! She wished he'd fall down in the long, wet weeds and never get out until morning. And she hoped Sister would fall down too—or anyway, that some one would catch her—saying so impatiently, as if it didn't matter:

"Oh, Dorrie doesn't know how to play this!"

"I do! I do know how to play! I've played it lots of times. Haven't I, Robert?"

And she had, but a little kids' Run-Sheep-Run, in the afternoon or just after supper—not the perilous, mysterious, exciting glory of the real Run-Sheep-Run at night. This one, one night —oh, she couldn't bear not having them decide; her breath seemed to choke her with eagerness, and she was praying frantically inside again, to God or Jesus, either one or both—one of them ought to help her.

Red looked over at her standing alone.

"Aw, let her play," he said easily. "What does it matter? Come on, kid. You can be on our side."

Pete's side went out first. Pete was getting all the luck tonight. Red's bunch stayed at the goal. They were watching, guessing, surmising.

"They're going east!"

"Yes, but that doesn't mean anything!"

"Bet they're headed for the ravine."

"Too hard to get out of there."

Doris was dumb with happiness. It was enough just to be admitted. The Whaley kids were still staring from the edge of the lot, a stubborn, forlorn, unwanted little tribe. And she was one of the big kids! Well, anyway, they were letting her play with them.

Once Red looked at her and tweaked a lock of her hair. "Think you can run, kid?" he asked her.

She knew she could run! She would show them. Oh, how

she worshiped Red! She would do anything for Red. She would catch Sister for him. How wonderful if she could be the one to find where the other side was hidden! They would all be glad, then, that she had been chosen. She was a little bit afraid of that fast Robert Nichols. But maybe she could keep away from him in the dark.

How different the vacant lot was at night! She had crossed it this morning going to town—crossed it, watchful for snakes, by that little diagonal path all the neighborhood had trodden. Then it had lain bright under the morning sun, still a little shine of dew on the thin-stemmed weeds that left mouths all wryly full of knobby seeds when the children made "mustaches" with them. She had stooped down to pick a dandelion and blow the feathery top to see if her mother needed her—but to blow very softly, so that she would have a good excuse for lingering. In the afternoon, she and Elsie and Vinnie and Blythe had played Going-to-New-Orleans. She wouldn't play that now! Or any of those games played in the daylight with just a bunch of little kids.

Dark and significant stood the lone elm tree that they had chosen for the goal. Doris glanced at it nervously. Could she ever reach it when it was her turn to run? A thrill of delicious fear shot through her, making her hair prickle all over her head.

Red's bunch was getting impatient. The other side had been out a long time now. They were choosing a hard hiding-place. Common fear and danger drew the watchers close, the girls shivering and giggling, the boys stepping out on little scouting excursions as far as the rules would let them go.

"See anything of them?"

"Not a sign."

But it couldn't be long now.

"Listen here, kids." Red gathered them all about him. "We're going to run this thing right. We're going to catch just as many of that bunch as we can. Get me? We've got to beat that crowd tonight! It may be the last chance this summer. Now, I want every one of you to do exactly as I say."

They were in a cluster now in the dusk. Each could hear the other's breathing, catch the gleam of eyes—they all belonged to the same side. Red's voice was low, fierce and vibrating. It sent a shock through them. His shoulders were tense, his arms freckled and strong below the short white sleeves, his red hair burning even in the twilight. He was their captain, their leader. All their dependence was upon him.

"I want every person on this side to go after one guy and get him. Now, all of you listen! Let the easy ones go. It's the fast ones we're after. I want two of you to run down that Chink Watson and catch him if you have to break your gol-darned necks."

"Who are you going after, Red?"

Red said with a deep, slow satisfaction, "I'm going to get that Jessie Thompson!"

Doris tried to crowd in with the others. Her eyes looked up at Red with shining, utter worship. She begged him:

"Who shall I catch? Red! Who shall I?"

She would run—she didn't care if all her blood vessels burst, if she did really and truly run her legs off; she could run faster than any of the big kids, she felt now.

Somebody laughed. Red looked down at her. His eyebrows lifted in a funny way.

"Gee, I forgot we had you on our side!"

Some one—that horrid fat Mabel—said impatiently, "Don't let her run. She can't catch anybody."

If they should leave her out now!—they were all looking at her.

"Aw, she can run," Red said grandly. "What does it hurt? You run, kid. Go after anybody you see."

Some one said, "Sh!" They saw Pete coming. He was trailing around the edge of the lot, but that didn't mean anything. He thought he could fool them. Red drew them about him again with an imperious gesture and gave his last, low, hurried instructions.

"All follow me and all keep close watch—remember . . . and the minute Pete calls 'Run-Sheep-Run'—!"

Pete sauntered up to them, carefully nonchalant.

"We know where you've left them. We can go straight to them."

"Think so, do you?" Pete answered the jeers.

"Well, let's get off, gang!" Red said impatiently.

Red struck across the vacant lot, and his flock trailed after him. The long, wet grass swished stealthily about their shoes. Pete, still nonchalant, sauntered as far as he dared in the rear.

No one paid any attention to Doris. She trotted along. She kept her eyes on Red's white shirt ahead of her in the dusk. To be playing, actually playing Run-Sheep-Run with Sister's crowd! In the passion of her devotion to Red, she hated Pete and the other side. She felt as if she could be a heroine and bring in the whole other side as captives. But as they kept on their stealthy search, going Indian file, her heart began to trip faster and faster and the sound of her own breathing frightened her.

Pete sang out, "Blue! Blue!" That was the first of the signals.

"Colors, is it?" Red said. "All right, old boy, we'll soon know what your blue means."

"Sh!"

Pete bent down to pick a long weed and to show that he wasn't worried. They had left the vacant lot now. Red was taking them across Hibbard's lawn. At every little sound—a branch moving, a footstep on the walk—there was a nervous twitter from one of the girls. The other side might be anywhere—in the shadow of the porch, behind those lilac bushes . . .

"PURPLE!" Pete shouted suddenly.

At every one of those warnings a shock of fear went through Doris. Her knees trembled, and she wanted to run back to the goal. But she must stand it—she was one of Red's bunch. Next it would be her own side that was hiding—in the dark, left behind by their leader, all crouched and breathing together. She shivered with a thrilling terror.

"Lie low!"

The long cry sounded hoarsely above them and trailed away into a moan of warning. Then the others must be close about! The barn, with its perilous shadows? In the long grass of the orchard? There were glints of watchful eyes in the dusk—the frightened breathing all subdued—the feet treading softly through wet weeds. Doris's blood beat in her throat. Her little heart choked her. She saw Red's gesture of warning—his lifted head . . .

"RUN-SHEEP-RUN!"

Screams from the girls, a mad stampede—the wild, glorious terror of that shout! From behind White's barn next door they saw the dark figures running. "Get 'em! Go after 'em!" Bolting madly through the grass, leaping the walk, swishing through the lilac branches—they had all started before Doris knew which way to run. She went scudding wildly after them—after some

one, she didn't know whom, one of her side or one of the other
. . . Her breath ached in her straining throat, and her thin little
legs began to hurt and get weak at the knees. Oh, she couldn't
keep up! She must. Away off ahead of her she saw Red's white
shirt and Sister's light dress. Red was going after Sister, and she
had to help him. Her forehead pushed against the rush of cool
night air, and her hair blew back as she plunged madly through
darkness.

The cement walk, a long pale line glimmering in darkness
. . . and bang into two people! She tried to go on—they caught
her.

"What's this? Why, it's Dorrie!"

It was mama and papa!

"Let me go, papa, please! We're all playing Run-Sheep-
Run. I'm catching somebody."

Like a little fish, plunging and straining, she struggled in
their hands.

But they couldn't understand. "Why are you out here?" And
in the dark? Didn't she know how late it was?

"We're playing, mama! Let me go!"

Mama said, "Oh, no, you must come with us now."

She tried to explain through sobs. It was Run-Sheep-Run.
She was on Red's side. Red had chosen her. There wouldn't be
enough without her. The game would be spoiled if they took her
away. And her own side hadn't gone out yet—the game was just
starting!

But bearing her along between them, each grasping a little
hot hand, papa and mama just couldn't understand her. Even her
crying couldn't stop them, they were so comfortably sure—like
older people!—that they knew all about it and were right.

Stay and play? Oh no, it was too late. It was far too late for
her. The game would go on without her, they assured her. She
was too little, anyway. These big children didn't want her. How
she hated their comforting but relentless hands! She could just
see a play of dark figures about the elm tree—laughter, a girl's
shrill scream that sounded like Sister's—and she had to go home
with papa and mama!

All the way home they had tried to console her.

Mr. Thompson said, "You little kids have the vacant lot all to yourselves the whole day long. I saw you playing there when I came home to dinner."

What did they suppose those little games mattered—Old Witch and Statuary—when she had felt the wild taste of the chase in the darkness? She never wanted to play those little kids' games again.

But when they reached home and got into the light, and saw the woebegone tear-stains on the little face, the parents' hearts smote them. They tried all their comforts. Did she want mama to make her a nice glass of lemonade? She was so hot!—Mrs. Thompson sighed, pushing back the damp hair from the flushed forehead. Trying to keep up with those big children! Perhaps there was still a piece of that candy? Papa, look in the top drawer of the buffet. The candy for which she had begged this morning, which mama had watchfully secreted—she wouldn't even say she wanted that. She let mama put a piece of it into her hand, but she held it slackly and refused to look at it. She sat in forlorn isolation and let the tears stay thick in her lashes.

Now the parents were at a loss. Each wanted to say to the other that she might have been allowed to stay a little longer, if it mattered this much; but it seemed that such words wouldn't do. They must preserve the cheerful falsity of their omniscience.

They pleaded with her. "Don't you see, we have to bring you home, so that you can grow up and be a big kid?"

"You let Sister stay."

"But, darling, Sister's a big girl now!"

"So am I."

"Oh, no, you aren't." Mama tried to stroke her hair. She begged, "Don't you want to be our little girl any longer?"

Papa cried with false, hearty cheer, "Of course she does! Why, we couldn't get along without her. We'd be two old folks, if we had to have two big girls right away. Like Grandma and Grandpa Brewer. Don't you want to keep your parents young?"

But he couldn't make her smile at his little jokes.

"Sister," mama mourned, "will soon be too big a girl to play." She thought for a moment of Jessie, wishing that by some magic they could keep her playing there forever, but knowing it wouldn't be so. "After she's through," mama promised, "it will be your turn."

"I want it to be my turn now!"

That was all they could get out of her. Couldn't she see, they asked her, that if they let her stay so late now and play so hard, she couldn't do it when she did get big? If she got everything too soon, how could there be anything left? There would be plenty of other nights—plenty of time to play Run-Sheep-Run. Yes, but they wouldn't be *this* night. That was the answer which none of the consolations could console.

At last there was nothing left to do but carry her up to bed so that she could wake up happier in the morning.

Her little legs dangled and bumped, and she wouldn't put her arms around her father's neck. She permitted herself to be undressed, but she turned her face away from kisses. Stricken, the two guiltily righteous parents looked down at the desolate little figure, finding it small comfort themselves that what must be must be; and, admitting the failure of their own wisdom as consolation, withdrew in favor of the kitten. Mr. Thompson had called and chased the little rascal all through the back yard, plucking him finally by guile from a tree; and now came upstairs holding him by the furry middle with four helpless paws dangling. At sight of that, Doris held out her slack arms and took the kitten to her. She squeezed his softness against her cheek, in love of him and reproach of mama and papa, and at least had the comfort of crying her last few tears into the fluffy warmth of his fur.

The parents stole downstairs. They could set up no claims to rival the kitten's. There was nothing for them to do now but wait until Jessie chose to come home. Next time they would have to let Doris stay. They could not tell her the sweetness of having things before her instead of behind her; and wistfulness for the big child mingled with humorous remorse for the little one. The game was still going on. The cries came distantly through the clear, cool darkness with its sharp touch of autumn, that seemed to say this was the last night any of them would be playing Run-Sheep-Run. Jessie's voice sounded shrill above the others. The parents, sighing and waiting in the lighted room, could hear it from across the vacant lot, like the last sweet call of her childhood through the deepening summer night.

Upstairs in her own little room, Doris heard closer than the cries of the players the familiar stirring and brushing of the maple tree outside her window. She pressed the kitten's warm side to her and felt a mournful comfort in the tickle of his little whiskers.

But he didn't want to stay. He had been snatched from freshly discovered cat pleasures of his own out among the dark trees in the garden. No longer was it bliss enough for him to lie in his little mistress's arms and purr. He was motionless, then he began a mute struggle.

She begged, "Stay, kitty!"

Then, with mournful acquiescence, she opened her hands and heard the soft thump of his little body on the floor and the pitter-patter of his feet down the stairs.

SHARING YOUR IMPRESSIONS

1. Children of the same age often give each other a sense of belonging, while older children sometimes do not accept them. Describe several memories of age prejudice among children.
2. Give some reasons why young children need playmates their own age.
3. Give some reasons for having young children spend time with older kids.
4. Make some guesses about how age prejudice begins for most of us.
5. Recall some of the games you played as a child. Then identify the kinds of games you recommend for big and little kids who play together.
6. How does learning through games differ from learning by other methods?

3

THE VALENTINE BOX

Ruth Suckow

When Betty had her mind set on a story, it was just as well to give up at once.

"Mother's told you all the stories she knows. Long ago."

"No, you haven't." Betty's trust in her poor little repertoire was inexhaustible.

"Mother can't think of any new ones."

"An old one, then. I don't want a new one. I want to hear about when you were a little girl. When you were a little girl and thought you wouldn't get any valentine."

"That old story again?"

"Yes!"

"Mother hates to tell that."

But light little fingers stroked her hand, soft as feathers, insistent, merciless. The mother sighed helplessly, staring into the dusky, pretty room. Betty echoed her sigh, but with satisfaction. She settled securely against her pillow. Her eyes, too, took on the fixed and darkened look of her mother's, anticipating the sorrowfulness of this many-times-heard story, as she, too, stared into the dusk.

"Well, once on Valentine's Day—"

"No! That isn't the way you begin it."

"How does mother begin it?"

Betty set her right inexorably. " 'Once when mother was a little girl' . . . that's the way you must tell it to me."

"Oh, dear, then I suppose that's the way it must be! Well, once, when mother was a little girl grandpa sold his business, and we had to move away from the town where we were living and move to a different town. It was early in the winter, and grandma and grandpa said that mother must start into school again right away, so that she wouldn't get behind in her studies. And so she had to go all by herself to a new school where she didn't know any of the little girls or any of the little boys."

A sigh of gusty mournfulness from Betty.

"She had to leave her little chum—"

"Lois?"

"Yes, Lois. And she hadn't any little friend of her own."

"Tell about the first day at school."

"Well, and so, on the first day, mother had to go to the new school all alone."

"But why didn't grandma take you?"

"Because grandma was so busy getting the new house settled. And anyway, mother was supposed to be a big girl and not to mind going to school alone."

"But you did mind it."

"Yes, but grandma didn't know it. So mother started out."

"Tell about how you were dressed."

"She wore a little red plaid dress, and a little gray kitty hood that was tied with red ribbons."

Betty stroked her mother's hand, thinking mournfully of the kitty hood.

"Mother was very proud of that little hood. Well, grandma didn't know that in this town school started ten minutes earlier than it had in the other town, and so when mother got to the building, she found that she was tardy. All the other children had gone inside, and she had to open the big doors and go up the big stairway all by herself."

"And the stairway creaked!"

"Every single step of the way! And the worst of it was that mother didn't know where to find her own room, and she was such a silly little girl that she was afraid to ask anybody, and she thought that if she were to open the wrong door, and all the strange children were to look at her and know that she had made a mistake, she would die."

"But you did find the right room?"

"Oh, yes. Mother went on her tiptoes all through the long halls until at last she found Number Five."

She heard the small sigh of relief.

"But she had on her coat and hood, and she had to leave those in the cloakroom."

"Tell what it was like."

"It was a long room, and there was a row of hooks on each side, the girls' hooks on one side and the boys' hooks on the other."

"And all the hooks had numbers!"

"Yes, a number for every one. And the only vacant hook was Number Fifteen. I've always remembered that Number Fifteen. So mother had to take off her gray coat and her gray hood—"

"Your *kitty* hood!"

"—And hang them up on Number Fifteen. And then she made a dreadful discovery. In the town where mother came from, all the little girls her age were wearing kitty hoods just like hers; and grandma had crocheted this one for her at Christmas time, and it was fluffy and new, and mother thought it was beautiful. But that was a little town, and this was a big town! It had two railroads and a whole thousand more inhabitants. And here the little girls weren't wearing kitty hoods. They were wearing caps."

"Round caps?"

"Yes, round caps. Every hook had a coat, and above every coat hung a round cap. So mother felt worse than ever. But there was nothing else for her to do. So finally she took off her gray coat and hung it on hook Number Fifteen. And then she did something that made her ashamed. She took off her little, fluffy kitty hood, that was just as soft and gray as the kitten she'd had to leave behind in the other town—"

"Because this was too big a town to keep so many cats."

"That was what grandma and grandpa had told her . . . And she hid it away under her coat, so that not even the shiny red ribbons showed. Then she stood a long while. She couldn't go back, for then grandma would have been ashamed of her. So she gave a little knock on the door."

"Loud enough for the teacher to hear it?"

"It must have been, because the teacher came."

"Was the teacher nice?"

"Nice enough, I think, but I've forgotten now just what this teacher was like. Mother's had so many other teachers . . . And so—oh, there was a great deal to it, too much to tell, but at any rate the teacher decided that mother could stay in that room. But I remember that she had to stand at the desk while the teacher asked her questions, and looked at her report cards, and tried to find a seat for her—and all this time the children in the room were staring until the teacher said, 'Go back to your lessons, class.'

"She gave mother the one vacant seat and all morning long mother sat there. She didn't know what these children were doing. They were using different books, and they were studying different lessons, and even her tablet paper was the wrong kind—so all she could do was sit.

"When recess came, mother marched out to the playground with the other children. She watched, and did just what they did, and followed the other little girls. But none of them knew her. So she had to pretend she didn't care about their games, and sit down in one of the basement windows where no one could notice her, and watch the other children play. The rest of the morning went just the same, and when mother went home to the new house at noon, she cried and told grandma she wasn't ever going back to that school."

The mother laughed easily and yet with a slight ruefulness.

Betty reminded her, "But you did go back!"

"Indeed I did! Grandpa said that mother needn't go, but grandma wouldn't hear of such a thing."

"Was grandpa nicer than grandma?"

"Well—perhaps mother thought so then. But I don't know just what grandma and grandpa could have done with her if they hadn't sent her back to school. So she had her face washed, and grandma held a wet towel to her eyes and her little red nose, and in the afternoon back she went."

In silence Betty contemplated the story. "Now tell me about the Valentine Box."

But the mother was not quite through with her introduction. She laughed again, softly.

"Go on," Betty urged.

But she sat looking into the dusk. She was remembering too many things to be told—how her father had promised to take her uptown that very night after school, to the big stores that filled her with awe, and see that she got a round cap exactly like those the other girls wore; how her mother had agreed, if she would be willing to wear the kitty hood when she played outdoors on Saturdays; and how she herself had apologized and explained to the little kitty hood, in a moment of shamed remorse, when she had come home triumphant in her new round cap and put the hood away in a drawer . . .   .

"The Valentine Box, mother!"

Yes, of course, she must get to the real story. That could be told, and these were things faintly stirring the darkness of her remembrance that no one would ever know but herself. There was too much bound up in them. . . . She turned away.

She said severely, "But you know you always cry, Betty."

"I won't cry this time," Betty promised hopefully.

"Why did I ever tell you this story in the first place? Well . . . "

And she began, she rather hoped for the last time, to tell the story of the Valentine Box.

"So mother got her round cap, and the right books, and the right kind of tablet paper, and she even began to understand what the class was doing in arithmetic. But none of the little girls had ever spoken to her. At recess she had to go and sit alone in the basement window, and after school she stayed and asked questions of the teacher so that she wouldn't have to march out with the others and see the girls go skipping off together. Of course, they might have spoken to her if she hadn't been such a silly, bashful little girl—"

"You aren't silly!"

"I hope not so silly as I was then. Anyway, it was about the first of February, and one morning, when mother went to school,

she saw valentines in the drug-store window; and when she got to
school, a whole group of little girls were standing together in the
cloakroom and talking about valentines. After that, valentines
were all she saw or thought or heard of. Last Valentine's Day, she
had had the best time in the world. Lois had painted a little
valentine for her, and she had painted one for Lois. And there
had been a party, and a little boy named Dewey Boggs had given
her a candy heart that said 'Love me.' Mother had kept it because
it was too pretty to suck, and then finally it was too dirty!"

"Mother, Dewey Boggs wasn't *daddy?*"

The mother laughed. "Oh, no, he wasn't daddy! You know
what daddy's name is, you foolish child!"

"I know it. Now tell me about the valentines."

"But this year everything was so different, and mother
didn't want Valentine's Day to come."

She felt the soft clasp of Betty's arms, comforting her in
advance.

"Now, Betty, you promised not to cry."

"I remember." The little voice was doleful.

"Then you mustn't. Or mother can't tell the story at all. She
shouldn't anyway . . . but . . . Well, the worst of all was when
the little girls began talking about the Valentine Box. At first,
mother didn't know what they meant. She heard it in the cloakroom and on the playground and everywhere. 'Are we going to
have a Valentine Box?' 'What do you think you'll get in the
Valentine Box?' And finally one of the little girls—"

"That Gertie?"

"That Gertie it was! You remember, funny little midget,
don't you?"

"Yes, because I don't *like* that Gertie."

"Oh, Gertie probably wasn't so bad as mother thought she
was then."

"But she was *loud.*"

"She was. She had the loudest voice on the playground. And
when the little girls chose sides, she always had to be the first to
choose . . . Well, that Gertie began waving her hand in the
air—"

"Show me how, mother. Do it."

"Oh, like this."

Betty giggled delightedly.

"And when the teacher said, 'Well, Gertie, what is it?' she hopped up from her seat and said, 'Teacher, are we going to have a Valentine Box this year?'

"That was the first mother had ever heard of a Valentine Box. She wondered what it could be. She was so silly that at first she thought it meant the teacher was going to give valentines to all the children—and she took her arithmetic home every night, so that the teacher would like her and give her a nice one."

"What had the teacher said to Gertie?"

"I think she'd said, 'We'll see.' "

"The way *you* do, mother."

"Do I? Yes, I suppose I do, funny one. And the teacher meant just the same thing that mother does—that she didn't much want to have the Valentine Box, but she supposed she'd have to agree! Because a few days later, after school had begun, she rapped with her rule on the desk and said, 'Class, attention!' "

Betty wiggled into a listening attitude.

"And then she said: 'On Valentine's Day, next Friday, there will be a Valentine Box in this room. All of you may bring your valentines here, and put them in the box, and we will take a half-hour in the afternoon and distribute the valentines.' And all the room clapped and clapped."

"Did you clap, mother?"

"At first mother clapped, because all the rest did and because she thought it sounded lovely, too. But afterward, when she thought about it, it didn't seem so nice to her. She began to wonder who would give her a valentine. At first, she thought about it just a little bit. Because she didn't really believe such a thing as being the one to get no valentine could happen. Not to her. And when she went past the drugstore, she would think: 'That's a pretty one! What if I should get that in the Valentine Box?'

"But the nearer the day came, the more she thought about it. There was a pretty little girl in her room named Fidelia. She wished Fidelia would give her a valentine. But she was such a silly little girl, as I told you, that instead of trying to know Fidelia better, she was all the more shy of her now, for fear Fidelia would think it was just a valentine she wanted.

"There was the little boy who sat behind her and who

whispered to her and untied her hair ribbons. She even thought
he might give her one. It would probably be one of those dreadful
comics, but she didn't care, if only there was a valentine in the
box for her. But one of the boys said to this boy, 'Hey, you going
to give any valentines?' and he said, 'Naw, I ain't going to give
any old valentines.' And then both the boys laughed and swaggered. And the next time he untied her ribbon, she looked
fiercely at him and said, 'You stop that!'

"But there was Lois. Surely Lois would remember and send
her a valentine. She would give it to the teacher and say, 'My
little chum sent me this and said to put it in the Valentine Box.' It
would be all the nicer because it had a stamp on it and had come
through the mails.

"So mother went to grandpa's office and told him she
wanted a nickel to buy Lois a valentine.

"'Lois!' he said to her. 'Well, what about the little girls
here?'

"And he gave her a whole quarter! But what was she to do
with it? Grandpa thought she was the nicest little girl in the
world, and he would have been angry if he had supposed every
one else didn't think so, too. Mother had to take the quarter, and
kiss him, and go away wondering what she could do with it.

"But no letter from Lois came. Every day she ran home from
school, and every day there was nothing. She wouldn't ask
grandma about it, because she couldn't bear to have grandma
know. She had sent Lois a pretty valentine with a picture of a
gentleman with powdered hair handing roses to a lady in a
puffed-out skirt. Friday came nearer and nearer, and she didn't
know what she was going to do. She woke up in the night because
she had dreamed the teacher had a great big Valentine Box and
was calling out every name but her own. She couldn't stand it.
She went and sat on grandpa's lap, and she thought she would ask
him to put a valentine in the box for her. But she couldn't. Then
grandpa and grandma would know all about it, how she didn't
know anybody at school, and how even Lois had forgotten her,
and she hadn't told them a single word. So when grandpa said,
'What does this little girl want?' she told him, 'An apple.'

"Then it was Valentine's Day itself. It was the loveliest
bright winter day. The sun was shining, and the water was

dripping from the icicles, so that they looked like what mother and Lois used to call 'diamond fingers.' 'What are you going to have to eat at your party?' Lois would ask mother when they were on the way to school. And mother would say, 'I'm going to have snowsparkle pudding and diamond fingers.'"

Betty said, "That's what *I'm* going to have some day!"

"So that at first mother didn't know why she felt so funny. There was a funny feeling in her stomach."

"Why was it in your *stomach*, mother?"

"I don't know, but that's where it was."

"What was it like?"

"Oh goodness, Betty, mother can't stop to remember. It was there—and then mother knew it was because this was Valentine's Day. At first she thought she wouldn't go to school. When she went down to breakfast, she told grandma she didn't feel well enough to go to school today. But grandma said, 'Let me see your tongue!' And then she said that she guessed this was 'Friday sickness,' and mother would be all right when it came time to play tomorrow morning. And there wasn't any letter from Lois—"

"Why not?"

"Well, mother had been away a long time—several weeks—and there were so many other little girls in the school . . . All the way to school she wondered what could happen so she wouldn't have to go. Maybe a fairy would come with her wand and tap on the Valentine Box—or maybe one of the gods and goddesses would send a cloud to hide her. Of course, she knew none of these things would really happen. She still had part of her quarter unspent. And so, when she came to the drug store, she went in and said to the man, 'I want to buy a valentine.'"

"The pretty one you saw in the window?"

"Oh, no, that was gone long ago. But a pretty one, too, with paper embroidery all around the edge, and little hearts and cupids, and a verse that said the person who got this valentine was very pretty and some one's love. The man said, 'How's this one?' and she said, 'It's all right.' And she went through the alley, instead of through the street, and she looked to see that no one was coming, and first she shut her eyes tight and prayed, 'Oh, dear God, please let the teacher call out my name!' and then she wrote a name on the valentine. She kept it in her arithmetic all morning.

"But that afternoon she went to school very early. She told grandma she had to work on her diagrams. Nobody was in the room but the teacher. The teacher had on a pretty dress, and there, on her desk, was a great, big Valentine Box all covered with red crêpe paper and with a beautiful bow of white.

" 'See our Valentine Box!' the teacher said. 'Do you have any valentines to put in it?' Mother said, 'Yes, ma'am.' And she dropped in her valentine. Then she went to her seat and worked on her diagrams."

"Tell me how you felt, mother."

"Well, it was a very funny feeling."

"In your *stomach?*"

"No, little funny one, I think all over. It was too much of a feeling to be any one place."

"Now tell me the rest of it."

"Well, pretty soon the other children began coming into the room, and all the little girls brought in valentines and dropped them into the box."

"Didn't the boys bring in valentines, too?"

"Some of them did. But you see, it didn't matter so much if the boys didn't get any valentines."

"Why not, mother?"

"Well, darling—just because it doesn't! Anyway it was the little girls who cared.

"All afternoon none of the children wanted to get their lessons. They whispered and wiggled in their seats. Little girls wore their best dresses and best hair ribbons, and even that little boy who sat behind mother had slicked down his hair! And finally, at three o'clock, the teacher said, 'You may all put away your books.' "

Betty gave a deep sigh.

"And then when everything was quiet, the teacher opened the Valentine Box. It was all cram full of white envelopes and a great big sigh went over the room. The children craned their necks to see and they all wondered whose name would be the first one called."

"Whose was? Not yours, mother?"

"Oh, no, indeed it wasn't mother's name! Whose do you think it was? The teacher's! They had given her a beautiful, big valentine with lace paper and a red satin ribbon. The most beautiful valentine in the box. So every one was satisfied with that.

"But then came the other names. There were a few valentines for a few little boys—comic valentines, most of those, and you ought to have heard the children laugh! But most of them were for the little girls, and pretty soon it was the same names over and over again. 'Gertie' and 'Helen' and 'Fidelia,' and then 'Gertie' and 'Fidelia' and 'Helen' over again. Every time a name was called, up tripped the little girl to the desk, and back she came with her valentine. Pretty soon their desks were covered with white envelopes and bright pictures and paper lace. There was only one little desk that didn't have anything at all on it. All this time mother was listening—although she pretended not to—but the teacher never said 'Alice'!"

Betty's face was woebegone.

"At last the teacher came to the very bottom of the box. All the little heads were turning and waiting for the bell to ring. All the little girls were showing their valentines to each other. Every child in the room had one—even the little girl whose braids were tied with string and who lived on the other side of the railroad tracks. Every little girl but one—"

"Who?"

"You know who. Her heart was beating so queerly all this time. Her desk looked so empty that she took out her tablet and her books. She looked straight over all the heads and pretended not to see or hear anything. And then, just when it was time for the bell to ring, the teacher found the very last valentine and called 'Alice.'

"And then all the room stared while mother went up to the desk."

Betty gave a long, sobbing sigh. She settled back in her soft blankets. The mother hugged her tightly for a moment. Then her arms relaxed into a dreamy hold. Betty, struggling up a little shyly, saw the darkness in her eyes and a strange little smile on her lips. She burrowed her head against the warm shoulder, made little reminding sounds and movements. The mother

looked at her again, laid her cheek against the smooth head, and
the darkness in her eyes melted into tender brightness.

"I want to hear the rest of it, mother."

"But mother got her valentine. Isn't that the end?"

"No, I want to hear the rest of it."

"Well, then . . . "

She told it quickly, lightly, as if holding the story at a
distance from her, something careless and forgotten.

"Well, then, all the children in the room marched out with
their valentines. And as soon as they were out of the building
they began to talk about them. 'Who gave you this one?' and
'Who gave you that one?'—and Gertie said she had twenty-nine.
But they could all see that mother was carrying a valentine. She
walked like a proud, cool little girl and paid no attention to them
at all. They looked curious and respectful, as if they would like to
know her now, because it seemed that some one must like her
very much. You see, it was a very nice valentine. And when she
was going down the walk, that Gertie came up to her and said:

" 'Won't you let us see your valentine?'

"Mother took it out of the envelope. They all said it was very
nice. Fidelia said it was lovely. But mother, although she was
pleased, kept wanting to cry. And then Gertie said:

" 'Who gave it to you?'

"And mother said, 'I'm not going to tell.' And she marched
straight off home."

Betty was silent. Then she begged, "Is that *all* the story?"

"No, perhaps it isn't quite all. No, there was lots and lots
more to it than that."

The mother pinched and patted the little cheek. But there
was a tinge of bitterness in her voice. She smiled, too. She knew
what the little voice was pleading for.

"No, because when mother got home, she went up to her
room, and took the valentine out of the envelope again, and
looked at it. She knew that she was saved from being disgraced.
She knew that now Gertie and the other little girls were interested in her. They would ask her to play with them. But
somehow she didn't care so much about knowing them, after
this. It didn't seem so much to matter. She didn't care anything
about her valentine, and she went down and put it in the kitchen

stove, and when it was all burnt up, she got a book and read a story."

"Mother." The little voice was just a whisper. "Mother. Who gave you the valentine?"

"You know who gave it to me. Mother gave it to herself."

There was a sigh and a long silence. "And is *that* all?"

"Well—it's all of it as a story."

"But did the little girls play with you after that?"

"Oh, yes. They played with me."

"And *sometime* other people gave you valentines?"

"Lots of times. Oh, yes, indeed!" She hugged the little figure repentantly. "You mustn't feel sorry for mother after that."

"But why didn't *daddy* give you a valentine?"

"Because daddy didn't know mother then. And one year he did! She laughed. "An enormous big valentine, sent through the mail, in a box, not an envelope! A great, big valentine shaped like a banjo with golden strings. The biggest valentine he could buy!"

In silence Betty contemplated the splendor. She gave a sigh of satisfaction. Then her arms tightened again. Her voice breathed into her mother's ear.

"If *I'd* been there, *I'd* have given you a valentine. . . ."

SHARING YOUR IMPRESSIONS

1. Describe one of your own experiences with being a newcomer.
2. Speculate about the age of children as a factor in their adjustment to moving.
3. In what ways do the problems of belonging or adjusting in open classrooms differ from those in self-contained classrooms?
4. What suggestions do you have for teachers about how they can help students and faculty newcomers feel welcome?
5. In what ways can parents make the experience of moving less difficult for children?

6. When children are moved, is their most difficult adjustment to the other kids? The teacher? The curriculum? The
   neighborhood?
7. List some activities parents and teachers separately encourage that give children feelings of being left out instead of
   belonging.

4

SHOWIN' OFF

Stephen Crane

Jimmie Trescott's new velocipede had the largest front wheel of any velocipede in Whilomville. When it first arrived from New York he wished to sacrifice school, food, and sleep to it. Evidently he wished to become a sort of perpetual velocipede rider. But the powers of the family laid a number of judicious embargoes upon him, and he was prevented from becoming a fanatic. Of course this caused him to retain a fondness for the three-wheeled thing much longer than if he had been allowed to debauch himself for a span of days. But in the end it was an immaterial machine to him. For long periods he left it idle in the stable.

One day he loitered from school toward home by a very circuitous route. He was accompanied by only one of his retainers. The object of this détour was the wooing of a little girl in a red hood. He had been in love with her for some three weeks. His desk was near her desk in school, but he had never spoken to her. He had been afraid to take such a radical step. It was not customary to speak to girls. Even boys who had school-going sisters seldom addressed them during that part of the day which was devoted to education.

The reasons for this conduct were very plain. First, the more robust boys considered talking with girls an unmanly occupation; second, the greater part of the boys were afraid; third, they had no idea of what to say, because they esteemed the proper sentences should be supernaturally incisive and eloquent. In consequence, a small contingent of blue-eyed weaklings were the sole intimates of the frail sex, and for it they were boisterously and disdainfully called "girl-boys."

But this situation did not prevent serious and ardent wooing. For instance, Jimmie and the little girl who wore the red hood must have exchanged glances at least two hundred times in every school hour, and this exchange of glances accomplished everything. In them the two children renewed their curious inarticulate vows.

Jimmie had developed a devotion to school which was the admiration of his father and mother. In the mornings he was so impatient to have it made known to him that no misfortune had befallen his romance during the night that he was actually detected at times feverishly listening for the "first bell." Dr. Trescott was exceedingly complacent of the change, and as for Mrs. Trescott, she had ecstatic visions of a white-haired Jimmie leading the nations in knowledge, comprehending all from bugs to comets. It was merely the doing of the little girl in the red hood.

When Jimmie made up his mind to follow his sweetheart home from school, the project seemed such an arbitrary and shameless innovation that he hastily lied to himself about it. No, he was not following Abbie. He was merely making his way homeward through the new and rather longer route of Bryant Street and Oakland Park. It had nothing at all to do with a girl. It was a mere eccentric notion.

"Come on," said Jimmie, gruffly, to his retainer. "Let's go home this way."

"What fer?" demanded the retainer.

"Oh, b'cause."

"Huh?"

"Oh, it's more fun—goin' this way."

The retainer was bored and loath, but that mattered very little. He did not know how to disobey his chief. Together they followed the trail of red-hooded Abbie and another small girl.

These latter at once understood the object of the chase, and looking back giggling, they pretended to quicken their pace. But they were always looking back. Jimmie now began his courtship in earnest. The first thing to do was to prove his strength in battle. This was transacted by means of the retainer. He took that devoted boy and flung him heavily to the ground, meanwhile mouthing a preposterous ferocity.

The retainer accepted this behavior with a sort of bland resignation. After his overthrow he raised himself, coolly brushed some dust and dead leaves from his clothes, and then seemed to forget the incident.

"I can jump farther'n you can," said Jimmie, in a loud voice.

"I know it," responded the retainer, simply.

But this would not do. There must be a contest.

"Come on," shouted Jimmie, imperiously. "Let's see you jump."

The retainer selected a footing on the curb, balanced and calculated a moment, and jumped without enthusiasm. Jimmie's leap of course was longer.

"There!" he cried, blowing out his lips. "I beat you, didn't I? Easy. I beat you." He made a great hubbub, as if the affair was unprecedented.

"Yes," admitted the other, emotionless.

Later, Jimmie forced his retainer to run a race with him, held more jumping matches, flung him twice to earth, and generally behaved as if a retainer was indestructible. If the retainer had been in the plot, it is conceivable that he would have endured this treatment with mere whispered, half-laughing protests. But he was not in the plot at all, and so he became enigmatic. One cannot often sound the profound well in which lie the meanings of boyhood.

Following the two little girls, Jimmie eventually passed into that suburb of Whilomville which is called Oakland Park. At his heels came a badly battered retainer. Oakland Park was a somewhat strange country to the boys. They were dubious of the manners and customs, and of course they would have to meet the local chieftains, who might look askance upon this invasion.

Jimmie's girl departed into her home with a last backward glance that almost blinded the thrilling boy. On this pretext and

that pretext, he kept his retainer in play before the house. He
had hopes that she would emerge as soon as she had deposited
her schoolbag.

A boy came along the walk. Jimmie knew him at school. He
was Tommie Semple, one of the weaklings who made friends
with the fair sex. "Hello, Tom," said Jimmie. "You live round
here?"

"Yeh," said Tom, with composed pride. At school he was
afraid of Jimmie, but he did not evince any of this fear as he
strolled well inside his own frontiers. Jimmie and his retainer
had not expected this boy to display the manners of a minor chief,
and they contemplated him attentively. There was a silence.

Finally Jimmie said: "I can put you down." He moved
forward briskly. "Can't I?" he demanded.

The challenged boy backed away. "I know you can," he
declared, frankly and promptly.

The little girl in the red hood had come out with a hoop. She
looked at Jimmie with an air of insolent surprise in the fact that he
still existed, and began to trundle her hoop off toward some other
little girls who were shrilly playing near a nursemaid and a
perambulator.

Jimmie adroitly shifted his position until he too was playing
near the perambulator, pretentiously making mincemeat out of
his retainer and Tommie Semple.

Of course little Abbie had defined the meaning of Jimmie's
appearance in Oakland Park. Despite this nonchalance and
grand air of accident, nothing could have been more plain.
Whereupon she of course became insufferably vain in manner,
and whenever Jimmie came near her she tossed her head and
turned away her face, and daintily swished her skirts as if he were
contagion itself. But Jimmie was happy. His soul was satisfied
with the mere presence of the beloved object so long as he could
feel that she furtively gazed upon him from time to time and
noted his extraordinary prowess, which he was proving upon the
persons of his retainer and Tommie Semple. And he was making
an impression. There could be no doubt of it. He had many times
caught her eye fixed admiringly upon him as he mauled the
retainer. Indeed, all the little girls gave attention to his deeds,
and he was the hero of the hour.

Presently a boy on a velocipede was seen to be tooling down toward them. "Who's this comin'?" said Jimmie, bluntly, to the Semple boy.

"That's Horace Glenn," said Tommie, "an' he's got a new velocipede, an' he can ride it like anything."

"Can you lick him?" asked Jimmie.

"I don't—I never fought with 'im," answered the other. He bravely tried to appear as a man of respectable achievement, but with Horace coming toward them the risk was too great. However, he added, "*Maybe* I could."

The advent of Horace on his new velocipede created a sensation which he haughtily accepted as a familiar thing. Only Jimmie and his retainer remained silent and impassive. Horace eyed the two invaders.

"Hello, Jimmie!"

"Hello, Horace!"

After the typical silence Jimmie said, pompously, "I got a velocipede."

"Have you?" asked Horace, anxiously. He did not wish anybody in the world but himself to possess a velocipede.

"Yes," sang Jimmie. "An' it's a bigger one than that, too! A good deal bigger! An' it's a better one, too!"

"Huh!" retorted Horace, sceptically.

"'Ain't I, Clarence? 'Ain't I? 'Ain't I got one bigger'n that?"

The retainer answered with alacrity: "Yes, he has! A good deal bigger! An' it's a dandy, too!"

This corroboration rather disconcerted Horace, but he continued to scoff at any statement that Jimmie also owned a velocipede. As for the contention that this supposed velocipede could be larger than his own, he simply wouldn't hear of it.

Jimmie had been a very gallant figure before the coming of Horace, but the new velocipede had relegated him to a squalid secondary position. So he affected to look with contempt upon it. Voluminously he bragged of the velocipede in the stable at home. He painted its virtues and beauty in loud and extravagant words, flaming words. And the retainer stood by, glibly endorsing everything.

The little company heeded him, and he passed on vociferously from extravagance to utter impossibility. Horace was very sick of it. His defense was reduced to a mere mechanical grumbling: "Don't believe you got one 'tall. Don't believe you got one 'tall."

Jimmie turned upon him suddenly. "How fast can you go? How fast can you go?" he demanded. "Let's see. I bet you can't go fast."

Horace lifted his spirits and answered with proper defiance. "Can't I?" he mocked. "Can't I?"

"No, you can't," said Jimmie. "You can't go fast."

Horace cried: "Well, you see me now! I'll show you! I'll show you if I can't go fast!" Taking a firm seat on his vermilion machine, he pedaled furiously up the walk, turned, and pedaled back again. "There, now!" he shouted, triumphantly. "Ain't that fast? There, now!" There was a low murmur of appreciation from the little girls. Jimmie saw with pain that even his divinity was smiling upon his rival. "There! Ain't that fast? Ain't that fast?" He strove to pin Jimmie down to an admission. He was exuberant with victory.

Notwithstanding a feeling of discomfiture, Jimmie did not lose a moment of time. "Why," he yelled, "that ain't goin' fast 'tall! That ain't goin' fast 'tall! Why, I can go almost *twice* as fast as that! Almost *twice* as fast! Can't I, Clarence?"

The loyal retainer nodded solemnly at the wide-eyed group. "Course you can!"

"Why," spouted Jimmie, "you just ought to see me ride once! You just ought to see me! Why, I can go like the wind! Can't I, Clarence? And I can ride far, too—oh, awful far! Can't I, Clarence? Why, I wouldn't have that one! 'Tain't any good! You just ought to see mine once!"

The overwhelmed Horace attempted to reconstruct his battered glories. "I can ride right over the curbstone—at some of the crossin's," he announced, brightly.

Jimmie's derision was a splendid sight. " '*Right over the curbstone*'! Why, that wouldn't be *nothin'* for me to do! I've rode mine down Bridge Street Hill. Yessir! 'Ain't I, Clarence? Why, it ain't nothin' to ride over a curbstone—not for *me!* Is it, Clarence?"

"Down Bridge Street Hill? You never!" said Horace, hopelessly.

"Well, didn't I, Clarence? Didn't I, now?"

The faithful retainer again nodded solemnly at the assemblage.

At last Horace, having fallen as low as was possible, began to display a spirit for climbing up again. "Oh, you can do wonders!" he said laughing. "You can do wonders! I s'pose you could ride down that bank there?" he asked, with art. He had indicated a grassy terrace some six feet in height which bounded one side of the walk. At the bottom was a small ravine in which the reckless had flung ashes and tins. "I s'pose you could ride down that bank?"

All eyes now turned upon Jimmie to detect a sign of his weakening, but he instantly and sublimely arose to the occasion. "That bank?" he asked, scornfully. "Why, I've ridden down banks like that many a time. 'Ain't I, Clarence?"

This was too much for the company. A sound like the wind in the leaves arose; it was the song of incredulity and ridicule. "O—o—o—o—o!" And on the outskirts a little girl suddenly shrieked out, "Storyteller!"

Horace had certainly won a skirmish. He was gleeful. "Oh, you can do wonders!" he gurgled. "You can do wonders!" The neighborhood's superficial hostility to foreigners arose like magic under the influence of his sudden success, and Horace had the delight of seeing Jimmie persecuted in that manner known only to children and insects.

Jimmie called angrily to the boy on the velocipede, "If you'll lend me yours, I'll show you whether I can or not."

Horace turned his superior nose in the air. "Oh no! I don't ever lend it." Then he thought of a blow which would make Jimmie's humiliation complete. "Besides," he said, airily, " 'tain't really anything hard to do. I could do it—easy—if I wanted to."

But his supposed adherents, instead of receiving this boast with cheers, looked upon him in a sudden blank silence. Jimmie and his retainer pounced like cats upon their advantage.

"Oh," they yelled, "you *could*, eh? Well, let's see you do it, then! Let's see you do it! Let's see you do it! Now!" In a moment the crew of little spectators were gibing at Horace.

The blow that would make Jimmie's humiliation complete!

Instead, it had boomeranged Horace into the mud. He kept up a sullen muttering: " 'Tain't really anything! I could if I wanted to!"

"Dare you to!" screeched Jimmie and his partisans. "Dare you to! Dare you to! Dare you to!"

There were two things to be done—to make gallant effort or to retreat. Somewhat to their amazement, the children at last found Horace moving through their clamor to the edge of the bank. Sitting on the velocipede, he looked at the ravine, and then, with gloomy pride, at the other children. A hush came upon them, for it was seen that he was intending to make some kind of ante-mortem statement.

"I—" he began. Then he vanished from the edge of the walk. The start had been unintentional—an accident.

The stupefied Jimmie saw the calamity through a haze. His first clear vision was when Horace, with a face as red as a red flag, arose bawling from his tangled velocipede. He and his retainer exchanged a glance of horror and fled the neighborhood. They did not look back until they had reached the top of the hill near the lake. They could see Horace walking slowly under the maples toward his home, pushing his shattered velocipede before him. His chin was thrown high, and the breeze bore them the sound of his howls.

SHARING YOUR IMPRESSIONS

1. Describe your personal experience with show-offs.
2. Identify some ways in which parents and teachers encourage showing off.
3. How do boys and girls differ with respect to showing off?
4. At what age do you suppose bragging ought to be discontinued?
5. In what ways other than brute force can children meet their needs for recognition and power?
6. How do you feel about the play space available for your child or students?
7. Make some guesses about how a crowded home or neighborhood can affect child play and development.

2

PLAY
AND
CREATIVE
BEHAVIOR

5

THE GOSSAMER WORLD

Faith Baldwin

Pete was a farmer. He was the busiest farmer in eleven counties and the most absorbed. He had been a farmer only since after breakfast when, escaping from the house with Mr. Pettigrew at his heels, he had looked over the property with a calculating eye and decided upon the acreage north of the first big apple tree.

He had his implements with him: a small shovel, a tin pail, a twisted spoon and a fork with bent tines. He wore his faded blue jeans.

He looked, weather-wise, at the sky. It was flawless, the blue of early May. On the horizon a woolly lamb of a cloud. He said quietly to Mr. Pettigrew, "It'll rain before night."

Mr. Pettigrew barked.

"Well," said Pete firmly, "let's get going."

Mr. Pettigrew lay down and watched. He wondered if Pete had buried a bone? All that digging and scratching. It was, Mr. Pettigrew thought, yawning, singularly unproductive.

A pretty girl came rattling down the road in an ancient car. She had bright red curls. She swung into the short turn and stopped between the house and the garage. Mr. Pettigrew lolloped forth to meet her. Her arms were full of packages. She said, "Oof, Mr. Pettigrew, I wish you were as helpful as you are affectionate," and went into the house calling, "Anna—I'm home."

Anna padded out of the kitchen. She took the packages and said, glumly, "I forgot to say, butter. Well, we'll make do. Only, unless you want to go back to the Corners, no cupcakes."

"I'll go back," said Marjorie. "It's a lovely day. Where's Pete?"

"Haven't laid eyes on him since breakfast."

Marjorie strolled out of the house. Mr. Pettigrew loped along beside her and she perceived, under an apple tree, the blue-jeaned figure of her son.

"Hi," she said cheerfully.

"Hi," said Pete.

He had dug up a small space around him and was slowly and carefully drawing the fork through the resistant earth.

"What are you doing?" Marjorie inquired.

"Farmin'," Pete replied briefly.

"I see. What are you going to plant?"

She sat down beside him on her heels and watched. After a moment he answered, "Oh, corn and potatoes and flour and strawberries and celery and things."

"Pete—"

"I'm Mr. Palmer."

Mr. Palmer was the farmer up the road. Marjorie nodded. "Mr. Palmer—want to go the Corners with me? I forgot the butter."

"Busy," said Pete.

She looked at him with love and in wonder. He was five, going on six. He was small, slight, sturdy. His blond hair glinted in the sun, his eyes were bluer than blue. There were beads of sweat on his upper lip. His face and hands were very dirty.

Mr. Pettigrew flushed something in the adjacent bushes and ran around in circles, barking wildly. Pete dug and scratched. He looked at his mother and said, for he was a polite little boy, "Excuse me a minute."

He rose and went off. Mr. Pettigrew stopped barking to follow. Marjorie remained where she was, looking up through the rosy mass of apple blossoms to the blue sky. She was, perhaps, the luckiest woman in the world.

Mr. Pettigrew's barking aroused her from her almost mindless awareness of gratitude. She did not consciously say to herself, now or at any time, I am Marjorie, twenty-seven years old and healthy as a clam. I have Dan, with whom after seven years of marriage I am still romantically in love. We have Pete, belonging to us both and to himself. We'll have another baby. We have this house and eight acres of land. We have enough money to see us through illness or disaster, to take care of our daily needs. We have Anna in the kitchen and Mr. Pettigrew underfoot. We have friends we love and, even, relatives. We are wonderful, we are a family.

She rose and went toward the front of the house. There was Pete where he was expressly forbidden to be, right in the middle of the narrow twisting road, sitting down, his pail and shovel beside him.

Marjorie cried, "Pete—get up from there this minute, come *here* to me."

Pete got up. He looked up the road and down. He said, "Nothing coming."

Marjorie said, "Will you come here, Pete Watkins?"

"Mr. Palmer," corrected Pete.

She could shake him until his teeth fell out. She heard a sound around the road's bend, saw some drifting dust . . . "Pete," she cried, ran to the picket fence.

Pete picked up his pail and shovel and walked without haste. "There's lots of time."

Now he was inside the fence. She said, "How many times have I told you—?"

"Lots," said Pete. He looked at her frowning with intensity. "But," he explained, "a horse had passed by."

"Horse?" she repeated, puzzled, for he had given up being Gene Autry some time ago.

Pete was patient with her. He displayed the pail. "Manure," he said, "for the crops." He smiled suddenly, sweetly, and was gone, off to the apple tree to fertilize his field.

That evening, scrubbed, brushed and polished, he rode to the station with Marjorie to meet Dan. The train came chugging in and Pete was the engineer. He controlled the huffing and the puffing, he drove the engine through darkness and light, he was a great man, the engineer. Pete knew him; his name was Smith . . .

Maybe, he thought, I'm Mr. Smith.

Dan swung himself off the train. He was an average young man of thirty who did not appear average to his wife, his child or his parents. He worked in an office and would have a raise next year. He painted in his spare time. Some day he might have enough money to chuck his job for a year or two, during which time he would study and travel and paint, with of course Marjorie and Pete—next year, or the year after, or in ten years. A man can dream, can't he?

Meantime he liked his job.

"Hi, kids," he said, got in with them and kissed his wife's round cheek, which had mysteriously preserved its childlike heartbreaking curve. He clapped his son on the shoulder, feeling, with a pang of pure devotion, the bird bones, the smooth and meager flesh. "Well, Pete, how's tricks?"

"He's Mr. Palmer," said Marjorie.

"That so?" asked Dan. He inquired further, "How's crops?"

Pete sighed a little. He came close to his father's side, breathing with content the aura of masculinity, the strength and the wisdom. He said, "Maybe I'm Mr. Smith."

"Okay," Dan said, "so you're Mr. Smith."

All the way home Pete drove the engine.

After Pete's supper, after Marjorie had put him to bed in the corner room with the windows looking out to the apple trees and the distant hill, she and Dan had their dinner. The dining-room was small and Anna was big but she moved deftly around the table. All their friends envied them Anna. She had come to them shortly after their marriage; she had stayed, a big silent woman, with a mind of her own and a light hand with a cake.

It was still light afterward and Marjorie and Dan went walking. The earth upon which they trod was theirs. The house was theirs. It was not unusual, a square late Victorian farmhouse which needed paint. But it was their own.

"What's that?" asked Dan, regarding a little patch of earth, turned over, scratched, wet and obviously manured.

"Pete's farm," said Marjorie. "He's been Mr. Palmer all day."

The smallest farm in the world; you could kneel and put your arms around it.

She said, "He got the manure from the road, he lugged water from the house, pail after pail. And I thought I'd *never* get him clean!"

"What's he planted?"

"I don't know. He found some seeds in the garage. Lord knows what."

He put his arm around her and she leaned against him with contentment.

"Sometimes I worry about Pete," said Marjorie.

"Why?"

"He should have kids to play with—"

But there were none living on the dipping road; none of his age.

He said comfortably, "He'll have companionship next fall when he starts to school."

Marjorie sighed. She asked, "What will it be like, having him away all day too?"

Dan said, "Cheer up: in a manner of speaking, he's away all day as it is."

"Do you suppose all children are as imaginative? Sometimes it troubles me."

"Weren't you?" he asked.

"I can't remember."

"Neither can I," Dan admitted.

"Your mother," said Marjorie, "told me once that for a long time you had an imaginary dog. You used to take him walking. He was small, so you lifted him at the crossings. She said she would stand for minutes while you waited for him—at, for instance, hydrants."

"I hadn't thought of that for years," he said. "What *was* his name, now?" He thought hard. "Downy," he said in triumph.

She asked curiously, "When did you lose him?"

"I don't know . . ."

They walked back toward the house. Marjorie said suddenly, "I grew up in a houseful of sisters and brothers but I had a pretend-sister, as well."

"Good Lord, with four of flesh and blood?"

"I know. But I was the youngest. This one was a baby," she said, smiling in the darkness, "a baby who rarely cried. Dolls were stupid and predictable but Polly wasn't."

"Was that her name?"

"Yes. Before Pete was born I thought, if it's a girl, I'll call her Polly."

"Are you still of the same mind . . . if it's a girl?" he asked, laughing.

The awareness of another child was still very new. This would be a Christmas baby.

She said, "I suppose not. Maybe I'll let Pete name her. It's Dan if it's a boy, of course. I'll have to tell Pete soon."

"He won't notice anything for a long time."

"I know; but he'll want to know," she said earnestly.

During the summer Pete was Mr. Peters, the plumber, and Mr. Hannigan, the well driller. As Mr. Peters he spent a good deal of time in the bathroom and cellar but as Mr. Hannigan he worked outdoors. He drilled a deep well by the garage, making, as he worked, a steady grinding noise in his throat.

On very hot nights he was allowed to stay up and have supper with them on the screened porch. He reported one night, "Three hundred and fifty feet." He gravely warned his father, "Goin' to cost a lot of money."

"How much money, Mr. Hannigan?"

"Can't say. Might strike water tomorrow, might be next week. Better'n a cent a foot," said Pete.

Up the road the Carlsons were drilling a well and Pete, going the field way, had spent some time with Mr. Hannigan. Evidently someone had got his figures mixed.

"Our old well's pretty good," said Dan cautiously.

"Might not hold out," said Pete. He pushed a nonexistent cap back on his head and scratched thoughtfully. "It's a hell of a lot of work and you never know when you'll hit a vein," he added.

Marjorie grinned and then compressed her lips. Dan cleared his throat. Pete lived his role. But when he ceased to be Mr. Hannigan, he would also cease to bring hell into the conversation.

Pete was a singularly even-tempered little boy. He was amiable and as a rule obedient. But he had abundant spirit and he could argue the hind leg off an army mule. His parents gave him little trouble. They were slow and ponderous in their thinking, as befitted larger people, but generally they caught up with him. He didn't have to explain things more than twice. But the children he encountered, especially those older than himself, were difficult.

His cousins came to stay a week end; a boy and girl, nine and eleven, the children of his mother's sister. He did not especially like them. That week, having struck water at three hundred and sixty-two feet, his task was accomplished and he was himself, not Mr. Hannigan. But Mr. Pettigrew was a zebra. Pete had seen pictures of zebras and Marjorie had read him the text beneath the photographs. So Mr. Pettigrew became a zebra and was astonished to find Pete stalking him noiselessly over the African plains.

"What the heck you doing?" inquired his cousin, Charles.

"After a zebra," said Pete. He halted, holding his breath, "See?"

"That," said Charles, "is Mr. Pettigrew—silly name for a dog. Want to play catch?"

"No," said Pete.

"Okay," said Charles carelessly, "you're too little, anyway."

Pete threw a stone at him and connected. Charles yelped. A trickle of blood slid down one brown cheek.

"Why," inquired Marjorie, putting Pete to bed early and after a rationed supper, "why did you do it?"

Pete spoke with unusual anger. He said, "Mr. Pettigrew is a zebra."

She was conscious of delicate danger. She said gently, "Pete darling, Mr. Pettigrew's a zebra only for you. Don't you understand that? For Charles he's a cocker spaniel."

"I don't like Charles."

"But you can't throw stones at him just because he doesn't see things your way. Suppose I threw things at Aunt Laura."

Pete sat up in bed. He giggled. "You can't throw. You wouldn't hit her, ever."

"Suppose I tried? You'd be ashamed of me, wouldn't you? My own sister, in our house . . . just because we don't think alike."

"Don't you?" Pete asked, interested.

"Not always. But we don't throw things. We just let each other think as she pleases."

"What kind of thinks?"

"Well," said Marjorie, trying to reduce it to simple terms, "Aunt Laura likes to live in the city; I like to live in the country. And when it comes to politics . . ."

"What's politics?"

She gave up and drew the sheet over him. He kicked it off. "Tomorrow, before Charles leaves I wish you'd ask him to excuse you."

"For what?"

"For hitting him with the stone. It wasn't a friendly thing to do. And it was dangerous. You might have injured him seriously."

"I meant to," said Pete.

Children were another race, cruel and kind, generous and withholding. Marjorie went downstairs. Charles, a bit of adhesive on his cheek, was playing checkers with Dan. Feeling mendacious, she said, "Pete's sorry, Charles."

"He is not," said Charles from his own fount of wisdom.

"Oh, don't *fuss*," said her sister Laura. "I'm sure he didn't mean it."

"He did too," Charles contradicted. "And he's too little to fight with . . . worse luck."

Dan said equably, "Look, Charles, Pete lives in his own world. Maybe you did too at his age. In that world Mr. Pettigrew is a zebra. You could have pretended."

Laura looked up, a little sharply.

"Heck," said Charles, "what a silly game. Who wants to pretend?"

"You do," his older sister, Harriet, said smugly. "You pretend you're Mickey Mantle!"

"That's different," said Charles hotly, "and what about you and that dumb game you're always playing . . . movie stars?" He mimicked in a deep sultry voice. " 'Got a match?' "

"Oh," said Laura, "for goodness' sakes hush up, you two."

She turned to her sister. "At his age Charles is taken up with baseball and of course at her age Harriet thinks only of the movies," she said.

"Well?" said Dan in quiet triumph.

His sister-in-law shrugged. She said, "But that's quite normal, Dan . . . after all, baseball players and movie stars are *real!*"

"Zebras are real," said Dan and returned to his paper.

"He's as bad as Pete." Laura laughed. "I don't know why we're arguing. Pete will outgrow it, they'll all outgrow it."

"Maybe not always," said Marjorie, closing her eyes. She felt a little tired, somewhat dispirited. "Writers and artists find their imagination again. At the right time they grow back into it."

"Well," said Laura briskly, "don't count on a genius in the family."

"I don't." She added, a little astonished at herself, "I don't know what I'd want him to be. Geniuses must be very uncomfortable."

"To live with at any rate," Dan agreed, "or so I've heard."

Laura remarked, yawning, "Mercy, how *noisy* the country is at night. . . . Of course Pete's a bright little boy, being so much with older people."

"He's a dope," said Charles with shattering frankness. "He gives me a pain in the neck."

"Don't start *that* again," said Laura wearily. "After all, Pete's only a baby."

"Him and his zebras!" said Charles.

In August Marjorie went to bed and the doctor came every day. It wasn't exactly touch and go but she had to be quiet. Anna toiled up and down with trays, Dan took his vacation and prowled about uneasily, sitting and staring at her or asking in a husband tone, "Is there anything I can do for you?"

"Yes," she said finally, "you can amuse yourself. Get Bill to golf with you—he's always asking you to play. Or take Pete on a picnic. This is a miserable vacation for you."

"It's all right for me," he said, "as long as I'm near you . . . and Pete's busy."

"What now?"

"He's Dr. Alden."

"Yes, I know. He came up this morning, took my pulse and listened to my chest." She laughed, knowing she would soon be up and around again, going about her secret important business. "But what's he doing now?"

"He's off on calls," said Dan.

Marjorie was up before Dan's vacation ended and they had three days together, going slowly and carefully in the car to a place in the hills and staying there, alone. Pete was all right with Anna; they had left him with her before, if not often.

When they came back Anna made her report: Pete was fine. He had eaten well and gone to bed at his usual time. He'd had a little poison ivy on one finger but it hadn't spread. Mr. Pettigrew had been sick, something he ate. All right now. "The only thing," said Anna, "is the meals . . . setting the extra place and all . . . I don't like to waste food, I bring in as little as I can . . ."

"What place, what food?" asked Marjorie.

"Pete's new friend."

"New friend? Oh," cried Marjorie, "have people with children moved into the Newcombe place? I knew it was sold but I thought no one was moving in until autumn. How wonderful! But you shouldn't skimp, Anna," she said, "there's always enough."

Anna interrupted, "No one's moved into Newcombe's, ma'am. It's just another one of those . . ."

Pete explained, presently, as he looked down at his friend, who was very small, very clever and agile. His name was Distinction. Shun, for short.

"Oh *no*," said Marjorie privately to her huband. "And where did he get that?"

Shun's place was set at meals and the minute portions brought in. Pete was confident that Shun would be received as he received him. He talked to Shun at meals, argued and discussed projects with him. The rest of the summer he remained himself, for now he had a companion. Marjorie found it tiring at times.

"I didn't do it," he said, "Shun did."

"Pete, you *know* that isn't so."

"He was carrying the plate with the doughnuts," said Pete. "I didn't want him to. I said, 'You're too little.' But he's stubborn," Pete went on, using a word he had heard to describe himself, "and he carried it and somehow it dropped."

Shun was not the most lovable of guests. He was the whipping boy for Pete's forgetfulness, his tardiness, his every shortcoming. "I wanted to come, I did start but Shun was off somewhere; I had to find him . . ."

Marjorie said impatiently to Dan, "He can't grow up a buck passer, I won't have it. We'll have to put an end to Shun."

"I believe you dislike him."

"I'm beginning to. He scares me a little. Not just that Pete won't take the blame for anything, but because he's fond of him. . . . Good heavens, we talk as if he *existed!*"

"He'll unexist," prophesied Dan. "Suppose I have a talk with his dreamer-upper."

He took Pete aside and spoke to him, long and gravely. He ended, "It isn't like you not to take the blame for things you've done, Pete. I don't like it."

"But I don't," Pete began uneasily.

"Are you sure?"

Pete's eyes were remote. He said, "Shun does things."

"He's much smaller than you are," Dan reminded, "and younger. He hasn't the sense you have. So, in a way, if he does things you'd like to do but know you mustn't, aren't you to blame for letting him?"

Pete thought that over. After a while he said cautiously, "Maybe I am." He squared his shoulders, sharp and winglike. He said, "I'll have a talk with him, I guess."

Dan had heard that one before. He kept his mouth steady.

Shun behaved. In fact, he got all the credit. Pete, coming in with asters, cried, "Shun picked these." Pete, carrying packages, said, "Shun can't, they're too heavy, so he told me to."

"Some alter ego," commented Dan. "Wonder how he'll do in school?"

For Pete and Shun were preparing to go to school, getting their things together, pencil boxes and bits of paper. Pete and Shun talked it over, nights, with Mr. Pettigrew lying between them. What would school be like? Oh, they'd seen the building, of course, and the children at recess. They'd seen the children, in cars and on bikes, and in the bus, going and coming; but what was it *like?*

The very last week Pete forgot himself. He was Mr. Buzzini, the contractor who was doing over the Newcombe place. Shun was his helper. They spent considerable time, keeping out of Mr. Buzzini's way and watching, contemplating the erection of an office building on the far lot—so that Pete's father wouldn't have to go so far to work.

When school began they were to go by bus. This had long been argued in the family. Pete, who had never ridden on a bus, was insistent. Marjorie wanted to take him to school and bring him back in the car.

Dan decided. Pete was better off going by bus with the other children; he'd be more on his own. Also, later, Marjorie wouldn't be able to take him; it might turn stormy before Christmas; and afterward she couldn't, with a baby to look after.

It was time Pete heard about that baby.

Marjorie told him, a day or so before school opened. "And maybe by Christmas," she said, "when you hang up your stocking, maybe there'll be another stocking to hang . . ."

"Sure," said Pete. "Shun's."

"Yes, of course; but still another. You're going to have a brother or a sister. Will you like that, darling?"

"I don't need no one; not with Shun."

"I know. But this one will be different."

"How big?"

"At first, very small. A baby."

"A baby?" He lay and contemplated that with Mr. Pettigrew's ear trailing across his hand. "They yell."

"They have to, to get strong lungs."

"Your baby? Pop's?"

"Of course."

"Like I was, once?"

"You still are," she said lovingly.

"I'm not a baby." He stretched his growing legs, the ankles scarred with old bites and scratches. After a while he said, "I won't really mind if you don't."

"I won't. We'll none of us mind." She leaned to kiss him. "Good night, Pete."

"Mr. Buzzini," said Pete.

She watched him go off to school with the lunch box, the pads and pencil boxes, and saw that he walked slowly to the bus, not because he was afraid but because Shun's pace was slower, being so small. Yet her eyes were not seeing very well this morning. The bus was crowded with starched scrubbed children. Pete waved, a quick flip of his hand, which had once been very fat and creased and dimpled and was no longer. His haircut was very short, the nape of his neck hollowed and thin, and defenseless.

The bus drove off down the winding road.

Her neighbor, Mrs. Radford, who had a child in the bus and two in high school, came to stand at the picket fence. She said, "Well, Pete's first day at school. . . . I know how you feel, I don't get over it."

"It's silly," said Marjorie.

"No. You're always seeing children off somewhere, I suppose—grade school, high school, college; you see them off on wedding trips." She was silent. Her oldest son had gone to war. He had not come back. Her youngest had gone today, for the first time, to school.

She added, "You're always waiting, I guess: to bear a child, to wait until he comes home from somewhere . . ."

Pete came home that afternoon. He tumbled out of the bus and raced to the house. Marjorie went to meet him. She knelt down and put her arms around him. "How was it?"

"All right, I guess." He snorted. "The woman's silly."

"What woman?"

"The teacher. She keeps asking questions."

"That's what she's there for. You'll learn the answers."

Mr. Pettigrew came tearing out of the kitchen door, beside himself with welcome.

Marjorie asked, "How did Shun like school?"

"He didn't like it," said Pete, "they kept saying shush."

"You mustn't talk in class," she began.

But he was off, running to the back door, asking Anna, were there cookies? Could he have some milk?

Dan came home to find them waiting for him at the station. How was school, he wanted to know. It was silly, said Pete firmly. He guessed he wouldn't go back.

"Why not, Mr. Buzzini?"

Pete hooted with laughter. He said, "I'm not Mr. Buzzini. I'm Peter Watkins."

"Is that so?" said his father, astonished.

A week or two later Pete slid into his place at supper. Now he ate supper with his parents, unless they had guests and it became dinner, served at a later hour. He looked at the empty chair beside him and at the butter plate, with its tiny portion, which Anna set down. He asked, "What's that for?"

Anna looked at Marjorie and Marjorie looked at Dan.

"That's for Shun," said Dan, "or isn't he dining at home tonight?"

A flash of delight crossed Pete's face, luminous, revealing, secret with laughter and understanding. Then it was gone. He said, "Oh, that silly game. I don't play it any more." His face was alight again but differently. He asked, "Can I bring Jim home some afternoon, can I?"

"Who's Jim?" Marjorie inquired.

"He sits next to me," said Pete. "He lives in the Hollow. Can I bring him—"

· "Of course," said his mother. "What's his last name?"

"I dunno. At recess we played catch." He shoved his chair back and exposed a dingy knee. "I fell down," he said proudly.

Mr. Pettigrew barked outside.

"Jim's got a dog," said Pete. "He's a terrier, he catches rats and everything."

Anna took away the empty chair and carried off the little plate. Without sorrow Pete watched them go but his thoughts were elsewhere.

One of the pack now, eager to run with it, careful to conform.

Dan looked at Marjorie. He was not surprised to see that her eyes were full of tears. She thought, you're always watching them go away . . .

Gone the gossamer world. Whether it would ever return, she did not know.

Dan shook his head at her slightly. He spoke to her with his eyes: It doesn't matter, they have to outgrow things, don't they? Their swaddling clothes and their rompers, their dreams and their little world?

"Mom," said Pete, "can I have some more spinach?"

"Spinach?" cried Marjorie, shocked to the core. "But you hate it. You don't even like Popeye!"

"Oh, him," said Pete carelessly. "But Jim says spinach gives you muscles."

At her table the schoolboy wolfing his despised spinach; under her heart the sheltered infant, waiting his world.

And Dan said, smiling, "After supper, Pete, if there's a little light left I'll show you how to catch."

SHARING YOUR IMPRESSIONS

1. Give some reasons why you occasionally feel the need to be alone.
2. As a child, when were the times you played alone?
3. How do you feel when your child or student prefers to play alone instead of with others?
4. What do you suppose are the benefits of solitary play for children?
5. What are some materials that are appropriate for the solitary play of preschoolers? Elementary school children? Teenagers?
6. How can solitary-play time be integrated into the day-care and preschool facilities where some children spend most of their time?
7. "Some children classed as having learning disabilities or as 'problem children' are only normal children suffering from the need to spend some time alone." Give your reasons for agreeing or disagreeing with this assertion.

6

THE TOYS OF PEACE

H. H. Munro

"Harvey," said Eleanor Bope, handing her brother a cutting from a London morning paper of the 19th of March, "just read this about children's toys, please; it exactly carries out some of our ideas about influence and up-bringing."

"In the view of the National Peace Council," ran the extract, "there are grave objections to presenting our boys with regiments of fighting men, batteries of guns, and squadrons of 'Dreadnoughts.' Boys, the Council admits, naturally love fighting and all the panoply of war . . . but that is no reason for encouraging, and perhaps giving permanent form to, their primitive instincts. At the Children's Welfare Exhibition, which opens at Olympia in three weeks' time, the Peace Council will make an alternative suggestion to parents in the shape of an exhibition of 'peace toys.' In front of a specially pointed representation of the Peace Palace at The Hague will be grouped, not miniature soldiers but miniature civilians, not guns but ploughs and the tools of industry . . . It is hoped that manufacturers may take a hint from the exhibit, which will bear fruit in the toy shops."

"The idea is certainly an interesting and very well-meaning

one," said Harvey; "whether it would succeed well in practice—"

"We must try," interrupted his sister; "you are coming down to us at Easter, and you always bring the boys some toys, that will be an excellent opportunity for you to inaugurate the new experiment. Go about in the shops and buy any little toys and models that have special bearing on civilian life in its more peaceful aspects. Of course you must explain the toys to the children and interest them in the new idea. I regret to say that the 'Siege of Adrianople' toy, that their Aunt Susan sent them, didn't need any explanation; they knew all the uniforms and flags, and even the names of the respective commanders, and when I heard them one day using what seemed to be the most objectionable language they said it was Bulgarian words of command; of course it may have been, but at any rate I took the toy away from them. Now I shall expect your Easter gifts to give quite a new impulse and direction in the children's minds; Eric is not eleven yet, and Bertie is only nine-and-a-half, so they are really at a most impressionable age."

"There is primitive instinct to be taken into consideration, you know," said Harvey doubtfully, "and hereditary tendencies as well. One of their great-uncles fought in the most intolerant fashion at Inkerman—he was specially mentioned in dispatches, I believe—and their great-grandfather smashed all his Whig neighbours' hothouses when the great Reform Bill was passed. Still, as you say, they are at an impressionable age. I will do my best."

On Easter Saturday Harvey Bope unpacked a large, promising-looking red cardboard box under the expectant eyes of his nephew. "Your uncle has brought you the newest thing in toys," Eleanor had said impressively, and youthful anticipation had been anxiously divided between Albanian soldiery and a Somali camel-corps. Eric was hotly in favour of the latter contingency. "There would be Arabs on horseback," he whispered; "the Albanians have got jolly uniforms, and they fight all day long, and all night too, when there's a moon, but the country's rocky, so they've got no cavalry."

A quantity of crinkly paper shavings was the first thing that met the view when the lid was removed; the most exciting toys always began like that. Harvey pushed back the top layer and drew forth a square, rather featureless building.

"It's a fort!" exclaimed Bertie.

"It isn't, it's the palace of the Mpret of Albania," said Eric, immensely proud of his knowledge of the exotic title; "it's got no windows, you see, so that passers-by can't fire in at the Royal Family."

"It's a municipal dust-bin," said Harvey hurriedly; "you see all the refuse and litter of a town is collected there, instead of lying about and injuring the health of the citizens." In an awful silence he disinterred a little lead figure of a man in black clothes.

"That," he said, "is a distinguished civilian, John Stuart Mill. He was an authority on political economy."

"Why?" asked Bertie.

"Well, he wanted to be; he thought it was a useful thing to be."

Bertie gave an expressive grunt, which conveyed his opinion that there was no accounting for tastes.

Another square building came out, this time with windows and chimneys.

"A model of the Manchester branch of the Young Women's Christian Association," said Harvey.

"Are there any lions?" asked Eric hopefully. He had been reading Roman history and thought that where you found Christians you might reasonably expect to find a few lions.

"There are no lions," said Harvey. "Here is another civilian, Robert Raikes, the founder of Sunday schools, and here is a model of a municipal wash-house. These little round things are loaves baked in a sanitary bake-house. That lead figure is a sanitary inspector, this one is a district councillor, and this one is an official of the Local Government Board."

"What does he do?" asked Eric wearily.

"He sees to things connected with his Department," said Harvey. "This box with a slit in it is a ballot-box. Votes are put into it at election times."

"What is put into it at other times?" asked Bertie.

"Nothing. And here are some tools of industry, a wheelbarrow and a hoe, and I think these are meant for hop-poles. This is a model beehive, and that is a ventilator, for ventilating sewers. This seems to be another municipal dust-bin—no, this is a model of a school of art and public library. This little lead figure is Mrs. Hemans, a poetess, and this is Rowland Hill, who introduced the system of penny postage. This is Sir John Herschel, the eminent astrologer."

"Are we to play with these civilian figures?" asked Eric.

"Of course," said Harvey, "these are toys; they are meant to be played with."

"But how?"

It was rather a poser. "You might make two of them contest a seat in Parliament," said Harvey, "and have an election—"

"With rotten eggs, and free fights, and ever so many broken heads!" exclaimed Eric.

"And noses all bleeding and everybody drunk as can be," echoed Bertie, who had carefully studied one of Hogarth's pictures.

"Nothing of the kind," said Harvey, "nothing in the least like that. Votes will be put in the ballot-box, and the Mayor will count them—the district councillor will do for the Mayor—and he will say which has received the most votes, and then the two candidates will thank him for presiding, and each will say that the contest has been conducted throughout in the pleasantest and most straightforward fashion, and they part with expressions of mutual esteem. There's a jolly game for you boys to play. I never had such toys when I was young."

"I don't think we'll play with them just now," said Eric, with an entire absence of the enthusiasm that his uncle had shown; "I think perhaps we ought to do a little of our holiday task. It's history this time; we've got to learn up something about the Bourbon period in France."

"The Bourbon period," said Harvey, with some disapproval in his voice.

"We've got to know something about Louis the Fourteenth," continued Eric; "I've learnt the names of all the principal battles already."

This would never do. "There were, of course, some battles fought during his reign," said Harvey, "but I fancy the accounts of them were much exaggerated; news was very unreliable in those days, and there were practically no war correspondents, so

generals and commanders could magnify every little skirmish
they engaged in till they reached the proportions of decisive
battles. Louis was really famous, now, as a landscape gardener;
the way he laid out Versailles was so much admired that it was
copied all over Europe."

"Do you know anything about Madame Du Barry?" asked
Eric; "didn't she have her head chopped off?"

"She was another great lover of gardening," said Harvey
evasively; "in fact, I believe the well-known rose Due Barry was
named after her, and now I think you had better play for a little
and leave your lessons till later."

Harvey retreated to the library and spent some thirty or
forty minutes in wondering whether it would be possible to
compile a history, for use in elementary schools, in which there
should be no prominent mention of battles, massacres, murderous intrigues, and violent deaths. The York and Lancaster period
and the Napoleonic era would, he admitted to himself, present
considerable difficulties, and the Thirty Years' War would entail
something of a gap if you left it out altogether. Still, it would be
something gained if, at a highly impressionable age, children
could be got to fix their attention on the invention of calico
printing instead of the Spanish Armada or the Battle of Waterloo.

It was time, he thought, to go back to the boys' room, and
see how they were getting on with their peace toys. As he stood
outside the door he could hear Eric's voice raised in command;
Bertie's chimed in now and again with a helpful suggestion.

"That is Louis the Fourteenth," Eric was saying, "that one
in knee-breeches, that Uncle said invented Sunday schools. It
isn't a bit like him, but it'll have to do."

"We'll give him a purple coat from my paintbox by and by,"
said Bertie.

"Yes, an' red heels. That is Madame de Maintenon, that one
he called Mrs. Hemans. She begs Louis not to go on this expedi-
tion, but he turns a deaf ear. He takes Marshal Saxe with him,
and we must pretend that they have thousands of men with
them. The watchword is *Qui vive* and the answer is *L'état c'est
moi*—that was one of his favourite remarks, you know. They land
at Manchester in the dead of night, and a Jacobite conspirator
gives them the keys of the fortress."

Peeping in through the doorway Harvey observed that the

municipal dust-bin had been pierced with holes to accommodate the muzzles of imaginary cannon and now represented the principal fortified position in Manchester; John Stuart Mill had been dipped in red ink, and apparently stood for Marshal Saxe.

"Louis orders his troops to surround the Young Women's Christian Association and seize the lot of them. 'Once back at the Louvre and the girls are mine,' he exclaims. We must use Mrs. Hemans again for one of the girls; she says 'Never,' and stabs Marshal Saxe to the heart."

"He bleeds dreadfully," exclaimed Bertie, splashing red ink liberally over the facade of the Association building.

"The soldiers rush in and avenge his death with the utmost savagery. A hundred girls are killed"—here Bertie emptied the remainder of the red ink over the devoted building—"and the surviving five hundred are dragged off to the French ships. 'I have lost a Marshal,' says Louis, 'but I do not go back emptyhanded.' "

Harvey stole away from the room, and sought out his sister.

"Eleanor," he said, "the experiment—"

"Yes?"

"Has failed. We have begun too late."

SHARING YOUR IMPRESSIONS

1. Why do some parents object to children's playing with toy weapons?
2. Identify some needs of children that may be met by conflict toys and games.
3. Give your opinion about letting children choose their own playthings.
4. What do you suppose young children mean when they talk about killing and dying?
5. Discuss the issue of whether children should be allowed to bring toy weapons to school for play during recess.
6. Speculate about the influence toys have on a child's psychological development.
7. Suggest some possible ways of guiding children in our society toward a nonviolent approach to life.

7

THE VELDT

Ray Bradbury

"George, I wish you'd look at the nursery."

"What's wrong with it?"

"I don't know."

"Well, then."

"I just want you to look at it, is all, or call a psychologist in to look at it."

"What would a psychologist want with a nursery?"

"You know very well what he'd want." His wife paused in the middle of the kitchen and watched the stove busy humming to itself, making supper for four.

"It's just that the nursery is different now than it was."

"All right, let's have a look."

They walked down the hall of their soundproofed Happylife Home, which had cost them thirty thousand dollars installed, this house which clothed and fed and rocked them to sleep and played and sang and was good to them. Their approach sensitized a switch somewhere and the nursery light flicked on when they came within ten feet of it. Similarly, behind them, in the halls, lights went on and off as they left them behind, with a soft automaticity.

"Well," said George Hadley.

They stood on the thatched floor of the nursery. It was forty feet across by forty feet long and thirty feet high; it had cost half again as much as the rest of the house. "But nothing's too good for our children," George had said.

The nursery was silent. It was empty as a jungle glade at hot high noon. The walls were blank and two dimensional. Now, as George and Lydia Hadley stood in the center of the room, the walls began to purr and recede into crystalline distance, it seemed, and presently an African veldt appeared, in three dimensions, on all sides, in color, reproduced to the final pebble and bit of straw. The ceiling above them became a deep sky with a hot yellow sun.

George Hadley felt the perspiration start on his brow.

"Let's get out of this sun," he said. "This is a little too real. But I don't see anything wrong."

"Wait a moment, you'll see," said his wife.

Now the hidden odorophonics were beginning to blow a wind of odor at the two people in the middle of the baked veldtland. The hot straw smell of lion grass, the cool green of the hidden water hole, the great rusty smell of animals, the smell of dust like a red paprika in the hot air. And now the sounds: the thump of distant antelope feet on grassy sod, the papery rustling of vultures. A shadow passed through the sky. The shadow flickered on George Hadley's upturned, sweating face.

"Filthy creatures," he heard his wife say.

"The vultures."

"You see, there are the lions, far over, that way. Now they're on their way to the water hole. They've just been eating," said Lydia. "I don't know what."

"Some animal." George Hadley put his hand up to shield off the burning light from his squinted eyes. "A zebra or a baby giraffe, maybe."

"Are you sure?" His wife sounded peculiarly tense.

"No, it's a little late to be sure," he said, amused. "Nothing over there I can see but cleaned bone, and the vultures dropping for what's left."

"Did you hear that scream?" she asked.

"No."

"About a minute ago?"

"Sorry, no."

The lions were coming. And again George Hadley was filled
with admiration for the mechanical genius who had conceived
this room. A miracle of efficiency selling for an absurdly low
price. Every home should have one. Oh, occasionally they frightened you with their clinical accuracy, they startled you, gave you
a twinge, but most of the time what fun for everyone, not only
your own son and daughter, but for yourself when you felt like a
quick jaunt to a foreign land, a quick change of scenery. Well,
here it was!

And here were the lions now, fifteen feet away, so real, so
feverishly and startlingly real that you could feel the prickling fur
on your hand, and your mouth was stuffed with the dusty uphol-
stery smell of their heated pelts, and the yellow of them was in
your eyes like the yellow of an exquisite French tapestry, the
yellows of lions and summer grass, and the sound of the matted
lion lungs exhaling on the silent noontide, and the smell of meat
from the panting, dripping mouths.

The lions stood looking at George and Lydia Hadley with
terrible green-yellow eyes.

"Watch out!" screamed Lydia.

The lions came running at them.

Lydia bolted and ran. Instinctively, George sprang after
her. Outside, in the hall, with the door slammed, he was laughing and she was crying, and they both stood appalled at the
other's reaction.

"George!"

"Lydia! Oh, my dear poor sweet Lydia!"

"They almost got us!"

"Walls, Lydia, remember; crystal walls, that's all they are.
Oh, they look real, I must admit—Africa in your parlor—but it's
all dimensional, superreactionary, supersensitive color film and
mental tape film behind glass screens. It's all odorophonics and
sonics, Lydia. Here's my handkerchief."

"I'm afraid." She came to him and put her body against him
and cried steadily. "Did you see? Did you *feel*? It's too real."

"Now, Lydia . . ."

"You've got to tell Wendy and Peter not to read any more on
Africa."

"Of course—of course." He patted her.

"Promise?"

"Sure."

"And lock the nursery for a few days until I get my nerves settled."

"You know how difficult Peter is about that. When I punished him a month ago by locking the nursery for even a few hours—the tantrum he threw! And Wendy too. They *live* for the nursery."

"It's got to be locked, that's all there is to it."

"All right." Reluctantly he locked the huge door. "You've been working too hard. You need a rest."

"I don't know—I don't know," she said, blowing her nose, sitting down in a chair that immediately began to rock and comfort her. "Maybe I don't have enough to do. Maybe I have time to think too much. Why don't we shut the whole house off for a few days and take a vacation?"

"You mean you want to fry my eggs for me?"

"Yes." She nodded.

"And darn my socks?"

"Yes." A frantic, watery-eyed nodding.

"And sweep the house?"

"Yes, yes—oh, yes!"

"But I thought that's why we bought this house, so we wouldn't have to do anything?"

"That's just it. I feel like I don't belong here. The house is wife and mother now, and nursemaid. Can I compete with an African veldt? Can I give a bath and scrub the children as efficiently or quickly as the automatic scrub bath can? I cannot. And it isn't just me. It's you. You've been awfully nervous lately."

"I suppose I have been smoking too much."

"You look as if you didn't know what to do with yourself in this house, either. You smoke a little more every morning and drink a little more every afternoon and need a little more sedative every night. You're beginning to feel unnecessary too."

"Am I?" He paused and tried to feel into himself to see what was really there.

"Oh, George!" She looked beyond him, at the nursery door. "Those lions can't get out of there, can they?"

He looked at the door and saw it tremble as if something had jumped against it from the other side.

"Of course not," he said.

At dinner they ate alone, for Wendy and Peter were at a special plastic carnival across town and had televised home to say they'd be late, to go ahead eating. So George Hadley, bemused, sat watching the dining-room table produce warm dishes of food from its mechanical interior.

"We forgot the ketchup," he said.

"Sorry," said a small voice within the table, and ketchup appeared.

As for the nursery, thought George Hadley, it won't hurt for the children to be locked out of it awhile. Too much of anything isn't good for anyone. And it was clearly indicated that the children had been spending a little too much time on Africa. That *sun.* He could feel it on his neck, still, like a hot paw. And the *lions.* And the smell of blood. Remarkable how the nursery caught the telepathic emanations of the children's minds and created life to fill their every desire. The children thought lions, and there were lions. The children thought zebras, and there were zebras. Sun—sun. Giraffes—giraffes. Death and death.

That *last.* He chewed tastelessly on the meat that the table had cut for him. Death thoughts. They were awfully young, Wendy and Peter, for death thoughts. Or, no, you were never too young, really. Long before you knew what death was you were wishing it on someone else. When you were two years old you were shooting people with cap pistols.

But this—the long, hot African veldt—the awful death in the jaws of a lion. And repeated again and again.

"Where are you going?"

He didn't answer Lydia. Preoccupied, he let the lights glow softly on ahead of him, extinguish behind him as he padded to the nursery door. He listened against it. Far away, a lion roared.

He unlocked the door and opened it. Just before he stepped inside, he heard a faraway scream. And then another roar from the lions, which subsided quickly.

He stepped into Africa. How many times in the last year had

he opened this door and found Wonderland, Alice, the Mock
Turtle, or Aladdin and his Magical Lamp, or Jack Pumpkinhead
of Oz, or Dr. Doolittle, or the cow jumping over a very real-
appearing moon—all the delightful contraptions of a make-
believe world. How often had he seen Pegasus flying in the sky
ceiling, or seen fountains of red fireworks, or heard angel voices
singing. But now, this yellow hot Africa, this bake oven with
murder in the heat. Perhaps Lydia was right. Perhaps they
needed a little vacation from the fantasy which was growing a bit
too real for ten-year-old children. It was all right to exercise one's
mind with gymnastic fantasies, but when the lively child mind
settled on *one* pattern . . . ? It seemed that, at a distance, for the
past month, he had heard lions roaring, and smelled their strong
odor seeping as far away as his study door. But, being busy, he
had paid it no attention.

George Hadley stood on the African grassland alone. The
lions looked up from their feeding, watching him. The only flaw
to the illusion was the open door through which he could see his
wife, far down the dark hall, like a framed picture, eating her
dinner abstractedly.

"Go away," he said to the lions.

They did not go.

He knew the principle of the room exactly. You sent out
your thoughts. Whatever you thought would appear.

"Let's have Aladdin and his lamp," he snapped.

The veldtland remained; the lions remained.

"Come on, room! I demand Aladdin!" he said.

Nothing happened. The lions mumbled in their baked
pelts.

"Aladdin!"

He went back to dinner. "The fool room's out of order," he
said. "It won't respond."

"Or—"

"Or what?"

"Or it *can't* respond," said Lydia, "because the children
have thought about Africa and lions and killing so many days that
the room's in a rut."

"Could be."

"Or Peter's set it to remain that way."

"Set it?"

"He may have got into the machinery and fixed something."

"Peter doesn't know machinery."

"He's a wise one for ten. That I.Q. of his—"

"Nevertheless—"

"Hello, Mom. Hello, Dad."

The Hadleys turned. Wendy and Peter were coming in the front door, cheeks like peppermint candy, eyes like bright blue agate marbles, a smell of ozone on their jumpers from their trip in the helicopter.

"You're just in time for supper," said both parents.

"We're full of strawberry ice cream and hot dogs," said the children, holding hands. "But we'll sit and watch."

"Yes, come tell us about the nursery," said George Hadley.

The brother and sister blinked at him and then at each other. "Nursery?"

"All about Africa and everything," said the father with false joviality.

"I don't understand," said Peter.

"Your mother and I were just traveling through Africa with rod and reel; Tom Swift and his Electric Lion," said George Hadley.

"There's no Africa in the nursery," said Peter simply.

"Oh, come now, Peter. We know better."

"I don't remember any Africa," said Peter to Wendy. "Do you?"

"No."

"Run see and come tell."

She obeyed.

"Wendy, come back here!" said George Hadley, but she was gone. The house lights followed her like a flock of fireflies. Too late, he realized he had forgotten to lock the nursery door after his last inspection.

"Wendy'll look and come tell us," said Peter.

"She doesn't have to tell *me*. I've seen it."

"I'm sure you're mistaken, Father."

"I'm not, Peter. Come along now."

But Wendy was back. "It's not Africa," she said breathlessly.

"We'll see about this," said George Hadley, and they all walked down the hall together and opened the nursery door.

There was a green, lovely forest, a lovely river, a purple mountain, high voices singing, and Rima, lovely and mysterious, lurking in the trees with colorful flights of butterflies, like animated bouquets, lingering in her long hair. The African veldtland was gone. The lions were gone. Only Rima was here now, singing a song so beautiful that it brought tears to your eyes.

George Hadley looked in at the changed scene. "Go to bed," he said to the children.

They opened their mouths.

"You heard me," he said.

They went off to the air closet, where a wind sucked them like brown leaves up the flue to their slumber rooms.

George Hadley walked through the singing glade and picked up something that lay in the corner near where the lions had been. He walked slowly back to his wife.

"What is that?" she asked.

"An old wallet of mine," he said.

He showed it to her. The smell of hot grass was on it and the smell of a lion. There were drops of saliva on it, it had been chewed, and there were blood smears on both sides.

He closed the nursery door and locked it, tight.

In the middle of the night he was still awake and he knew his wife was awake. "Do you think Wendy changed it?" she said at last, in the dark room.

"Of course."

"Made it from a veldt into a forest and put Rima there instead of lions?"

"Yes."

"Why?"

"I don't know. But it's staying locked until I find out."

"How did your wallet get there?"

"I don't know anything," he said, "except that I'm beginning to be sorry we bought that room for the children. If children are neurotic at all, a room like that—"

"It's supposed to help them work off their neuroses in a healthful way."

"I'm starting to wonder." He stared at the ceiling.

"We've given the children everything they ever wanted. Is this our reward—secrecy, disobedience?"

"Who was it said, 'Children are carpets, they should be stepped on occasionally'? We've never lifted a hand. They're insufferable—let's admit it. They come and go when they like; they treat us as if we were offspring. They're spoiled and we're spoiled."

"They've been acting funny ever since you forbade them to take the rocket to New York a few months ago."

"They're not old enough to do that alone, I explained."

"Nevertheless, I've noticed they've been decidedly cool toward us since."

"I think I'll have David McClean come tomorrow morning to have a look at Africa."

"But it's not Africa now, it's *Green Mansions* country and Rima."

"I have a feeling it'll be Africa again before then."

A moment later they heard the screams.

Two screams. Two people screaming from downstairs. And then a roar of lions.

"Wendy and Peter aren't in their rooms," said his wife.

He lay in his bed with his beating heart. "No," he said. "They've broken into the nursery."

"Those screams—they sound familiar."

"Do they?"

"Yes, awfully."

And although their beds tried very hard, the two adults couldn't be rocked to sleep for another hour. A smell of cats was in the night air.

"Father?" said Peter.

"Yes."

Peter looked at his shoes. He never looked at his father any more, nor at his mother. "You aren't going to lock up the nursery for good, are you?"

"That all depends."

"On what?" snapped Peter.

"On you and your sister. If you intersperse this Africa with a little variety—oh, Sweden perhaps, or Denmark or China—"

"I thought we were free to play as we wished."

"You are, within reasonable bounds."

"What's wrong with Africa, Father?"

"Oh, so now you admit you have been conjuring up Africa, do you?"

"I wouldn't want the nursery locked up," said Peter coldly. "Ever."

"Matter of fact, we're thinking of turning the whole house off for about a month. Live sort of a carefree one-for-all existence."

"That sounds dreadful! Would I have to tie my own shoes instead of letting the shoe tier do it? And brush my own teeth and comb my hair and give myself a bath?"

"It would be fun for a change, don't you think?"

"No, it would be horrid. I didn't like it when you took out the picture painter last month."

"That's because I wanted you to learn to paint all by yourself, son."

"I don't want to do anything but look and listen and smell; what else *is* there to do?"

"All right, go play in Africa."

"Will you shut off the house sometime soon?"

"We're considering it."

"I don't think you'd better consider it any more, Father."

"I won't have any threats from my son!"

"Very well." And Peter strolled off to the nursery.

"Am I on time?" said David McClean.

"Breakfast?" asked George Hadley.

"Thanks, had some. What's the trouble?"

"David, you're a psychologist."

"I should hope so."

"Well, then, have a look at our nursery. You saw it a year ago when you dropped by; did you notice anything peculiar about it then?"

"Can't say I did; the usual violences, a tendency toward a slight paranoia here or there, usual in children because they feel persecuted by parents constantly, but, oh, really nothing."

They walked down the hall. "I locked the nursery up,"

explained the father, "and the children broke back into it during the night. I let them stay so they could form the patterns for you to see."

There was a terrible screaming from the nursery.

"There it is," said George Hadley. "See what you make of it."

They walked in on the children without rapping.

The screams had faded. The lions were feeding.

"Run outside a moment, children," said George Hadley. "No, don't change the mental combination. Leave the walls as they are. Get!"

With the children gone, the two men stood studying the lions clustered at a distance, eating with great relish whatever it was they had caught.

"I wish I knew what it was," said George Hadley. "Sometimes I can almost see. Do you think if I brought high-powered binoculars here and—"

David McClean laughed dryly. "Hardly." He turned to study all four walls. "How long has this been going on?"

"A little over a month."

"It certainly doesn't *feel* good."

"I want facts, not feelings."

"My dear George, a psychologist never saw a fact in his life. He only hears about feelings; vague things. This doesn't feel good, I tell you. Trust my hunches and my instincts. I have a nose for something bad. This is very bad. My advice to you is to have the whole damn room torn down and your children brought to me every day during the next year for treatment."

"Is it that bad?"

"I'm afraid so. One of the original uses of these nurseries was so that we could study the patterns left on the walls by the child's mind, study at our leisure, and help the child. In this case, however, the room has become a channel toward—destructive thoughts, instead of a release away from them."

"Didn't you sense this before?"

"I sensed only that you had spoiled your children more than most. And now you're letting them down in some way. What way?"

"I wouldn't let them go to New York."

"What else?"

"I've taken a few machines from the house and threatened them, a month ago, with closing up the nursery unless they did their homework. I did close it for a few days to show I meant business."

"Ah, ha!"

"Does that mean anything?"

"Everything. Where before they had a Santa Claus now they have a Scrooge. Children prefer Santas. You've let this room and this house replace you and your wife in your children's affections. This room is their mother and father, far more important in their lives than their real parents. And now you come along and want to shut it off. No wonder there's hatred here. You can feel it coming out of the sky. Feel that sun. George, you'll have to change your life. Like too many others, you've built it around creature comforts. Why, you'd starve tomorrow if something went wrong in your kitchen. You wouldn't know how to tap an egg. Nevertheless, turn everything off. Start new. It'll take time. But we'll make good children out of bad in a year, wait and see."

"But won't the shock be too much for the children, shutting the room up abruptly, for good?"

"I don't want them going any deeper into this, that's all."

The lions were finished with their red feast.

The lions were standing on the edge of the clearing watching the two men.

"Now *I'm* feeling persecuted," said McClean. "Let's get out of here. I never have cared for these damned rooms. Make me nervous."

"The lions look real, don't they?" said George Hadley. "I don't suppose there's any way—"

"What?"

"—that they could *become* real?"

"Not that I know."

"Some flaw in the machinery, a tampering or something?"

"No."

"I don't imagine the room will like being turned off," said the father.

"Nothing ever likes to die—even a room."

"I wonder if it hates me for wanting to switch it off?"

"Paranoia is thick around here today," said David McClean. "You can follow it like a spoor. Hello." He bent and picked up a bloody scarf. "This yours?"

"No." George Hadley's face was rigid. "It belongs to Lydia."

They went to the fuse box together and threw the switch that killed the nursery.

The two children were in hysterics. They screamed and pranced and threw things. They yelled and sobbed and swore and jumped at the furniture.

"You can't do that to the nursery, you can't!"

"Now, children."

The children flung themselves onto a couch, weeping.

"George," said Lydia Hadley, "turn on the nursery, just for a few moments. You can't be so abrupt."

"No."

"You can't be so cruel."

"Lydia, it's off, and it stays off. And the whole damn house dies as of here and now. The more I see of the mess we've put ourselves in, the more it sickens me. We've been contemplating our mechanical, electronic navels for too long. My God, how we need a breath of honest air!"

And he marched about the house turning off the voice clocks, the stoves, the heaters, the shoe shiners, the shoe lacers, the body scrubbers and swabbers and massagers, and every other machine he could put his hand to.

The house was full of dead bodies, it seemed. It felt like a mechanical cemetery. So silent. None of the humming hidden energy of machines waiting to function at the tap of a button.

"Don't let them do it!" wailed Peter at the ceiling, as if he was talking to the house, the nursery. "Don't let Father kill everything." He turned to his father. "Oh, I hate you!"

"Insults won't get you anywhere."

"I wish you were dead!"

"We were, for a long while. Now we're going to really start living. Instead of being handled and massaged, we're going to *live*."

Wendy was still crying and Peter joined her again. "Just a moment, just one moment, just another moment of nursery," they wailed.

"Oh, George," said the wife, "it can't hurt."

"All right—all right, if they'll just shut up. One minute, mind you, and then off forever."

"Daddy, Daddy, Daddy!" sang the children, smiling with wet faces.

"And then we're going on a vacation. David McClean is coming back in half an hour to help us move out and get to the airport. I'm going to dress. You turn the nursery on for a minute, Lydia, just a minute, mind you."

And the three of them went babbling off while he let himself be vacuumed upstairs through the air flue and set about dressing himself. A minute later Lydia appeared.

"I'll be glad when we get away," she sighed.

"Did you leave them in the nursery?"

"I wanted to dress too. Oh, that horrid Africa. What can they see in it?"

"Well, in five minutes we'll be on our way to Iowa. Lord, how did we ever get in this house? What prompted us to buy a nightmare?"

"Pride, money, foolishness."

"I think we'd better get downstairs before those kids get engrossed with those damned beasts again."

Just then they heard the children calling, "Daddy, Mommy, come quick—quick!"

They went downstairs in the air flue and ran down the hall. The children were nowhere in sight. "Wendy? Peter!"

They ran into the nursery. The veltland was empty save for the lions waiting, looking at them. "Peter, Wendy?"

The door slammed.

"Wendy, Peter!"

George Hadley and his wife whirled and ran back to the door.

"Open the door!" cried George Hadley, trying the knob. "Why, they've locked it from the outside! Peter!" He beat at the door. "Open up!"

He heard Peter's voice outside, against the door.

"Don't let them switch off the nursery and the house," he was saying.

Mr. and Mrs. George Hadley beat at the door. "Now, don't be ridiculous, children. It's time to go. Mr. McClean'll be here in a minute and . . ."

And then they heard the sounds.

The lions on three sides of them, in the yellow veldt grass, padding through the dry straw, rumbling and roaring in their throats.

The lions.

Mr. Hadley looked at his wife and they turned and looked back at the beasts edging slowly forward, crouching, tails stiff.

Mr. and Mrs. Hadley screamed.

And suddenly they realized why those other screams had sounded familiar.

"Well, here I am," said David McClean in the nursery doorway. "Oh, hello." He stared at the two children seated in the center of the open glade eating a little picnic lunch. Beyond them was the water hole and the yellow veldtland; above was the hot sun. He began to perspire. "Where are your father and mother?"

The children looked up and smiled. "Oh, they'll be here directly."

"Good, we must get going." At a distance Mr. McClean saw the lions fighting and clawing and then quieting down to feed in silence under the shady trees.

He squinted at the lions with his hand up to his eyes.

Now the lions were done feeding. They moved to the water hole to drink.

A shadow flickered over Mr. McClean's hot face. Many shadows flickered. The vultures were dropping down the blazing sky.

"A cup of tea?" asked Wendy in the silence.

SHARING YOUR IMPRESSIONS

1. Deliberations about life in the future should include an em-

phasis on leisure. What do you foresee as the most desirable changes in education for leisure?

2. What kinds of concerns do you recommend that the parents of a young child consider when deciding how much time they should spend playing with their child?

3. In your opinion, how much of the school-time schedule should be devoted to education for leisure?

4. In principle, how do you react to allowing fathers and mothers of preschoolers to spend half of their job time at home (with pay) on condition that the time is devoted to parent-child play and other forms of education?

5. Discuss the consequences for the family of children's dependence on television.

6. Think of some recommendations for parents who want to use television as an educational influence.

7. How do you feel about forbidding children to watch certain television programs?

8

THE SAND CASTLE

Mary Lavin

John was the oldest. He had straight black hair and a pale face. Emily came next. She had bright hair. Every summer they got gold freckles, but in the winter they went away. Alexander was the youngest. His freckles never went away, but Alexander did not mind. He did not mind about being fat, either, as long as he was getting big, one way or another.

One summer they went to stay in Howth, a small seaside resort. It had a silver bay and a bright green boat-slip, a silver strand and a cold white harbor. There were things to do, every hour of the day, and the nights fell even faster there than they fell at home. When the tide was out, you could dig for cockles and go down so deep with the spade that you came to jet-black clay underneath the silver sand. You could skim stones on the shallow waters. When the sea was full and high, you could fish from the pier with a string and a pin. You could vault over the old pier stakes that stuck up in the sand like stunted trees. You could sit on the slimy boat-slip and talk to the fishermen as they mended their nets. You could pile up big stones and try to knock them down again with smaller stones. You could walk out to the end of the cold white harbor wall and look down over the sides at the great green tongues of the sea that licked up the walls. You could do This. You could do That.

Emily and John quarreled all day long because they could not decide between This and That. Even Alexander was independent in his ideas, for a four-and-a-half-year-old.

"What will we play today?" he asked, on their second day there, as they sat at their lunch in the window alcove of the hotel.

"You can do what you like," said Emily. "You won't play with us!"

"Why?" said Alexander. "Why won't I play with you?"

"You're too small," Emily said.

Alexander could not accept this familiar insult. He stared at his plate. The tears splashed onto the surface of the shining porcelain.

"Alexander is not as small as you think," said Nurse. "He walked to the end of the pier yesterday afternoon, all by himself." She looked anxiously at Alexander, whose tears were now falling on his plate, with the loud, steady fall of the first raindrops that herald a thunderous downpour. "Tell them about your walk, Alexander!"

Alexander looked up, with such a jerk that two tears sped into the air on either side of him. He entered at once upon the narrative with a vigorous faith in the fact that it would vindicate him from future charges of being too small to play with the others.

"I walked to the end of the pier," he said, "all by myself. Nurse sat on a lobster pot. I walked to the very end, and when I got there I sat down on a seat." As he spoke he was impressed by the exactitude of his memory, but when his narrative was over he became aware of a certain paucity of detail. Moreover, when he looked at his audience, he realized that he had held their attention to no purpose, for the story was ended and his audience clearly expected more.

"Well?" said Emily.

"What happened then?" said John.

Alexander was humiliated. Desperately he tried to remember further incidents about the walk, but, although he could call up a picture of the pier, it was a cold, straight pier, without turns or steps, and all he could see on it was himself, walking along toward the seat at the far end, and a solitary, dull sea bird. Alexander was forced to fasten upon the sea bird. "While I was sitting on the seat," he said, taking up the narrative after the most fragmentary and imperceptible pause, "a big bird came along and sat beside me."

"Did you catch him?" John asked with a spurt of interest.

Fearing that he might be expected to produce evidence if he answered in the affirmative, Alexander shook his head.

"Before I had time to catch him," he said, earnestly staring at his listeners, "he ran away."

"You mean he flew away." Emily was beginning to look incredulous.

"No, he ran away," Alexander said, having learned that it is best to stick to one's first story even if it is a poor one. Emily looked at John.

John fixed Alexander with a fierce and unblinking stare. "How many legs had he?"

"He had four legs, of course," Alexander said, indignantly, but immediately he began to doubt his statement, and when at that moment a sea gull flew past the window, with no legs visible at all, his doubts became more serious.

"A sea gull with four legs!" said John, and he began to laugh.

"I knew he was lying all the time," said Emily.

Nurse looked up. "Emily! That is not a nice way to speak about your little brother."

"Make him tell the truth then!" said Emily, turning to Nurse.

"Tell the truth, Alexander," Nurse said, frowning.

Alexander began again, but this time his voice was humble and his story was interrupted by apologetic sniffling. "It's true that I walked to the end of the pier," he said, "but it's not true about the bird. There was a bird, but he just stood on the ground."

"Did you sit on the seat?" John asked.

"I did."

"Did the bird come near the seat?"

Alexander did not reply for a minute, and then he straightened up. "No," he said, "but he looked at me." And proudly, putting his own head to one side and shutting an eye, he showed how the bird looked when it looked at him. "I am going to walk down the pier again today," he said, after he had opened his eye and straightened his neck again.

"You are not," said Emily.

"I am," said Alexander.

"You will do as we say," said Emily.

The tears came into Alexander's eyes again. Nurse frowned and bit her lip. Nurse was pale, and there was a dark stain under the lashes of her young blue eyes. "Why are you children so difficult?" she said. "Why aren't you like other children? Why are you always quarreling?" She paused, and then she brightened. "Why don't you build a nice big sand castle?"

"A sand castle!" John was almost speechless with indignation.

"The sand is dirty," said Emily. "I heard a lady say that she saw fleas in it, hopping up and down!"

"Emily!" Nurse looked around hastily to see if there was anyone within earshot. "There are some things that are not mentioned at table."

There was silence then for a few minutes, and Nurse looked out between the stiff lace curtains at the far blue sea, and the gray beach lit along its length with bright cockle streams catching the silver sunlight. When she spoke again it was softly, as if to herself. "Very few people can build a good sand castle. It takes skillful planning. It takes a strong steady hand."

Alexander looked rapidly from Emily to John and from John to Emily, no doubt regretting that he could not look in two directions at one time. Emily and John were looking at Nurse. But Nurse still looked at the sea.

"I could build the best castle that was ever built," John said.

Nurse continued to look at the sea. She said nothing, but she allowed a faint and supercilious smile to fashion itself at the corners of her mouth.

John addressed the smiling mouth. "I'll show you!" he said, angrily, and he beckoned to Emily. "Are you coming?" he said to her, and he strode out of the room. Emily strode after him.

Alexander had some difficulty descending from his chair,

and so he could not stride out after them with the arrogance he would have liked to show, because they were already going through the swinging glass doors of the vestibule, and he had to run or he would have been left behind altogether.

Outside the hotel, the air was bright and challenging. The wind shook the red geraniums that stood in glaringly white urns on the terrace and threatened to dash their petals all over the green grass.

Alexander caught up with Emily. He drew a deep breath and pulled her by the skirt. "Wait for me," he said, mysteriously, and disappeared around the corner in the direction of the hotel. When he came back he carried a rusty, corrugated bucket. He had seen it sometime previously but had been unable to devise a use for it.

"Where did you get that?" Emily asked, enviously, stretching out her hand for it.

"Finders, keepers!" Alexander said, retreating a pace or two, putting the bucket behind his back.

"Oh, keep it!" Emily said, tossing her hair angrily. She ran after John. Alexander ran after her.

They caught up with John in the long dune grasses that separated the hotel lawn from the flat sand on the lower shore.

"Here is a good place to build the castle," Alexander said, setting down his bucket. The soft white sands lifted into streamers on the air. John looked at Alexander with contempt.

"Is that all you know about building?" he said, as he strode ahead, his feet sending up branching sprays from the sand, as a clipper sends up sea spray.

"What is the matter with this place?" Alexander asked Emily, in a whisper.

"You have to have wet sand to make the walls firm," Emily said.

"I could get water from the sea to wet the sand." Alexander held up the bucket, and looked out through the handle at the tempting blue waters with which he would fill it.

"The sea is too far away from here," Emily said.

Alexander put the bucket on his head, tilted it forward, and put the handle under his chin as a chin strap.

"If we were playing soldiers," he said, with infinite regret, "I could be the General."

"You know John is always the General," Emily said, scathingly.

Down on the hard, damp, corrugated ripples of the lower shore, John had taken off his coat. Emily sat down with her legs spread out. Alexander sat on his upturned bucket. For a time John dug in the sand silently, mounting it high. Then he looked up and glanced around at the shell-strewn shore.

"Get me an oyster shell, Emily," he ordered.

Emily poked Alexander in the ribs.

"Get him an oyster shell," she said, pointing to the cockle beds that were rippling with shallow water, blown by the wind. Alexander sped for the shallows. The other two watched him as he went, and listened with satisfaction to the flat flapping sound that his feet made as he ran through the waters of the cockle stream and reached the far side where shells littered the sand. In a few minutes they saw him bend and pick up something, and then they saw him turn and run back across the flat and empty beach, starting a flurry among the feeding gulls and splashing water up each side of himself.

"Is this right?" he shouted, holding up a great shell.

John put out his hand and took the shell without speaking.

"Do you want anything else?" said Alexander, panting.

John did not hear him.

Alexander turned to Emily. "Will I get another shell for him?" he asked, politely.

But Emily was sitting with her legs spread out wide, and she was absorbed in the task of taking a lollipop out of her pocket. She had run into difficulty because the lollipop had melted and become somewhat stuck to the inside of her pocket. She did not answer. Alexander, however, had forgotten his question in the intensity of watching for the lollipop to emerge. His eyes opened wider and wider. As the lollipop came unstuck at last, he clapped his hands.

"Can I have a lick?"

Emily took a long steady lick of the lollipop and said nothing.

"Just one lick?" said Alexander.

"Go away," Emily said, taking two short licks and one long, defiant one.

"Please!" Alexander said humbly.

"Don't bother me!" said Emily. "Go away!" and she took up a fistful of sand and threw it at the pleading Alexander . Alexander pursed his lips. He made a dive upon the sand to gather a fistful of retaliation, when a more effective method of achieving his object occurred to him. He glanced up at the dunes to see that the setting was right, and seeing, as he had hoped, that Nurse was sitting there, within earshot under her striped sunshade, he threw back his head, and putting his hands to his face, gave a long, thin, penetrating wail of anguish.

"There's sand in my eye!" he wailed. "Oh, oh! there's sand in my eye. I'm blinded." And he began to stagger, very blindly, up the beach.

"Come back, Alexander," Emily said urgently, and she pulled John by the sleeve. "What will I do?" she said. "He'll tell Nurse that I threw it at him."

"You did!" John said, without looking up.

"We'll be kept in after tea!" Emily warned.

John looked up. "Give him the lollipop," he directed. "That's what he wants."

Alexander had paused momentarily in his blind stagger forward, and his wailing had grown less loud because it interfered somewhat with his hearing. When Emily made no move to give him the lollipop, however, he set off once more and threw back his head with a view to louder wailing.

"Alexander." Emily stood up. "Alexander," she called, running after him. "Will you stop crying if I give you my lollipop?"

Alexander turned around slowly, and came back with his tear-wet hand outstretched. He took the lollipop and sat down on the sand. Emily sat with her back to him. John resumed his work.

"I am going to dig the moat now," John said after a while, and he began to dig around the castle with both hands, throwing up the sand on all sides.

Wildly the sand rose in the air. Lightly it floated downward again. It lay like a fine mist of rain on Emily's bright hair. And it drifted all over Alexander, but he sat in beatific unconcern of it, although the fastly falling grains settled upon the sticky lollipop and impeded the progress of his bright, industrious tongue, that licked and licked and licked.

"This will be the best castle that was ever built," John declared, and he wiped his hand across his mouth, leaving a whisker of sand upon his chin.

"Oh, look," Alexander said. "John has a beard. John has a beard." And throwing away the lollipop stick, clean as if it had been licked by the briny tongues of the sea, he lifted a fistful of sand and began to decorate his own sticky chin with blond whiskers.

"Stop that," said John, "we have no time to waste." He picked up Alexander's bucket where it lay on its side forgotten, and put it into Alexander's hand. "Get me water for the moat," he said.

"The bucket is leaking," Emily said, disparagingly.

"He can run quick, so the water won't have time to leak out," said John.

Alexander ran off like mad toward the thin sea waves, with his battered bucket swinging in his hand. Every time he let it down to chase a sea gull, or to poke his finger into a pool, John called out to him, and the sea birds rose in a flurry, and he picked up the battered bucket again and ran toward the waves with fresh vigor.

In a short while he was racing back, with all the fury of a full-blown wave racing for the shore.

"Is it spilling? Is it spilling?" he shouted, as he ran, not daring to take time to look behind him.

"Hurry! Hurry!" John and Emily shouted together, and they stood up and cheered him, as he dashed through the last cockle stream an inch ahead of the racing drops of water that seemed to be chasing him like a swarm of silver bees.

John rushed forward and caught the bucket from him and dashed the remaining water into the moat. Triumphantly the three of them flung themselves face-down on the sand and leaned over the edge of the moat to gaze with pride and admiration. But in a few minutes the water had stolen out of sight between the grains of sand, and soon there were defiant gleams of granite as the sand dried out again to a pale silver color. Then there was nothing left of the perilous water but a few iridescent bubbles.

"The water is gone!" Alexander said, and the statement of this truth seemed to be more bitter than the truth itself, for the tears welled into his eyes.

"What will we do?" said John, looking at Emily.

"We'll think of something," said Emily, and she got down on her knees and inspected the bottom of the moat. "Perhaps if we put stones along the bottom it might keep the water from leaking away."

Alexander got up and moved a bit away. He sat down on his hunkers and began to root in his pockets. After a minute he produced a ball of silver paper, and began to tear off pieces of the thin tinfoil and lay them along the bottom of the moat.

"Look at the water!" he said, pulling Emily by the sleeve.

"It's just like water," said John, and he got down on his knees. "Give me some, Alexander," he said. "It's just as good as water. You'd think it was water," and he began to line the moat upon the opposite side from Alexander until the whole circle of the dike around the castle shone with fake silver water.

So, gradually, although at first he wanted to work at the castle alone, John allowed the others to offer suggestions and give him help. When the artist first begins to shape his creation he is filled with a pride in himself and cannot bear to think that any hand but his could shape the perfection of the dream behind his brain, but as the dream emerges into a tangible form his selfish pride in his own power fades before a pure, unselfish pride in the thing he has created. Then he is willing and anxious to accept help from others, and is even ready, if necessary, to make the tragic abnegation of abandoning his task to other hands if those hands seem better fitted than his own to consummate the task.

Emily pinned back her hair. Alexander took off his shoes. Sitting with their legs spread out, all three of them worked without talking. They patted and dug, they mounded the sand, they smoothed it, and they piled it high. And soon a noble castle, with a noble crenelated tower, rose out of the sand and stood between them and the sun. It rose so high, so proud, so tall, that it cast a deep blue shadow on the pale sand.

"What kind of doors will we have?" said John. "We could have real wood for doors."

"We could have real glass in the windows," said Emily.

"I'll get the wood," said Alexander. "I'll get the glass." And he ran up to a bank of seaweed, higher up on the shore, where broken china, bits of glass, splinters of driftwood, tin, pearl buttons, shells, and empty bottles were tangled in the mesh of seaweed. He ran back with his arms filled and let fall a flittering cascade of treasures.

John began to pick out suitable pieces of glass, but all at once Emily clapped her hands. "I have an idea," she said. "We could have real doors and windows; that you could see through!" And picking up a shell she began to dig a hole in the side of the sturdy wall.

"Be careful," warned John. But the idea gripped him, and picking up another shell he began to tunnel into the castle upon the opposite side from Emily. "Be careful," he called out, from time to time. "We are nearly meeting!" And indeed, even as he spoke he felt something alive stirring within the castle, and a minute later he felt Emily's hot fingers underneath his own.

"Hurrah!" said John, and throwing himself on his face he peered into the tunnel. "Can you see me?" he yelled in delight as he caught sight of Emily's blue eyes at the other end.

"Can you see me?" screamed Emily.

Alexander jumped up and down. "Can I have a look? Can I have a look?" he yelled, but without much hope of being heard. All the same he continued to jump up and down.

When at last the furious ecstasy of creation had wasted his strength John sat back and drew a deep breath of renewal.

"What do you think of it, Alexander?" he asked patronizingly.

But Alexander was speechless. He jumped up and down more furiously, and all he could say, as he stared at the castle, was "Gosh." "Gosh," cried Alexander, "Gosh! Gosh! Gosh!"

But as Alexander said "Gosh," a faint voice in his ears whispered it back again, slyly. "Gosh."

Alexander stopped jumping up and down. Emily and John stared at him suspiciously.

"Gosh," said Alexander, once more, bravely, but while he spoke he put out a hand, edging near to Emily, and caught at her skirt. "Gosh," said the small white voice behind him, "Gosh, gosh, gosh."

They all swung around, with their lips apart, their hands

groping out for each other. There, at their feet, were the thin white lips of the cold sea waves, saying over and over again, without even waiting, now, for Alexander, "Gosh—" and then, "Gosh." "Gosh—" and then, "Gosh—"

John looked at Alexander; Alexander's ears were sticking out with excitement. His chin was pulled in tight. He was staring at the waves, mesmerized with their words. The castle was forgotten behind him. But when John looked at Emily her lips were pressed tightly together. John pressed his own lips together. Stronger than the bitter odor of the sour seawater that stole into his nostrils was the first bitter foretaste of human impotence. "What will we do?" he cried. "Our castle will be destroyed!" But as he spoke a combative spirit woke within him. "We will fight back the sea!" he cried. "We will rout the enemy. Arm yourselves, my men! Arm yourselves." And taking up stones he led his men. "I am the king of the castle!" he cried.

Missile after missile was hurled into the water, breaking the faces of the pale waves but unable to silence their chuckles of triumph or stem their relentless advance. The green regiment outnumbered even the stones on the shore, and soon the defenders had to lay down arms as the castle keep began to collapse with a slow sliding of grain after grain.

Big tears ran down Alexander's red cheeks. But Emily's eyes were dry, and they seemed to have taken on the agate color of the sea.

"There is one thing we can do!" she said, and she bit her lip and looked at the castle. She turned around and looked at the boys. "I am queen of the castle!" she said then, in a loud voice, and raising her arms like a bird lifting his wings for flight, she leapt into the air, and landed with both feet upon the crenelated tower. The castle crumbled around her feet.

Her feet sank into streaming sand. She raised them heavily, one after another, and rivers of sand ran lightly over the white knobs of her ankles. Her dress belled out like a tulip. Her bright hair blazed. "Now you can't have our castle!" she cried to the greedy reaching waves.

Uncomprehendingly, John and Alexander looked on for a moment. Then they, too, ran forward and, jumping into the air, landed upon the castle with a shout, and began to leap up and down. "Gosh!" said Alexander. "Gosh! Isn't this great? Isn't this the best game ever?"

They jumped and jumped, all three of them, while the waters stole around their feet, with swirling foam, and writhing seaweed, and millions of grains of sand restlessly traveling.

And soon they forgot the reason why they were jumping and they began to see who could jump the highest, and who could make the biggest splashes in the rising water. And as they rose up and down, in their hearts also there rose and broke, and rose again, and broke, the silent waves of a wild intuition that was carrying them forward, nearer and nearer to the shores of adult knowledge—those bright shores of silt.

SHARING YOUR IMPRESSIONS

1. How do you react when children destroy something they've made?
2. Recall a childhood experience in which you were the youngest and least capable in a group venture.
3. What are some advantages and disadvantages for children of having surrogates spend extended time with them?
4. What are some advantages and disadvantages for parents of having their children spend extended time with surrogates?
5. How can parents and teachers make greater use of play as a means of teaching children?
6. Although elementary teachers feel that peer play is valuable, recess duty is an unpopular assignment. This is your chance to invent a better role for whoever must supervise recess.

3

FEARS
AND
ANXIETIES

9

BE NICE TO MR. CAMPBELL

Robert Lowry

1

She was fixing the salad when her cowboy came back from next door.

"Dear, do you *always* have to slam the screendoor like that?"

He opened the refrigerator and brought out the ice cream he hadn't finished at lunch.

"You'll spoil your dinner, puddin. You're going to have such a nice dinner."

But he wasn't having any of her; he was searching in the drawer for a spoon. With a terrible rasping noise he dragged a chair over to the table and began to eat. He had a spot of chocolate on the end of his button nose now, and a dribble ran down from the corner of his wide, pink mouth, past his chin.

"Look, you're getting it all over yourself. You've just *got* to keep yourself clean, sweetheart. We're having company tonight."

He went ahead shoving big spoonfuls of ice cream into his mouth, his long-lashed eyes staring down at the plate. There was

Reprinted from *Prize Stories of 1950*, edited by Herschel Brickell. Copyright 1950 by American Mercury. Reprinted by permission of American Mercury, Box 1306, Torrance, CA 90505.

simply no use talking to him when he was in this mood; she'd already shouted herself hoarse finding that out. But in the end she couldn't resist. "Wipe your mouth off, for goodness sake!" She went toward him with a towel, and for the first time he looked up at her, his round blue eyes flat with resistance. "Take this and wipe your mouth off, Joey."

He caught the towel, jerked it from her hand and threw it on the floor. "No."

She felt her hands grip; her heart began pounding. "No? Just what do you mean saying no to your mother, Joey?"

"I mean no," Joey said. "N–O. And I'm not going to keep clean, either." He was mashing the ice cream into a soupy mess with his spoon.

"Then you won't be allowed to eat with us, dear. You'll just have to take your dinner in the kitchen."

"I don't care," he said sullenly. "I'd rather have it in the kitchen anyway. I don't want to eat with Mr. Campbell." He was stirring the ice cream now, slopping some of it over the side of the dish. "He's too fat."

She could only stand there staring down at him, at his round mussed towhead bent over the dish, his ears stuck out in a way she could never understand since she'd always bought him hats that fitted, his cowboy suit already dirty with that one spot of chocolate on the vest. She avoided hearing more about Mr. Campbell by saying, "You ought to try to keep your cowboy suit clean, darling. You'll want to wear it Saturday when your father takes you to the circus."

He looked up at her, his moist underlip belligerent. "My father bought me this suit."

"Of course your father bought it for you." She went back to the salad and began shredding in the carrots. "That's all the more reason to keep it clean, so you'll look nice when he sees you in it."

"You didn't buy it, my father bought it. You never buy me anything as good as a cowboy suit."

"But your father went out West, Joey," she said. "You can only buy nice cowboy suits like yours out West."

"Why don't *you* ever take me out West? If I lived with Daddy *he'd* take me."

She slid the salad bowl into the refrigerator and washed her hands at the sink. She tried to think of the proper answer to this question, but each answer seemed wrong. The books—she could go back to the books and see what they advised. But she already knew: they never had anything encouraging to say about a child of divorced parents; it was all an uphill struggle, a series of compromises, a forced string of compliments about the absent member of the family which only seemed to make the child long more for him. "Let's not go through all that again," she said lamely. "Just go wash your face and hands now."

He surprised her by actually walking over to the sink and obeying her.

"And will you promise Mommy you'll be nice to Mr. Campbell when he comes?"

She jumped when the screendoor slammed. He'd gone out into the yard to play again.

2

You have got to love a woman, Tony Campbell thought, to go out this far to see her. He was taking the river drive and keeping his speed five miles over the limit. The river looked plenty busy out there. A string of coal barges going by, some people fishing off their houseboat, a paddle-wheeler pushing upstream along the far shore. It's funny how you never think how many people make their living off the river, he thought, and he remembered a piece in the paper this morning that had surprised him by giving figures showing there was more river traffic now than ever before. You wouldn't think that, Tony Campbell thought.

Well, he couldn't fool himself about Lois, he liked her even if she did live ten miles from town and own the worst brat in the U. S. My God, he thought, I *must* like her, when you consider I never get anything more for my trip out here than the privilege of sitting in that living room all evening, afraid even to hold hands because the brat might poke his nose in. Let's see, he'd known her almost a month now. And during the whole period he'd been really alone with her exactly two times—once after the party where he'd first met her (she'd escaped from her friend, that dame who made the ceramics, so he could take her home), and once when the kid had spent the night at his father's apartment. The rest of the time they'd had to sit in that damn living room playing records low and hardly able to talk for fear the kid would wake up and come down and start his scene again. Three nights ago, when he'd been out here for dinner, the kid had refused even to shake hands—and had topped everything by going upstairs and pounding on the floor with a hammer, pretending he was building something. Lois acts like she's afraid of him, Tony thought. She's too soft with him, that's the main trouble. What he needs is a good walloping.

But I better watch myself, he added, or that's the way I'll be spending my evenings all the rest of my life—walloping that kid. Or no, she probably wouldn't even let me talk back to him. If I hitched up with her, it would be just like it is now. The kid would be in charge of everything; our whole life would have to be built around his whims. . . . Too bad, he thought. A real knockout of a girl, too. And she certainly was gazing at him out of the softest, dampest eyes in history every time he saw her. Only she'd better come through with more than that pretty soon, if she wanted him to go on making this pilgrimage every other night or so. He was getting a little tired of her acting as though even a kiss with the brat in the same house was some sort of sin. After all, she'd been married, she knew her way around. She ought to be wise to the fact that acting aloof all the time didn't make a woman more attractive.

He turned off the drive into a suburban street lined with trees and small frame houses. Just why that snafu husband of hers had wanted to move her 'way out here to the end of the world, he couldn't figure out. He must have been a real goof, Tony thought. No wonder she divorced him—ten thousand dollars a year or no ten thousand dollars a year.

He pushed on the brake and turned off the motor. As he slammed the door he noticed the two kids digging a hole in the side yard—Joey hardly recognizable in sombrero, chaps, and high-heel boots.

"Hello there, Buffalo Bill," Tony said.

The kid didn't answer or even look up. Tony mounted the porch steps and the door opened.

"Somebody's had his car polished," she said.

"That's me," Tony said. "Always clean and respectable."

He noticed that she didn't touch him till they were inside the house with the door closed. Then she put her arms around him and kissed him very lightly on the mouth, in order not to spoil her lipstick. The softness and smell of her made him feel better about the drive out. He had a beauty here, all right—big slanted blue eyes, wide full mouth, creamy complexion, and dark heavy hair that swept back off her heart-shaped face. A little thin, but that wasn't really noticeable because her breasts and hips were good. She looked younger than any girl of thirty had a right to. No wonder when he'd met her at that party he'd never guessed she was already a mother with a seven-year-old kid on her hands.

"Anybody hungry?" she asked. "Or could you stand a drink first?"

3

They mixed martinis in the kitchen and carried them through the dining room, where he noticed ominously that three places were set at the table, into the living room.

"I spoke to Joey when I came in," he said. "But he didn't bother to answer."

"Oh, he probably didn't hear. He's so intense when he's playing."

He didn't say anything to that. There was no use making a big thing out of criticizing the kid, she always got excited then and went through the whole list of his merits—report cards, bright sayings, examples of politeness to strangers, and all the rest. Well, it was probably true, the kid might be all right to other people. It's like she says, Tony thought. Joey just resents me because he doesn't want anybody to take his father's place. And yet he couldn't drive the notion out of his head that even if the kid were grown up and they met casually somewhere without any past connections, they still wouldn't like each other. The kid was too sullen and too loud-mouthed both at the same time.

Lois had moved over closer to him. It gave him a sense of power to put his arm around her narrow shoulders like this.

"Does anybody love anybody?" she asked, flashing up her eyes.

She was kind of rushing it this evening. "Somebody loves

you," he said, a sinking feeling in the pit of his stomach because he knew where this kind of talk, cold sober before dinner might lead him.

"Then don't I rate a kiss?"

He looked down at her amazed—she'd always been so stingy with her kisses while the kid was still awake. He leaned over her, the smell of her heavy in his nostrils, and kissed her mouth. Rich—a deep kiss. He couldn't remember kisses any better, and he guessed he'd had his share. He slid his hand up to her breast, but she stiffened and sat up straight, pushing urgently against his chest.

For Christ sake, he thought, if she'd make up her—

And then he saw that Buffalo Bill was standing in the doorway staring at them.

"Did Sammy go home?" Lois asked breathlessly.

"Yes," Joey said. "I chased him home."

"Why, that's not nice, dear." She leaned forward and brushed the spray of blond hair off his forehead, but it fell back into place again. "That's no way to treat your friends."

"He laughed at me when I hurt my knee," Joey said. "He's not going to laugh at *me*."

After holding his face away and making a somewhat furtive attempt to wipe off the lipstick, Tony finally looked up. He had to raise up on one buttock to stuff the handkerchief back in his pocket—must be picking up a little weight since he'd bought this suit last winter. "What were you digging out there?" he asked. "A hole to China?"

Joey sat down and began to kick his legs against the chair. He didn't look at Tony. "You can't dig a hole to China. What do you know about digging?"

Tony tried to laugh. "Oh, I've had my share of digging, all right." He winked at Lois. "I thought I'd never get through digging foxholes when I was in the Army."

"You weren't either in the Army," Joey said, kicking harder and staring straight ahead. "You're too fat."

"Stop swinging your legs, dear. And you mustn't dispute Mr. Campbell's word."

"My father was in the Army but *he* wasn't. He wasn't anywhere. He's too fat to go anywhere."

"If you talk like that any more, Joey, you're going to be sent out of the room."

"I will not! I can stay here as long as I feel like it. Why don't you send *him* out of the room?"

A blind flash of anger brought Tony to his feet. "Well, if that's the alternative—"

"Please sit down, Tony," Lois said, grabbing his hand and smiling up at him. "Joey doesn't really mean what he's saying. He's been playing all afternoon and he's awfully tired."

Tony let himself be persuaded to sit down again. He lit a cigarette, adding fire to the fire that was already in his face. Why the hell, he wondered, did I come all the way out here just to get myself involved in something like this?

Joey's face was white and implacable. "You like *him* better than my father, don't you?" Joey said.

"For Christ sake," Tony said, "if we have to go through all that again—"

"Please." Lois put her hand on his arm. "Joey's going to bed right after dinner if he keeps talking like this. And he won't have any stories read to him for an entire week."

"I am *not* going to bed right after dinner. I'm going to stay up as long as he's here."

Lois jumped up: Tony was shocked at how witchlike her face could look when she was angry. "You're going to bed right now if you keep this up!" she shouted. "You'll eat your dinner right this minute and go straight to bed without another word!"

With a fine sense of diplomacy, Joey got off the chair and left the room, and Lois sank back down on the sofa. She tried to force her strained face into a smile, but without much success. "Do you have a cigarette, darling?" When he gave her one and lit it, she continued, "And how's the printing business these days?"

"Inky," Tony said, and in spite of the fact that he made his joke without much heart, she threw back her head and laughed elaborately—a kind of nervous release from the tension she'd just endured, he decided. "I had one customer today who said that the red we used on his job wasn't red enough."

"Oh, I love that!" Lois laughed.

"So I told him that next time I'd drain a pint of my blood into it and try to improve it."

"Oh, Tony, you didn't!"

"Sure I did," Tony said, suddenly realizing that it was a better line than he'd guessed it was this morning—especially since old Weaver hadn't cracked a smile. "You can't please some people no matter how hard you try, least of all in the printing business."

They sat quietly for a while, contemplating in silence the profound humor of Tony's answer, and then Lois pushed her soft shoulder against his chest and murmured, "Oh, darling, I don't know *what* I'd have done if you hadn't come out tonight. You *are* getting to be a habit, you know."

"Good or bad?"

She arched her eyebrows and took a deep drag on her cigarette before she smudged it out. "Smoking's my only *bad* habit."

He ran his hand down her ribs. "Could we try that kiss again?"

She leaned forward to listen. "I think that he's out in the kitchen, darling."

"For God's sake, do we have to go through this same watching-and-waiting game every time I see you?"

She turned her hurt face to him then, showing him moist eyes. He felt like a heel.

"It's just that we're never alone," Tony said. "I always feel I have an enemy in the house—even when he's sleeping."

She sighed, and let herself go limp against the back of the sofa. "But you just don't understand him, darling. You think he doesn't like you, and, believe me, that isn't true. Why, only yesterday he was after me to know when you were coming out again. Don't you see how much of a shock for him it must be to know that someone else is claiming some of my affection? You really can't expect a child to react any other way."

"Oh, I expect it all right," Tony said. "But how long is it going to keep up?"

She sat staring at the door through which Joey had disappeared. "He'll get over it soon," she said hopefully. "Really, darling, he's a *very* sweet and affectionate child. And polite, too. Did I tell you that his teacher sent a note home with his report saying how well mannered he is?"

4

He couldn't bring himself to cross her—she was a mother with her child. And it was obvious enough the kind of split-up person the kid was, trying to be the man of the house now that his father was gone. Yet the intense hatred that brewed in him wasn't easy to get rid of. It had been years since he'd felt this way about anybody.

"Let's get back to that kiss," she murmured. And this time *she* came to him—pushing her breasts against him hard and letting her mouth cover his. He closed his eyes, setting himself for something special, noting as he did so that she was acting more in love with him tonight than she ever had before. He ran his hand up her back, thinking, If she's willing to kiss like this here with the kid still awake, maybe tonight after—

"I want to listen to my radio program."

She jerked away from him. Joey stood blank-faced in the doorway, holding a white portable radio in his hands; he acted as though he hadn't seen a thing.

"Your radio program is off now," Lois said shrilly. "Go wash your face and hands, we're going to have dinner in a minute."

"It is *not* off! It's only six o'clock." He came on into the room and put the radio on the desk. "I want to know where it is on the dial." He began turning the knob around, bringing in an assortment of raucous noises.

"Which program are you talking about?"

"You know which one! The Flying Demon."

"Is that program still on the air?" Tony asked.

"You shut up!"

"You'd better be the one to shut up," Tony said, abashed because he'd really only asked the question to show Lois that he wasn't mad at the kid. "For God's sake, Lois, doesn't he have any manners at all?"

"I have more manners than you have! Fat Stuff!"

Tony was off the sofa and reaching for the kid before he realized it. But after he'd grabbed the tiny wrist he couldn't do anything except hold on, and the kid was shouting, "Take your hands off me! I'll tell my father on you!" He let him go and stood staring down at him, wishing he didn't have to glance over and see the look on Lois' face.

Joey slid off the chair and ran around to the sofa. Now he was sitting in the exact spot where Tony had been sitting, beside his mother.

"Fat Stuff!" Joey said. "Fat Stuff! Fat Stuff! Fat Stuff!"

Tony went into the dining room and picked up his hat from the chair.

"Upstairs this minute!" he heard Lois saying. "And no more movies for a whole month!"

"I don't care, he hit me," Joey was saying. "He can't hit me and get away with it."

"He *didn't* hit you, he merely grabbed you when you drove him to exasperation. Button up your shirt."

Tony went to the living-room door. "Think I'll take a run up the street and get some cigarettes; I'm all out," he said.

"But I have cigarettes somewhere," Lois said, glancing around the room. "You don't have to go out for them, I'll find some—I think upstairs."

He turned away. "I'll be back in a minute."

As he was opening the car door he heard her call from the house, "I'll have dinner on the table when you get back." He didn't look around; he started the motor.

5

"You're eating your dinner and then you're going to bed," Lois said. "I don't want any more nonsense out of you. You ought to be ashamed of yourself."

"I don't care, he started it."

"Just be quiet now and sit down and eat your dinner. We've heard enough out of you for one evening."

Suddenly docile, he sat down at the table and quietly devoured the roast beef and vegetables she brought him. She felt that she had triumphed after all, because he ate everything without objections, refusing nothing. And he did look darling sitting there—poor confused little thing. Certainly it wasn't his fault that he acted this way. It was the fault of his parents . . . of unfortunate circumstances for which she felt partly responsible. But the circumstances had been unavoidable. Even during the first months of her marriage she'd realized that she'd made a mistake; that under Arthur's likable exterior there was a steel barrier which kept him from communicating with people, from experiencing any of the carefree pleasantries which made living with another person possible. They'd had nothing to say to each other, that was the truth of the matter. He'd settled her out here far from town and driven home every evening to eat, read the paper and go to bed. And when Joey had arrived, he'd reacted like a spoiled child. He'd been positively *jealous* of her interest in her baby; had refused to pay the slightest attention to him. Of course, now that Joey was growing up he was showing more interest. He could swoop down at any moment and take him off to glamorous week ends whenever he chose to, spend piles of money, lavish gifts on him—no wonder Joey thought his father was some sort of god while she looked like the drab everyday reality. And there was no explaining to Arthur that this was the worst possible thing for the child—that *she* had to live with him every day of the week, not just a few hours a month like his father. As for the divorce, she had no regrets about it. Who could say whether it would be better for a child to grow up in a frigid, unfriendly atmosphere, rather than as the adored object of a mother and father who were separated? And besides, everyone knew that seven was a difficult age for any youngster.

"Come on now, cowboy," she said, taking his hand. "Let's toddle off to bed."

"I got to get something." He jerked away from her and flew into the living room, coming back in a moment carrying the white radio. She was going to object, but felt too worn out, and merely took him by the hand and led him up the stairs.

In the room he sat down on the bed while she knelt at his feet and took off his shoes and socks. Looking up at him, she saw a face so small, so wronged, so innocent, that it hurt her to look at him. He was the child of a love that was dead, wasn't he? So how could he be expected to react like anything except a lost creature? She was all he really had to depend on now, and she must never fail him in any way. Hugging him to her suddenly, she wanted to kiss him, but he pushed her away.

"Don't you want Mommy to kiss you?" she asked. "Mommy loves her little boy-baby."

"You can kiss me if you read me a story."

But she rebelled at that. "No story tonight," she said.
"You've been naughty to Mr. Campbell. You shouldn't be
naughty like that to one of Mother's friends."

"I don't like him. I don't want him coming around here."

"But *why* don't you like him, Joey? He's very nice to you."

"He's too fat, that's why."

"You mean you only like thin people? It would be a strange
kind of world if there were only thin people in it."

He was in bed now, propped up against the pillow. "Is Mr.
Campbell coming back?" he asked, the wide blue long-lashed
eyes that hurt her heart staring blankly at her.

"Of course he's coming back, dear."

"When?"

"In a few minutes."

"That's why you won't read me a story, isn't it?"

"No, of course it isn't. I won't read you a story because
you've been naughty today. Naughty little boys don't deserve
stories."

He turned his face to the wall. "No, you're not telling me the
truth. You won't read me a story because you'd rather be downstairs with Mr. Campbell."

She moved over closer to him. "Give Mommy a good-night
kiss."

"I want a story," he said without turning.

She stared for a while at his back—at the form of his little
body in the blue pajamas. Finally, she asked, resignedly, "If I
read you one page will you go right to sleep?"

"*The Little Red Fire Engine,*" he said jumping up and pulling the book from the bookcase.

And after she'd read the page, he was very good, he put his
arms around her neck and kissed her. "Lie down with me for a
minute, Mommy," he said. "Just till Mr. Campbell comes back."

She lay down beside him, her arms around him, her cheek
against his, her ear alert for the sound of Tony's footsteps on the
porch. When Joey's breathing became regular she gently disen-
gaged herself from him, got up, and tucked the covers snugly up
around his chin. After one last lingering glance at the way a spray
of blond hair, like a small hand, persisted in falling over his
forehead, she turned off the light and went downstairs.

6

In the kitchen, the roast, a few slices cut off the end, rested on top of the stove. The grease in the bottom of the pan had cooled and turned white.

In the dining room, the two unused plates and the carefully arranged silverware around them gleamed in the darkness on either side of the small vase of red roses, which were beginning to wilt.

In the living room, Lois lay curled in the corner of the sofa like a small animal seeking protection from the weather. She had been sleeping like this, her shoes knocked off on the floor and her silk-stockinged legs curled under her, for over an hour, but even now, awakening slowly, she didn't change her position.

Tony wasn't the first. Six months after her separation there had been Herb, too tall for her, too impossibly quiet for her, too much of a snob for her—a news announcer on the local radio station. Herb had called the whole thing off after he'd grown angry because she wouldn't go on a week-end trip to the Indianapolis auto races with him. She could hear his voice on the phone even now saying, "You're just going to have to learn to separate yourself from that kid of yours once in a while, Lois, or you'll never have any life of your own." He hadn't called again —and she'd hoped nobody would ever call again. But then, a month later, she'd met Ted, the brother-in-law of a neighbor of hers, and he'd taken up some of her evenings in the period immediately after her divorce had come through, leaving quite suddenly, with no promises for the future, when his company had transferred him to its Chicago office. And just now there had been Tony; she could already prepare herself to start looking back on Tony. It annoyed her a little when she realized that, of these three men, she'd chosen to sleep only with Herb; and he had certainly attracted her least of all. But perhaps it had happened like that because he'd been the first man to come into her life after her marriage had broken up, and she had slept with him in a kind of nihilistic rejection of everything that was finished with and behind her.

She had really begun to care about Tony; it wouldn't have been very much longer till they would have had a real affair. And now he was gone. In the first hour of waiting here for his return she'd tried to worry herself with the thought that perhaps something terrible had happened to delay him. But it hadn't worked; she needed only to think about the huffy way he'd left to know that he had probably not even stopped at the drugstore for cigarettes, but had driven straight on back to town.

She felt utterly alone. She wanted to go up to bed, but couldn't force her legs to move off this sofa. She longed for a cigarette and stiffened in resentment at the thought that he hadn't even bothered to bring her a pack before he left for good. These two stale martini glasses here before her: she wanted to sweep them off the table with the back of her hand. And yet she only sat here—stagnant, alone, slightly ill.

She came alert when she thought she heard Joey say something upstairs. He might only be talking in his sleep, but . . . So she roused herself at last and went out through the living room. She was already on the stairs when the phone began to ring.

"Hello, Lois?"

Should she just hang up or should she listen to what he had to say? She listened.

"Yes, Tony, what is it?"

"Lois . . . I'm drunk."

"Yes, that's quite evident, Tony."

"I couldn't come back tonight, Lois. I meant to come back . . . but a man can take just so much."

She hardened. "So much of what, Tony?"

He was too drunk to pay any attention to her question. "You'll let that kid ruin your life, Lois. If I hadn't had a few drinks I wouldn't be telling you this, but somebody ought to tell you. You're not doing Joey a favor or yourself either when you let him take advantage of you like that. You're still young enough to have some fun, Lois. You ought to— Look, why don't you get a baby sitter tonight?"

"What?"

"Get a baby sitter tonight and I'll come around with the car in about fifteen minutes and pick you up."

She couldn't help the short laugh that escaped her. "A baby sitter!" she said, and all her sudden hatred for him seemed to form a knot in her forehead. "So that's your solution—Fat Stuff!"

It had slipped out unconsciously, and she noted the unbe-
lieving pause at the other end before she jammed down the
receiver and went upstairs.

Joey lay on his side now, his right arm raised above his head
as though he were throwing a baseball in his sleep. The warmth
and meaning of her life flowed back into her veins as she went on
into the room and stood gazing down at him.

He awoke with a start when she tucked the sheet up around
him. "Mommy," he said, stretching up his arms.

She leaned over and let him embrace her.

"Mommy," he said sleepily, "stay here with me. Will you
sleep with me tonight, Mommy, please?"

"Of course I will, darling," she whispered.

And when she came back from the bathroom and lay down
beside him, she felt her spirit envelop him and embrace him, in
the way that her arms were doing, and she felt the world outside
slipping farther and farther away from her.

SHARING YOUR IMPRESSIONS

1. If you come from a broken home or have friends who do, share
   some of the adjustments that had to be made.
2. Make some guesses about the anxieties and fears you would
   expect to be common among children of divorce.
3. What can parents and children do to help one another
   through a divorce?
4. How can a divorced parent help children with their feelings of
   anxiety toward a potential step-parent?
5. In what ways should parent education be different for single
   persons who are rearing children by themselves?
6. What do you suppose are today's dominant fears among children? Adolescents? Young adults? Middle-age persons? The
   elderly?
7. What have you found to be the best way of coping with fears?
8. What are some examples of anxieties that are faced by most
   students? Teachers? Parents?
9. What anxieties do you suppose are most prominent among
   parents who are divorced? Unmarried? Widowed?

10

BLACK BOY

Richard Wright

Hunger stole upon me so slowly that at first I was not aware of what hunger really meant. Hunger had always been more or less at my elbow when I played, but now I began to wake up at night to find hunger standing at my bedside, staring at me gauntly. The hunger I had known before this had been no grim, hostile stranger; it had been a normal hunger that had made me beg constantly for bread, and when I ate a crust or two I was satisfied. But this new hunger baffled me, scared me, made me angry and insistent. Whenever I begged for food now my mother would pour me a cup of tea which would still the clamor in my stomach for a moment or two; but a little later I would feel hunger nudging my ribs, twisting my empty guts until they ached. I would grow dizzy and my vision would dim. I became less active in my play, and for the first time in my life I had to pause and think of what was happening to me.

"Mama, I'm hungry," I complained one afternoon.

"Jump up and catch a kungry," she said, trying to make me laugh and forget.

"What's a *kungry*?"

"It's what little boys eat when they get hungry," she said.

From pp. 13–16 in *Black Boy*, by Richard Wright. Copyright 1937, 1942, 1944, 1945 by Richard Wright. Reprinted by permission of Harper & Row, Publishers, Inc., Jonathan Cape Ltd., and Mrs. Ellen Wright.

"What does it taste like?"

"I don't know."

"Then why do you tell me to catch one?"

"Because you said that you were hungry," she said smiling.

I sensed that she was teasing me and it made me angry.

"But I'm hungry. I want to eat."

"You'll have to wait."

"But I want to eat now."

"But there's nothing to eat," she told me.

"Why?"

"Just because there's none," she explained.

"But I want to eat," I said, beginning to cry.

"You'll just have to wait," she said again.

"But why?"

"For God to send some food."

"When is He going to send it?"

"I don't know."

"But I'm hungry!"

She was ironing and she paused and looked at me with tears in her eyes.

"Where's your father?" she asked me.

I stared in bewilderment. Yes, it was true that my father had not come home to sleep for many days now and I could make as much noise as I wanted. Though I had not known why he was absent, I had been glad that he was not there to shout his restrictions at me. But it had never occurred to me that his absence would mean that there would be no food.

"I don't know," I said.

"Who brings food into the house?" my mother asked me.

"Papa," I said. "He always brought food."

"Well, your father isn't here now," she said.

"Where is he?"

"I don't know," she said.

"But I'm hungry," I whimpered, stomping my feet.

"You'll have to wait until I get a job and buy food," she said.

As the days slid past the image of my father became associated with my pangs of hunger, and whenever I felt hunger I thought of him with a deep biological bitterness.

My mother finally went to work as a cook and left me and my

brother alone in the flat each day with a loaf of bread and a pot of tea. When she returned at evening she would be tired and dispirited and would cry a lot. Sometimes, when she was in despair, she would call us to her and talk to us for hours, telling us that we now had no father, that our lives would be different from those of other children, that we must learn as soon as possible to take care of ourselves, to dress ourselves, to prepare our own food; that we must take upon ourselves the responsibility of the flat while she worked. Half frightened, we would promise solemnly. We did not understand what had happened between our father and our mother and the most that these long talks did to us was to make us feel a vague dread. Whenever we asked why father had left, she would tell us that we were too young to know.

One evening my mother told me that thereafter I would have to do the shopping for food. She took me to the corner store to show me the way. I was proud; I felt like a grownup. The next afternoon I looped the basket over my arm and went down the pavement toward the store. When I reached the corner, a gang of boys grabbed me, knocked me down, snatched the basket, took the money, and sent me running home in panic. That evening I told my mother what had happened, but she made no comment; she sat down at once, wrote another note, gave me more money, and sent me out to the grocery again. I crept down the steps and saw the same gang of boys playing down the street. I ran back into the house.

"What's the matter?" my mother asked.

"It's those same boys," I said. "They'll beat me."

"You've got to get over that," she said. "Now, go on."

"I'm scared," I said.

"Go on and don't pay any attention to them," she said.

I went out of the door and walked briskly down the sidewalk, praying that the gang would not molest me. But when I came abreast of them someone shouted.

"There he is!"

They came toward me and I broke into a wild run toward home. They overtook me and flung me to the pavement. I yelled, pleaded, kicked, but they wrenched the money out of my hand. They yanked me to my feet, gave me a few slaps, and sent me home sobbing. My mother met me at the door.

"They b-beat m-me," I gasped. "They t-t-took the m-money."

I started up the steps, seeking the shelter of the house.

"Don't you come in here," my mother warned me.

I froze in my tracks and stared at her.

"But they're coming after me," I said.

"You must stay right where you are," she said in a deadly tone. "I'm going to teach you this night to stand up and fight for yourself."

She went into the house and I waited, terrified, wondering what she was about. Presently she returned with more money and another note; she also had a long heavy stick.

"Take this money, this note, and this stick," she said. "Go to the store and buy those groceries. If those boys bother you, then fight."

I was baffled. My mother was telling me to fight, a thing that she had never done before.

"But I'm scared," I said.

"Don't you come into this house until you've gotten those groceries," she said.

"They'll beat me; they'll beat me," I said.

"Then stay in the streets; don't come back here!"

I ran up the steps and tried to force my way past her into the house. A stinging slap came on my jaw. I stood on the sidewalk, crying.

"Please, let me wait until tomorrow," I begged.

"No," she said. "Go now! If you come back into this house without those groceries, I'll whip you!"

She slammed the door and I heard the key turn in the lock. I shook with fright. I was alone upon the dark, hostile streets and gangs were after me. I had the choice of being beaten at home or away from home. I clutched the stick, crying, trying to reason. If I were beaten at home, there was absolutely nothing that I could do about it; but if I were beaten in the streets, I had a chance to fight and defend myself. I walked slowly down the sidewalk, coming closer to the gang of boys, holding the stick tightly. I was so full of fear that I could scarcely breathe. I was almost upon them now.

"There he is again!" the cry went up.

They surrounded me quickly and began to grab for my hand.

"I'll kill you!" I threatened.

They closed in. In blind fear I let the stick fly, feeling it crack against a boy's skull. I swung again, lamming another skull, then another. Realizing that they would retaliate if I let up for a second, I fought to lay them low, to knock them cold, to kill them so that they could not strike back at me. I flayed with tears in my eyes, teeth clenched, stark fear making me throw every ounce of strength behind each blow. I hit again and again, dropping the money and the grocery list. The boys scattered, yelling, nursing their heads, staring at me in utter disbelief. They had never seen such frenzy. I stood panting, egging them on, taunting them to come on and fight. When they refused, I ran after them and they tore out for their homes, screaming. The parents of the boys rushed into the streets and threatened me, and for the first time in my life I shouted at grownups, telling them that I would give them the same if they bothered me. I finally found my grocery list and the money and went to the store. On my way back I kept my stick poised for instant use, but there was not a single boy in sight. That night I won the right to the streets of Memphis.

SHARING YOUR IMPRESSIONS

1. What do you remember from your childhood about peers who picked on you and the way you coped with them?
2. What responsibility do teachers have to the victims of a bully? To the bully?
3. What should parents teach their children in order to help them deal with those who victimize them?
4. In what ways can siblings and other children help reduce peer abuse?
5. What is it about some children that makes them victims of bullies more often than other children?
6. What are the obligations of neighbors to other people's children?
7. How do you deal with mischievous children in your neighborhood?

11

THE NIGHT ENOCH SLEPT DOWNSTAIRS BY THE FIRE

Alan Sillitoe

Enoch's parents parted in a singular way. He was eight years of age at the time.

It happened one morning after he had gone to school, so that he didn't know anything about it till coming home in the evening.

Jack Boden got up as usual at seven o'clock, and his wife, who was Enoch's mother, set a breakfast of bacon and eggs before him. They never said much, and they spoke even less on this particular morning because both were solidly locked in their separate thoughts, which, unknown to each other, they were at last intending to act on.

Instead of getting a bus to his foundry, Jack boarded one for the city center. He sought out a public lavatory, where for the price of a penny he was able to draw off his overalls; he emerged with them under his arm. They were wrapped in the brown paper he had put into his pocket before leaving the house, a sly and unobtrusive movement as he called from the scullery: "So long, love. See you this afternoon."

Now, wearing a reasonable suit, he walked to the railroad station. There he met Rene, who had in her two suitcases a few of his possessions that he had fed to her during clandestine meetings over the past fortnight. They worked in the same factory and had, as many others who were employed there saw, "fallen for each other." Rene wasn't married, so there seemed nothing to stop her going away with him. And Jack's dull toothache of a conscience had, in the six months since he'd known her, cured itself at last.

Yet they got on the train to London feeling somewhat alarmed at the step they had taken, though neither liked to say anything in case the other should take it as a sign of wanting to back out. Hardly a word was spoken the whole way. Rene wondered what her parents would say when they saw she'd gone. Jack thought mostly about Enoch, but he knew he'd be safe enough with his mother, and that she'd bring him up right. He would send her a letter from London to explain that he had gone—in case she hadn't noticed it.

No sooner had Jack left for his normal daylight stint at the foundry than his wife Edna attended to Enoch. She watched him eat, standing by the mantelpiece for a good view of him during her stare. He looked up, half out of his sleep, and didn't smile back at her.

She kissed him, pushed sixpence into his pocket and sent him up the street to school; then she went upstairs to decide what things to take with her. It wasn't a hard choice, for though they had plenty of possessions, not many of them were movable. So it turned out that two suitcases and a handbag held all she wanted.

There was ample time, and she went downstairs to more tea and a proper breakfast. They'd been married ten years, and for seven, at least, she'd had enough. The trouble with Jack was that he'd let nothing worry him. He was so trustworthy and easygoing, he got on her nerves. He didn't even seem interested in other women, and the worst thing about such a man was that he hardly ever noticed when you were upset. When he did, he accused you of upsetting him.

There were so many things wrong that now that she was about to leave she couldn't bring them to mind, and this irritated her and made her think it had been even worse than it was, rather than the other way round. As a couple they had given up tackling any differences between them by the human method of talking. It was as if the sight of each other struck them dumb. On first meeting a dozen years ago they had been unable to say much—which, in their mutual attraction, they had confused with love at first sight. And they no longer tried to talk to each other about the way they felt because neither of them thought it would do any good. The only thing left was to act. It wasn't that life was dull, exactly, but they had nothing in common. If they had, maybe she could have put up with him no matter how bad he was.

For a week she'd been trying to write a letter, to be posted from where she was going, but she couldn't get beyond: "I'm leaving you for good, so stop bothering about me any more. Just look after Enoch, because I've had my bellyful and I'm off." After rereading it, she put it back in her handbag and closed it.

Having decided to act after years of thinking about it, she was now uncertain as to what she would do. A sister lived in Hull, so her first plan was to stay there till she found a job and a room. This was something to hang on to, and beyond it she didn't think. She'd just have to act again, and that was that. Once you started, there was probably no stopping, she thought, not feeling too good about it now that the time had come.

An hour later she turned the clock to the wall and walked out of the house for good, safe in knowing that shortly after Enoch came in from school his father would be home to feed him. They had lavished a lot of love on Enoch—she knew that. Maybe too much, some of which they should have given to each other but had grown too mean and shy to do.

She left the door unlocked so that he could just walk in. He was an intelligent lad who'd be able to turn on the gas fire if he felt cold. When Mrs. Mackley called from her back door to ask if she was going on her holidays, Edna laughed and said she was only off to see Jack's mother at Netherfield, to take her some old rags to cut up and use for rug clippings.

"Mam!" Enoch cried, going in by the back door. "Mam, where's my tea?"

He'd come running down the road with a pocketful of marbles. His head, in fact, looked like one of the more psychedelic ones, with a pale, round face, a lick of brilliant-ginger hair down over his forehead and a streak of red toffee stain across his mouth.

Gossiping again, he thought scornfully, seeing the kitchen empty. He threw his coat, still with sleeves twisted, over to the settee. The house did have more quiet than usual; he didn't know why. He turned the clock to face the right way and then went into the scullery and put the kettle on.

The tea wasn't like his mother made. It was too weak. But it was hot, so he put a lot of sugar in to make up for it and then sat at the table to read a comic.

It was early spring, and as soon as it began to get dark he switched the light on and went to draw the curtains. One half came over easily but the other only part of the way, leaving a foot-wide gap of dusk, like a long, open mouth going up instead of across. This bothered him for a while, until it got dark, when he decided to ignore it and switch the television on.

From hoping to see his mother he began to wonder where his father was. If his mother had gone to Aunt Jenny's and missed the bus home, maybe his father at the foundry had had an accident and fallen into one of the molds—from which it was impossible to get out alive, except as a skeleton.

Jam pot, butter dish, knife and crumbs were spread over the kitchen table when he got himself something to eat. Not that it bothered him that his father might have been killed, because when they had left him for an hour on his own a few months ago he had wondered what he would do if they never came back. Before he had had time to decide, though, they opened the door to tell him to get a sandwich and be off to bed sharp; otherwise he'd be too tired to get up for school in the morning. So he knew they'd be back sooner than he expected. When Johnny Bootle's father was killed in a lorry last year he'd envied him, but Johnny Bootle himself hadn't liked it very much.

Whether they came back or not, it was nice being in the house on his own. He was boss of it, could mash another pot of tea if he felt like it and keep the gas fire burning as long as he liked. The telly was flickering but he didn't want to switch it off, even though heads kept rolling up and up, so that when he looked at it continually for half a minute it seemed as if they were going round in a circle. He turned to scoop a spoonful of raspberry jam out of the pot and to swallow some more of the cold tea.

He sat in his father's chair by the fire, legs stretched across the rug, but ready to jump at the click of the outdoor latch and be back at the table before they could get into the room. His father wouldn't like him being in his chair, unless he was sitting on his knee. All he needed was a cigarette, and though he looked on the sideboard and along the shelf, there were none in sight. He had to content himself with trying to whistle in a thick, manly style. Johnny Bootle had been lucky in his loss because he'd had a sister.

If they didn't come back tonight, he wouldn't go to school in the morning. They'd shout at him when they found out, but that didn't matter if they were dead. It was eight o'clock, and he wondered where they were. They ought to be back by now, and he began to regret that he'd hoped they never would be, as if God's punishment for thinking this might be that He'd never let them.

He yawned, and picked up the clock to wind it. That was what you did when you yawned after eight in the evening. If they didn't come soon, he would have to go upstairs to bed, but he thought instead he would get some coats and sleep on the sofa down here, with the gas fire shining bright, rather than venture to his bedroom alone. They'd really gone for a night out, and that was a fact. Maybe they were late coming back because they'd gone for a divorce. When the same thing had happened to Tom Brunt it was because his mam had gone to fetch a baby, though he was taken into a neighbor's house next door before he'd been alone this long.

He looked along the shelf to see if he had missed a cigarette that he could put into his mouth and play at smoking with. He had good eyes and no need of glasses, that was true, because he'd been right the first time. In spite of the bread and jam he still felt hungry, and went into the scullery for some cheese.

When the light went, taking the flickering telly with it, he found a flashlight at the back of a dresser drawer and looked for a shilling to put in the meter. Fortunately the gas fire gave off enough pink glow for him to see the borders of the room, especially when he shone the flashlight beam continually around the walls as if it were a searchlight looking for enemy planes.

"It's a long wait to Tipperary"—as he had sometimes heard his father sing while drunk, but his eyes closed with the piece of cheese still in his hand. He hoped he would drop off before they came in so that they'd be sorry for staying out so late and wouldn't be able to be mad at him for not having gone to bed.

He walked across the room to the coat hooks in the recess, but his mother's and father's coats had gone, as he should have known they would be, since neither of them was in. There was nothing to put over himself when he went to sleep, but he still wouldn't go upstairs for a blanket. It would be as bad as going into a wood at night. He had run across the road once when a bus was coming and seen Frankenstein once on the telly, but he wouldn't go into a wood at night, even though lying Jimmy Kemp claimed to have done so.

Pushing one corner at a time, he got the table back against the sideboard. There was an oval mirror above the mantel, and he leaned both elbows on it to get as good a look at himself as he could in the wavering pink light—his round face and small ears, chin in shadow and eyes popping forward. He distorted his mouth with two fingers and curled his tongue hideously up to his nose to try to frighten himself away from the bigger fear of the house, which was threatening him with tears.

It was hard to remember what they'd done at school today, and when he tried to imagine his father walking into the house and switching on the light it was difficult to make out his face very clearly. He hated him for that, and hoped one day to kill him with an ax. Even his mother's face wasn't easy to bring back, but he didn't want to kill her. He felt his kneecaps burning from being too close to the gas bars, so he stood away to let them go cool.

When he was busy rolling up the carpet in front of the fire and was away from the mirror, his parents suddenly appeared to him properly, their faces side by side with absolute clarity, and he wished they'd come back. If they did, and asked what the bloody hell he thought he was doing, rolling up the carpet, he'd say, Well, what else do you expect me to do? I've got to use something for a blanket when I go to sleep on the settee, haven't I?

If there was one skill he was glad of it was that he could tell the time. He'd learned it properly only six months ago, so it had come just right. You didn't have to put a shilling in the clock, so that was still ticking, at least, except that it made him feel tired.

He heaved at the settee to swivel it around in front of the fire, a feat that convinced him that one day he'd be as strong as his father—wherever he was. There was certainly no hope of the gas keeping on till the morning, so he turned it down to number two. Then he lay on the settee and pulled the carpet over him. It smelled of stone and pumice, and of soap that had gone bad.

He sniffed the cold air and sensed there was daylight in it, though he couldn't open his eyes. Weaving his hand as far as it would go, he felt that the gas fire had gone out, meaning that the cooking stove wouldn't work. He wondered why his eyelids were stuck together. Then he thought of chopping up a chair to make a blaze, but the grate was blocked by the gas fire. This disappointed him, because it would have been nice to lean over a fire, warming himself as the bottom of the kettle got blacker and blacker till it boiled at the top.

When his eyes mysteriously opened, old Tinface the clock said it was half past seven. In any case there were no matches left to light anything. He went into the scullery to wash his face.

He had to be content with a cup of milk with a spoonful of sugar in it, and more bread and cheese. People were walking along the back yards on their way to work. If they've gone for good, he thought, I shall go to my grandma's, and I'll have to change schools because she lives at Netherfield, miles away.

His mother had given him sixpence for sweets the morning before, and he already had twopence, so he knew that this was enough to get him half-fare to Netherfield.

That's all I can do, he thought, turning the clock to the wall. He wondered whether he ought to put the furniture right in case his parents came in and got mad that it was all over the place, though he hoped they wouldn't care, since they'd left him all night on his own.

Apart from not wanting to spend the sixpence his mother had given him till she came back, he was sorry at having to go to his grandma's because now he wouldn't be able to go to school and tell his mates that he'd been all night in a house on his own.

He pushed a way to the upper deck of the bus, from which

height he could look down on the roofs of cars and see level into the top seats of other buses passing them through the town. You never know, he thought; I might see 'em—going home to put a shilling each in the light and gas for me. He gave his money to the conductor.

It took a long time to get clear of traffic at Canning Circus, and he wished he'd packed up some bread and cheese before leaving the house. Men were smoking foul fags all around, and a gang of boys going to People's College made a big noise until the conductor told them to stop it or he'd put them off.

He knew the name of his grandmother's street but not how to get there from the bus stop. A postman pointed the direction for him. Netherfield was on the edge of Nottingham, and huge black cauliflower clouds with the sun locked inside came over on the wind from Colwick Woods.

When his grandmother opened the back door he was turning the handle of the old mangle outside. She told him to stop and then asked in a tone of surprise why he was there at that time of morning.

"Dad and Mam have gone," he said.

"Gone?" she cried, pulling him into the scullery. "What do you mean?"

He saw the big coal fire and smelled the remains of bacon that she must have done for Tom's breakfast—the last of her sons living there. His face was distorted with pain.

"No," she said, "nay, you mustn't cry. Whatever's the matter for you to cry like that?"

The tea she poured was hot, strong and sweet, and he was sorry at having cried in front of her.

"All right now?" she said, drawing back to watch him and see if it was.

He nodded. "I slept on the couch."

"The whole night! And where can they be?"

He saw she was worried. "They had an accident," he told her, pouring his tea into the saucer to cool it. She fried him an egg and gave him bread and butter.

"Our Jack's never had an accident," she said grimly.

"If they're dead, Grandma, can I live with you?"

"Aye, you can. But they're not, so you needn't worry your little eyes."

"They must be," he told her, feeling certain about it.

"We'll see," she said. "When I've cleaned up a bit, we'll go and find out what got into 'em."

He watched her sweeping the room, then stood in the doorway as she knelt down to scrub the scullery floor, a smell of cold water and pumice when she reached the doorstep.

"I've got to keep the place spotless," she said with a laugh, standing up, "or your Uncle Tom would leave home. He's bound to get married one day, though, and that's a fact. His three brothers did, one of 'em being your daft father."

She held his hand back to the bus stop. If Uncle Tom does clear off, it looks like she'll have me to look after, he thought. It seemed years already since he'd last seen his mother and father, and he was growing to like the adventure of it, provided they didn't stay away too long. It was rare going twice across town in one day.

It started to rain, so they stood in a shop doorway to wait for the bus. There wasn't so many people on it this time, and they sat on the bottom deck because his grandma didn't feel like climbing all them steps.

"Did you lock the door behind you?"

"I forgot."

"Let's hope nobody goes in."

"There was no light left," he said. "Nor any gas. I was cold when I woke up."

"I'm sure you was," she said. "But you're a big lad now. You should have gone to a neighbor's house. They'd have given you some tea. Mrs. Upton would, I'm sure. Or Mrs. Mackley."

"I kept thinking they'd be back any minute."

"You always have to go to the neighbors'," she told him when they got off the bus and walked across Ilkeston Road. Her hand had warmed up now from the pumice and cold water. "Don't kick your feet like that."

If it happened again, he would take her advice. He hoped it wouldn't, though next time he'd sleep in his bed and not be frightened.

They walked down the yard and in by the back door. Nothing was missing; he could have told anybody that, though he didn't speak. The empty house seemed dead, and he didn't like that. He couldn't stay on his own, so he followed his grandmother upstairs and into every room, half expecting her to find them in some secret place he'd never known of.

The beds were made and wardrobe doors closed. One of the windows was open a few inches, so she slammed it shut and locked it. "Come on down. There's nowt up here."

She put a shilling in the gas meter and set a kettle on the stove. "Might as well have a cup of tea while I think this one out. A bloody big one it is, as well."

It was the first time he'd heard her swear, but then, he'd never seen her so worried, either. It made him feel better. She thought about the front room, and he followed her.

"They kept the house clean, any road up," she said, touching the curtains and chair covers. "That's summat to be said for 'em. But it ain't everything."

"It ain't," he agreed, and saw two letters lying on the mat just inside the front door. He watched her broad back as she bent to pick them up, thinking now that they both were dead, for sure.

SHARING YOUR IMPRESSIONS

1. Describe a neglected or abused child whom you have known.
2. Make some guesses about what the adults involved in child abuse have in common. Then suggest some ways to minimize child abuse.
3. Children sometimes announce that they're going to run away from home, but until recently parents seldom did so. How do you account for the reported rise in missing mothers and fathers?
4. In your opinion, how does lack of communication between parents affect their children?
5. Since current statistics show that divorce is a reality in the lives of many elementary school children, what should the schools be doing to help children understand something about the causes and meaning of divorce?

6. Parent education now focuses almost exclusively on pre-school. Give some reasons for supporting the education of parents at other levels of a child's development.
7. Parent education is still in the formative stage. How should it differ from the education of certified teachers in terms of content and procedures?
8. Give some examples supporting the assertion that the United States is becoming an anti-child society. Then provide some reasons for being optimistic about the future of today's children.

12

THE FIRST DAY OF SCHOOL

R. V. Cassill

Thirteen bubbles floated in the milk. Their pearl transparent hemispheres gleamed like souvenirs of the summer days just past, rich with blue reflections of the sky and with shadowy greens. John Hawkins jabbed the bubble closest to him with his spoon, and it disappeared without a ripple. On the white surface there was no mark of where it had been.

"Stop tooling that oatmeal and eat it," his mother said. She glanced meaningfully at the clock on the varnished cupboard. She nodded a heavy, emphatic affirmation that now the clock was boss. Summer was over, when the gracious oncoming of morning light and the stir of early breezes promised that time was a luxury.

"Audrey's not even down yet," he said.

"Audrey'll be down."

"You think she's taking longer to dress because she wants to look nice today?"

"She likes to look *neat*."

"What I was thinking," he said slowly, "was that maybe she didn't feel like going today. Didn't feel *exactly* like it."

Reprinted from *The Happy Marriage*, by R. V. Cassill. Copyright © 1966, Purdue Research Foundation, West Lafayette, Indiana, U.S.A. Reprinted by permission of the author and publisher.

"Of course she'll go."

"I meant she might not want to go until tomorrow, maybe. Until we see what happens."

"Nothing's going to happen," his mother said.

"I know there isn't. But what if it did?" Again John swirled the tip of his spoon in the milk. It was like writing on a surface that would keep no mark.

"Eat and be quiet. Audrey's coming, so let's stop this here kind of talk."

He heard the tap of heels on the stairs, and his sister came down into the kitchen. She looked fresh and cool in her white dress. Her lids looked heavy. She must have slept all right—and for this John felt both envy and a faint resentment. He had not really slept since midnight. The heavy traffic in town, the long wail of horns as somebody raced in on the U. S. highway holding the horn button down, and the restless murmur, like the sound of a celebration down in the courthouse square, had kept him awake after that. Each time a car had passed their house his breath had gone tight and sluggish. It was better to stay awake and ready, he had told himself, than to be caught asleep.

"Daddy gone?" Audrey asked softly as she took her place across the table from her brother.

"He's been gone an hour," their mother answered. "You know what time he has to be at the mine."

"She means, did he go to work today?" John said. His voice had risen impatiently. He met his mother's stout gaze in a staring contest, trying to make her admit by at least some flicker of expression that today was different from any other day. "I thought he might be down at Reverend Specker's," John said. "Cal's father and Vonnie's and some of the others are going to be there to wait and see."

Maybe his mother smiled then. If so, the smile was so faint that he could not be sure. "You know your father isn't much of a hand for waiting," she said. "Eat. It's a quarter past eight."

As he spooned the warm oatmeal into his mouth he heard the rain crow calling again from the trees beyond the railroad embankment. He had heard it since the first light came before dawn, and he had thought, Maybe the bird knows it's going to rain, after all. He hoped it would. *They won't come out in the rain*, he had thought. Not so many of them, at least. He could wear a raincoat. A raincoat might help him feel more protected on the walk to school. It would be a sort of disguise, at least.

But since dawn the sun had lain across the green Kentucky trees and the roofs of town like a clean, hard fire. The sky was as clear as fresh-washed window glass. The rain crow was wrong about the weather. And still, John thought, its lamenting, repeated call must mean something.

His mother and Audrey were talking about the groceries she was to bring when she came home from school at lunch time. A five-pound bag of sugar, a fresh pineapple, a pound of butter . . . .

"Listen!" John said. Downtown the sound of a siren had begun. A volley of automobile horns broke around it as if they meant to drown it out. "*Listen* to them."

"It's only the National Guard, I expect," his mother said calmly. "They came in early this morning before light. And it may be some foolish kids honking at them, the way they would. Audrey, if Henry doesn't have a good-looking roast, why then let it go, and I'll walk out to Weaver's this afternoon and get one there. I wanted to have something a little bit special for our dinner tonight."

So . . . John thought . . . she wasn't asleep last night either. Someone had come stealthily to the house to bring his parents word about the National Guard. That meant they knew about the others who had come into town, too. Maybe all through the night there had been a swift passage of messengers through the neighborhood and a whispering of information that his mother meant to keep from him. Your folks told you, he reflected bitterly, that nothing is better than knowing. Knowing whatever there is in this world to be known. That was why you had to be one of the half dozen kids out of some nine hundred colored of school age who were going today to start classes at Joseph P. Gilmore High instead of Webster. Knowing and learning the truth were worth so much they said—and then left it to the hooting rain crow to tell you that things were worse than everybody had hoped.

Something had gone wrong, bad enough wrong so the National Guard had to be called out.

"It's eight twenty-five," his mother said. "Did you get that

snap sewed on right, Audrey?" As her experienced fingers ex-
amined the shoulder of Audrey's dress they lingered a moment
in an involuntary, sheltering caress. "It's all arranged," she told
her children, "how you'll walk down to the Baptist Church and
meet the others there. You know there'll be Reverend Chader,
Reverend Smith, and Mr. Hall to go with you. It may be that the
white ministers will go with you, or they may be waiting at
school. We don't know. But now you be sure, don't you go
farther than the Baptist Church alone." Carefully she lifted her
hand clear of Audrey's shoulder. John thought, Why doesn't she
hug her if that's what she wants to do?

He pushed away from the table and went out on the front
porch. The dazzling sunlight lay shadowless on the street that
swept down toward the Baptist Church at the edge of the colored
section. The street seemed awfully long this morning, the way it
had looked when he was little. A chicken was clucking conten-
tedly behind their neighbor's house, feeling the warmth, settling
itself into the sun-warmed dust. Lucky chicken.

He blinked at the sun's glare on the concrete steps leading
down from the porch. He remembered something else from the
time he was little. Once he had kicked Audrey's doll buggy down
these same steps. He had done it out of meanness—for some silly
reason he had been mad at her. But as soon as the buggy had
started to bump down, he had understood how terrible it was not
to be able to run after it and stop it. It had gathered speed at each
step and when it hit the sidewalk it had spilled over. Audrey's
doll had smashed into sharp little pieces on the sidewalk below.
His mother had come out of the house to find him crying harder
than Audrey. "Now you know that when something gets out of
your hands it is in the Devil's hands," his mother had explained
to him. Did she expect him to forget—now—that that was always
the way things went to smash when they got out of hand? Again
he heard the siren and the hooting, mocking horns from the
center of town. Didn't his mother think *they* could get out of
hand?

He closed his eyes and seemed to see something like a doll
buggy bump down long steps like those at Joseph P. Gilmore
High, and it seemed to him that it was not a doll that was riding
down to be smashed.

He made up his mind then. He would go today, because he had said he would. Therefore he had to. But he wouldn't go unless Audrey stayed home. That was going to be his condition. His bargaining looked perfect. He would trade them one for one.

His mother and Audrey came together onto the porch. His mother said, "My stars, I forgot to give you the money for the groceries." She let the screen door bang as she went swiftly back into the house.

As soon as they were alone, he took Audrey's bare arm in his hand and pinched hard. "You gotta stay home," he whispered. "Don't you know there's thousands of people down there? Didn't you hear them coming in all night long? You slept, didn't you? All right. You can hear them now. Tell her you're sick. She won't expect you to go if you're sick. I'll knock you down, I'll smash you if you don't tell her that." He bared his teeth and twisted his nails into the skin of her arm. "Hear them horns," he hissed.

He forced her halfway to her knees with the strength of his fear and rage. They swayed there, locked for a minute. Her knee dropped to the porch floor. She lowered her eyes. He thought he had won.

But she was saying something and in spite of himself he listened to her almost whispered refusal. "Don't you know anything? Don't you know it's harder for them than us? Don't you know Daddy didn't go to the mine this morning? They laid him off on account of us. They told him not to come if we went to school."

Uncertainly he relaxed his grip. "How do you know all that?"

"I listen," she said. Her eyes lit with a sudden spark that seemed to come from their absolute brown depths. "But I don't let on all I know the way you do. I'm not a . . . ." Her last word sunk so low that he could not exactly hear it. But if his ear missed it, his understanding caught it. He knew she had said "coward."

He let her get up then. She was standing beside him, serene and prim when their mother came out on the porch again.

"Here, child," their mother said to Audrey, counting the dollar bills into her hand. "There's six, and I guess it will be all right if you have some left if you and Brother get yourselves a cone to lick on the way home."

John was not looking at his sister then. He was already turning to face the shadowless street, but he heard the unmistakable poised amusement of her voice when she said, "Ma, don't you know we're a little too old for that?"

"Yes, you are," their mother said. "Seems I had forgotten that."

They were too old to take each other's hand, either, as they went down the steps of their home and into the street. As they turned to the right, facing the sun, they heard the chattering of a tank's tread on the pavement by the school. A voice too distant to be understood bawled a military command. There were horns again and a crescendo of boos.

Behind them they heard their mother call something. It was lost in the general racket.

"What?" John called back to her. "What?"

She had followed them out as far as the sidewalk, but not past the gate. As they hesitated to listen, she put her hands to either side of her mouth and called to them the words she had so often used when she let them go away from home.

"Behave yourselves," she said.

SHARING YOUR IMPRESSIONS

1. What are some of the ethnic prejudices you were led to believe as a child?
2. Disclose some of the racial prejudices that are still with you.
3. Compare the ethnic prejudice of your children or students with that of boys and girls when you were growing up.
4. Share your thinking about busing as a means to achieve racial balance within schools.
5. What do you see as the best ways of helping children to grow up without racial prejudice?
6. What are your feelings about the worthwhileness of children's having playmates of different races?

4

MODELS
AND
OBSERVERS

13

A DIFFERENT WORLD

Robert M. Coates

Jim Barnett held the apartment door open with his foot while he took the key out of the lock and dropped it into his pocket. Then he stepped inside and let the door slam behind him. "Hi!" he said. "Anybody home?" There was no answer, and in a way he hadn't expected any; from where he stood in the little entrance hall he could see into the living room, with its white painted walls and carefully placed furniture and the chill end-of-the-afternoon light coming in from the two windows, and the very air of the place seemed empty. It was Della's day off, he remembered; probably Helen had Jamie out in the Park, or somewhere. Jim was a young man, under thirty, with a bony, brown, handsome face, dark eyes, and a wide mouth beneath a small black mustache. He had on a gray overcoat and a carelessly crumpled felt hat, and he had a brown paper parcel, wrapped tightly enough to define the shape of two bottles, under his arm.

He put the parcel down on the telephone table in the hall and walked into the living room. The doors of both bedrooms were standing open and—not that he expected to find any notes propped on dressing tables or anything; that would have been silly—he walked past each and looked in. His and Helen's was neat as usual, the bed made up, his pajamas put away, the counterpane drawn into place. Jamie's was the customary jumble: toys, picture books, games and fragments of games overflowing the big catchall box in the corner; a scooter propped against a chair; and, spread out on the play table, a half-dozen cardboard rectangles of the kind they use to keep shirts in shape, all of these now covered with scrawls of colored crayon. He stood looking at it a moment. "A different world," he said, for some reason aloud. "Well, the laundry came anyway, I see." He turned back to the living room.

With no one in it and no noise or voices stirring, it looked bare. The morning's *Times* lay folded on one end of the sofa, and bunched on the seat of the easy chair in the window corner were three or four pairs of silk stockings rolled up in balls. Helen's wooden workbasket, that was shaped like a Shaker cradle and that she'd had for God knows how many years—long before she'd had him, anyway—was standing on the floor beside the chair. He picked up one of the stocking balls and looked at it. It was rolled so that all you saw was the hem, doubled back in a kind of bag in which the rest of the stocking lay bunched, and the top of the bag was loose and wrinkly; he couldn't help thinking how humdrum and unattractive the thing looked compared to the way a stocking looked on a woman's leg.

If Helen ever really left, he thought, it wouldn't be without her workbasket. He tossed the ball back onto the chair, aiming for the others in the group and overshooting a little. He went to the hall and, taking off his overcoat and hat, hung them in the closet, then walked into the kitchen, picking up the parcel and unwrapping it as he went. It contained two bottles of rye. He opened one, got some ice from the refrigerator and the bottle of Italian vermouth from the liquor shelf, and mixed himself a Manhattan. Then he went into the living room and, pushing the stockings to one side, sat down in the easy chair. He had hardly settled himself there before he heard the scrape of a key in the lock. It was Helen and Jamie; he could hear Jamie's high, excited voice saying something and Helen replying, laughing, as she opened the door. Then they both came in.

They came in in a kind of tangle, Helen pulling at Jamie's toboggan cap and he squealing and trying to get past her, and at first they didn't notice the man in the chair. Then he said, "Well, what ho!" and they both turned around.

"Oh, look, Mummy, look! Daddy's home!" Jamie shouted, and ran over to him. He was about five, with his mother's pale skin and bright-blue eyes, and he was holding something small and red in his hand and waving it. "Daddy, look!" he said, but the man didn't pay much attention. He put his hand on the boy's head and rubbed it absently. He was looking at Helen. "Sure, kiddo," he said. "Sure, sure."

Helen hadn't moved. "Jamie!" she said sharply, and stopped, and then for a second she didn't say anything. She had on her black caracul jacket and the little black matching fur hat, and her cheeks were flushed and fresh-looking from the cold air outside. She wasn't laughing now. Her face had gone set and expressionless, and after that first quick glance of surprise she hadn't really looked at him at all. "Well," she said finally. "You're home early."

He took a sip from his glass, his eyes watching her over the rim. "You don't seem too pleased," he said.

"About what?"

Jamie was leaning over the side of the chair, pulling at his father's sleeve. "Daddy, look," he kept saying. Jim stiffened his arm and held him away. "Just a minute, kid. Don't spill my drink now," he said. "About my being home, of course."

"Should I be?" she said coolly. She hung her things in the closet and shut the door. "Jamie. Better take off your snow suit now. Before you get hot."

"But Daddy hasn't looked yet."

Helen sighed. "It's that little dump truck he lost the other day in the Park. Another boy found it and gave it to him. You might look at it."

Jim looked at it and then at the boy. Jamie was staring up at him with that clear, intent gaze a child's eyes can assume. "It was Stevie Albright that found it," he explained. He had captured his father's attention at last and he didn't want to relinquish it, but he felt the pull of his mother's command, too, and it made him talk faster and faster, his eyes wide and his voice excited. "He found it in the sand pile where I losted it and he took it home and his mummy told him it was mine, so he brought it right back and he gave it to me. Today."

"Well, well," the man said.

Helen was standing by the couch. "Jamie. Come," she said.

This time he obeyed. He went over to the couch and climbed on it, dangling his legs so she could pull off his galoshes. "It was Stevie Albright, Mummy," he repeated.

"I know," she said. He sat fingering the loose stuff of her dress at the shoulder and looking past her at his father. "Wasn't Stevie nice to find my truck for me, Daddy?" he demanded.

"He sure was, kid."

"I'll have to give *him* something next time, I guess."

"I suppose you will." The man got up and walked over to where Helen was kneeling in front of the couch. She didn't look around. "I got some rye," he said. "Would you like a drink?"

"Not just now, thanks."

He stood looking down at her. "You still sore about last night?" he asked.

"How did you think I would feel?"

A sort of stubborn look came over his face, but he kept his voice even. "Because that's why I came home. I thought maybe the way we were talking last night—I mean I got to thinking about it. I really do feel lousy about the whole business, Helen. I wanted you to know that."

"Look," she said. "Let's just not talk now, shall we? While someone's here?"

Jim glanced at Jamie, and Jamie smiled. But his father's glance went right back to his mother's head again. His mother had her head bent down. "I just wanted to say I was sorry, that's all," his father said. "There's no harm in anyone hearing that."

"I suppose not. There's no harm in anyone hearing anything, I guess."

Suddenly his father's face got dark red. "Well, you'd rather hear about things like that than not be told anything, wouldn't you?" he demanded. "God almighty! That's what we always agreed on anyway, isn't it? And then when I do tell you—"

"Please, for God's *sake!*" she cut in, "I said not *talk* about it." She pulled off Jamie's ski pants and then gave him a pat as he slid off the couch. "Jamie, run into your room and play there, will you?" she said. Then she turned to face his father. "And it's not what *I* hear that bothers me," she went on. Her face had got white and her lips tight. "It's what everybody else will hear. If you'd done it with some stranger, some woman you were never going to see again. But doing it with a woman we both know, and in such a way—so you'd disgrace me and her and everybody, as well as yourself. No. This time it's really too much. This is really the end."

Jamie stood watching them both. He could tell by his father's expression that he was really angry, and though he couldn't see his mother's face now, he could tell by her voice that something was wrong with her too; her voice was so high and uneven that it sounded almost as if she were crying, and at the thought of that, though he had no idea what could be troubling her, such a feeling of insecurity and dread went through him that for a moment he wanted to cry too. "Mummy," he started to say, but as soon as he spoke she turned on him, and he saw at least that she wasn't crying; her eyes were bright and hard. "Jamie," she said, in a strange, tense voice that he'd never heard her use before, "I told you to go into your room." His father didn't say anything; he just turned abruptly away and walked over to look out the window.

"Can I take my truck too?" Jamie said.

"Yes, of course you can," she said, and gave him a little push toward the door. As Jamie walked away he heard his father start back toward his mother. "Now, listen," his father said, but then they both went into the other bedroom, and when they got there they shut the door. He could still hear them talking, but he couldn't make out the words, and anyway he was forgetting about all that now; there was so much here that was interesting. He liked his room and everything in it, and the way things were scattered around represented no disorder to his mind; if you wanted something you picked it up, and if you tired of it you put it down, and if they all got mixed up, as they did in the box in the corner, it only meant more surprises later when you started digging among them. In that way every toy was almost a new toy every time you found it.

But now he wanted to do something with the dump truck, and after he had looked around for a moment he went over to the play table and pushed the shirt boards off onto the floor. This made the table a clean, level place where anything might happen, and he began pushing the dump truck tentatively around its edge. Gradually ideas occurred to him. It was a policeman's car that he was driving down a street past a great many stores, and at each store he had to stop and back the car into the curb and park it and buy things and load them in and then drive away again. There was a long scratch that had been made in the table top once long ago. Where it crossed the street it became a river, and that made it the river they had all crossed in the ferry, his mother and father and he, and he sitting on his mother's lap because the back was all loaded down with suitcases and bundles.

That was when they had gone to the beach last summer. He drove on and when he reached the beach the car became a dump truck again, because a dump truck goes where they have a lot of sand. He raised his head suddenly. He was wondering why it was that, all through last summer, he had never once seen a dump truck coming to the beach for sand, and he almost started into the other room to ask someone, his mother or his father, why that was.

But just as he was almost going to do so, the door of their bedroom slammed and his father walked rapidly across the living room, and then he heard him yank at the clothes closet and the outer door slammed too. He sat for a moment, thinking. It had struck him that maybe the trucks only came to the beach at night, when no people were there, and in that case he'd have to have headlights and this truck didn't have any headlights. But then he began to forget about the sand problem and he went back to pushing the toy around again. It could just as well not be the beach at all. It could be that place up the street where they had torn the building down and all the steam shovels were working. There were plenty of trucks around there.

SHARING YOUR IMPRESSIONS

1. How did your parents feel about conducting conflict in your presence when you were a child? An adolescent? An adult?
2. How do you feel about arguing or expressing differences with another adult in front of your children or students?
3. Why do you suppose so many of us tend to fear interpersonal conflict?

4. We seldom view the conflicts of children in terms of possible benefit. Identify some types of conflict that youngsters experience, and consider how these encounters can support personality development.
5. Identify some topics of parent conflict that children should be spared exposure to.
6. How can parents and teachers help young children better understand the place of conflict in human relations?
7. Today we hear a great deal about child abuse. How common do you suppose the tragedy of battered women has become?

14

BOYS ARE AFRAID OF GIRLS

John De Meyer

Nancy was presumably doing her homework, but when Walter Fenton left his beloved tulips and walked into the house, what he saw in the living room caused his mouth to fall open. His fifteen-year-old daughter was draped across an overstuffed chair, she had on faded dungarees, a tired sweat shirt, antique saddle shoes, her pony hairdo was tied with a limp red ribbon and she had an enormous dish of ice cream in her lap. She was also reading a magazine, the television set was on full blast and the radio was apparently doubling in brass for the entire neighborhood.

"Nancy!" Walter Fenton exploded.

Nancy sighed. "Yes, father?"

Walter Fenton recognized the sigh as his daughter's the-rebellion-is-here-so-let's-see-how-bad-it-is-before-we-get-excited question mark. Which didn't help his feelings a bit. When his daughter had first become fifteen and had made the glorious discovery that there were boy creatures in the world, he had gone by the familiar "daddy." But now that Nancy was an elderly fifteen and wise to the ways of catching boy creatures, she had suddenly taken to the more formal "father." At first Walter Fenton, starved for dignity within his own household, had been pleased. Then he had discovered the enormous number of implications to the word "father." The word could imply everything from woebegone poverty, dire exhaustion which required automobile transportation to school, acquiescence, tolerance and a need for assistance with her homework, to impatience, lofty scorn, forbearance, martyrdom, renunciation, sacrifice and a complete resignation to the utter impossibility of ever being able to cope with retarded parents.

"What about your homework?" Walter Fenton demanded.

Nancy reached behind her for a notebook. "See, father?"

Like most fathers, Walter Fenton hated to be confronted with a *fait accompli* in the face of parental indignation. Fortunately, there was still the ice-cream, magazine, radio and television ensemble.

"Nancy, shut your eyes and tell me what's on television!" he ordered.

Nancy shut her eyes and licked ice cream from her spoon. "The kidnaper in the checkered shirt is sneaking up on Roy Rogers; on the radio Our Miss Brooks is saying no again, on account of she wants more time to think; the story in the magazine is about a juvenile delinquent with obtuse parents, and the judge has just told the father to give up golf if he wants to save his boy; and this ice cream is chocolate, lemon and lime, orange sherbet and peppermint stick. Is there anything else you want to know, father?"

"No," said Walter Fenton, deflated.

The telephone rang.

"Will you please pass me the phone, father?"

"Nancy! How can you possibly know the phone is for you?"

"I bet it is."

"Well, I bet it isn't!" said Walter Fenton.

He answered the phone and a young female voice said, "May I speak to Nancy, please?" Dismally, Walter Fenton handed the phone to Nancy.

"Thank you, father," Nancy said.

Which caused Walter Fenton to stomp out of the house. Something undefinably baffling and exasperating had come into his life and he intended to find out what it was.

He found his wife, Emily, raking up the debris he had left from weeding his tulips. "Emily, will you tell me what's going on around here?" he said. As usual, he approached Emily with the

indirect, for after seventeen years of married life he had learned
that the outcome of approaching Emily directly was unpredict-
able; he was always in danger of winding up arguing against his
own premise.

Emily handed him the rake. "You dug these weeds; you
rake 'em," she said.

"I asked you a question, Emily."

"Isn't her homework done?"

Walter Fenton flapped his hands helplessly. "Yes," he
sighed.

"Well? She can't get much better than straight A's, you
know."

"But she's in there dressed like a queen of the hoboes!"

"Last month when the females of this house bought a few
frocks, you howled like a banshee."

"And she's eating a gallon of ice cream, reading a magazine,
listening to the radio and watching television, all at the same
time!"

"Poor kid."

"How about poor me?" Walter Fenton cried. "Emily, my
own daughter is beginning to treat me like a backward child!"

"You should talk," said Emily. "She tells me I'm getting
old-fashioned yet."

One thing Walter Fenton could not imagine was Emily's
getting old-fashioned. "Emily, what's wrong with her?" he said
in alarm.

Emily looked at him steadily. "Don't you know?"

"No, Emily, I don't."

Emily sniffed.

"It couldn't be boy trouble, Emily! If there is any scheme
under the sun that child hasn't used to lure boys into captivity, I
haven't heard of it."

Emily placed her hands akimbo. "Walter Fenton," she said,
"don't you know that there comes a time in every girl's life when
there's a difference between chasing a boy and having a boy
chase her?"

"What has that got to do with ice cream, magazines, radio
and television?"

"Right now your daughter is scared to death."

Walter Fenton shook his head blankly. "I absolutely can't see why, Emily."

"Because Nan is waiting and nobody is chasing, that's why."

They were having supper and Walter Fenton had only a vague idea of what he was eating. He was thinking of his own painful and accidental boyhood, when, to him, girls had been mysterious and unattainable creatures. Good girls, that is. Good girls like Emily. And he would never fully understand the miracle that had happened to him when Emily had first smiled upon him. Nor would he ever forget the wonder of her first kiss. Even today he choked at the memory of it.

Suddenly he heard a wistful gee-I-wish-parents-weren't-such-a-burden sigh. He looked up quickly.

"I wish you wouldn't burp the way you do, father."

"Emily!" Walter Fenton glared.

"Good thought," said Emily.

Then Walter Fenton noticed that he was eating corned beef and cabbage for supper. "Cabbage is sneaky," he said.

"You must be eating an awful lot of sneaky things lately, father."

Walter Fenton pushed his plate back and borrowed some dignity. "Is there anything else that's troubling you about my make-up?"

Nancy sighed. "I wish you wouldn't tell such big fibs about the fish you catch, father."

Fishing was a tender subject with Walter Fenton. "I do not lie about the fish I catch!" he retorted.

"You have an awful loud imagination, father."

Walter Fenton fumed in baffled silence. Then he said stiffly, "Your mother is perfect, I presume?"

Nancy glanced uneasily at her mother. She hesitated. "She's getting pretty dowdy."

Emily stifled a gasp.

"Are you going to stand for that, Emily?" Walter Fenton shouted.

"I'm going to eat my supper," said Emily.

With the knowledge that there was time later for an explosion, Walter Fenton controlled himself.

"Emily!" he exploded later in their bedroom. "You can't tell me that burping on account of cabbage has anything to do with boys chasing girls!"

"No?" Emily turned away from brushing her hair with a glint in her eye. "Maybe it's time you learned something about girls."

"I don't need any courses in birds and bees, Emily! Not after seventeen years, I don't!"

"There might be a difference of opinion about that."

"Cabbage has nothing whatever to do with the birds and the bees, Emily!"

"It has a lot to do with waiting for the Boy from the Blue though."

"I don't understand you, Emily."

"Waiting for Lochinvar to come out of the west, then."

"Since when has Lochinvar been coming out of the west in this day and age?" Walter Fenton snorted.

Emily smiled thinly. "For your information, Lochinvar has been coming out of the west ever since girls were born. And, so far as I know, the situation hasn't changed a bit."

"Emily," Walter Fenton croaked, "does Nancy believe that kind of junk?"

"That kind of junk, as you put it, is proof absolute to a girl that she is both wanted and desirable. And for girls, the times that Lochinvar doesn't come out of the west are a form of torture beside which the rack, thumbscrews, lead in the veins and burning at the stake are mere trivialities.

"Walter Fenton, when Lochinvar doesn't come out of the west, a girl wants to know why. Does she have pimples? No, she doesn't have pimples. Isn't she pretty? Yes, she's pretty. Are her legs crooked? No, her legs aren't crooked. What you don't understand, Walter Fenton, is that a girl has to find some reason why the Boy hasn't come out of the Blue. Right now I'm dowdy and you burp when you eat cabbage. What the reason will be tomorrow I haven't the slightest idea. But I can tell you this: until the Boy does come out of the Blue, you and I will be brought up all over again. Somebody has to take the blame, and it's right that they should."

Walter Fenton had never heard Emily talk so much before. Emily was ordinarily given to crisp sentences and rejoinders. He shook his head in bewilderment. "Emily, were you like this when you were a girl?"

"None of your business," said Emily. "Go see what your daughter is doing in her bedroom right now."

"She'll be reading a magazine, eating a gallon of ice cream and listening to her radio, and on challenge she'll be able to tell me the details of all three!"

"Go see."

And Walter Fenton did. He crept stealthily to Nancy's door and opened it a bare crack.

Nancy was parading in front of her mirror in a new frock. Her hair was no longer done up in the familiar pony hairdo. It was tightly done up and seemed to peak at the top. She was twisting and turning. Smiling and frowning. Suddenly her lips trembled and she snatched for another frock from a pile on her bed.

Even in his masculine denseness, Walter Fenton knew that Nancy was trying to convince herself that the Boy from the Blue would come someday. He closed the door softly and crept back to his room.

"Emily, there must be some solution to this!"

"If there is," said Emily tightly, "there are several hundred million mothers in the world who would like to know about it."

Walter Fenton slept fitfully that night. He was plagued by a hideous contradiction. All during his own boyhood, girls had been princesses, and just as remote. He could still remember his wild, improbable dreams of rescuing girls from terrible distress, dreams of unheard-of prowess in any number of desperate circumstances. Through the years he had come to realize that those dreams had been born of his own fearful belief that he would never be noticed by a girl. But now his own daughter in her girlhood was plagued by the very same fears that had made his own boyhood a nightmare.

As usual when he was troubled, Walter Fenton quickly busied himself in the morning. He shaved, he dressed, he shined his shoes, he tried another tie. But his thoughts were racing.

And Emily was taking more pains than usual, but he didn't notice at first. "Emily, I think we could help her," he said.

"Don't be silly," said Emily. "We don't even have a boy to start on."

Walter Fenton heaved a sigh. "Well, at least it isn't a tragedy, Emily. After all, she's only fifteen."

"Did you ever hear of Romeo and Juliet?" said Emily.

"Everybody's heard of Romeo and Juliet!"

"Juliet was fourteen," said Emily.

Walter Fenton vaguely resented the fact that somehow Shakespeare had understood tragedy could happen so early in life. Then he noticed Emily.

"What are you getting all dressed up for, Emily?" he said blankly.

"I'm dowdy," said Emily.

"But you're going to get breakfast, I hope!"

"Breakfast is no time to look dowdy," said Emily.

Walter Fenton watched in mild astonishment as Emily applied make-up. The years seemed to slip away from her. In spite of himself, he planted a kiss on the nape of Emily's neck.

"I love you, Emily," he murmured.

"Habit," said Emily.

"Emily, my love for you is not habit!"

"It is too."

"Do you love me, Emily?"

"No," said Emily.

"Emily!"

"Let's go and make breakfast," said Emily.

And Walter Fenton trotted down the stairs after her, very much as he had during their honeymoon.

Nancy was late for breakfast and she was suspiciously red-eyed. Apparently she had not slept well either. But when she saw her mother, her eyes rounded in horror. "Mother!" she cried in betrayal.

Walter Fenton glanced, bewildered, from his daughter to Emily. As far as he could see, Emily looked every bit as desirable as she had the day he married her.

But there was a worried look in Emily's eyes. "Did I forget something, Nan?"

"Mother!" Nancy wailed. "I don't want you to look like my sister-r-r-r!"

Fortunately, the telephone rang, but Walter Fenton was too stunned to answer it. With a reproachful glance at her mother, Nancy answered.

"Hello. . . . Oh, hi, Dibs. . . . No, I never met your brother. . . . You want me to what? Wha-a-at did you say?" Nancy glanced sharply at her mother. "Oh, I s'pose I'd have to ask my mother. Wait a minute."

Nancy cupped her hand over the mouthpiece. "Mother," she said lifelessly, "Dibbie Williams' brother's date, Posy White, stood him up on account of Posy's got the chicken pox, and he doesn't have anybody to go to the Auditorium dance with tonight, and his dance card is all filled up, and Dibbie wants to know if——"

Emily's smile was strangely sad. "Do you want to go, Nan?"

"He would be kind of secondhand, mother."

"A boy is a boy," said Walter Fenton.

"That used to be my line!" Emily snapped. Then she said, "Do you really want to go, Nan?"

Nancy hesitated and her chin trembled. "It's awfully secondhand, mother."

"You go!" Walter Fenton ordered.

Walter Fenton went to work that morning with a spring in his step. Now that Nancy had a boy again, he was certain his domestic life would return to normal. He could not have been more mistaken.

That night he found Nancy and Emily knee deep in dresses. Nancy was close to tears.

"But I don't want to wear that dress, mother!"

"Nancy, behave yourself!" Walter Fenton ordered.

Suddenly and furiously, Emily was upon him, hauling him out of hearing. "Walter Fenton," she stormed, "if you let one more peep out of you, I'm moving into the guest room!"

Walter Fenton stared in masculine bewilderment. "But she's going to a dance, isn't she?"

"At this moment she'd rather die."

"But——"

"Walter Fenton, can you ever get it into your head that a

boy who has been stood up by chicken pox is not precisely a Lochinvar riding out of the west?"

"But he's a boy, Emily."

"Who will undoubtedly be hideously glad when this dance is over and he has dumped Nan on the front doorstep!"

"He asked her, Emily."

"His sister asked her, and that boy is probably beating his sister's brains out right now."

Walter Fenton flushed loyally. "Then that boy is an idiot!"

"And so are you!" said Emily, tripping back to Nancy.

So it was another dreary supper for Walter Fenton. Somehow he knew that he would never understand women. Not even Emily.

Just then Nancy pounded her little fist on the table. "Mother, I don't want to go!"

"I don't blame you," said Emily with pressed lips.

After supper, Walter Fenton tried to seek solace from a mystery story. Next to Emily and his beloved tulips, a mystery story was Walter Fenton's most cherished delight. But the adventures of a mayhem-minded old maid were neither mystifying nor entertaining. He was interrupted by Emily's angry steps tripping down the stairs.

"If you want to see what a mess you've made of things, go upstairs," Emily gritted.

Emily's tone was not one to be trifled with, and Walter Fenton neither protested nor commented. He trudged heavily up the stairs and into Nancy's room.

Walter Fenton knew very little about fabrics, especially girl fabrics. All he knew was that Nancy was a shimmering dream as she sat on the edge of her bed, and that the tears were streaming down her cheeks. A flood of sobless tears.

"Nan."

"Please go away, daddy."

Walter Fenton tried again, "Nan."

As the tears streamed, Nancy was staring straight ahead. "I wouldn't care, daddy, if I thought he'd ask me again. But he won't."

Walter Fenton had never felt so inadequate in his life. And suddenly he knew he was going to say something he had never believed he would say to a living soul. He knelt by the bed.

"Nan, did you ever hear about your mother and me?"

"I know you were very fortunate to get her, daddy."

"Did she ever tell you how it happened?"

"She said you chased her within an inch of her life."

"I was too scared to chase a girl, Nan."

For the first time, Nancy stopped staring. "Scared? You, daddy?"

"Boys get scared, too, Nan."

"Not the way girls do, daddy." Nancy's shoulders heaved. "No girl wants to go where she isn't wanted."

"Nan, when I was a boy I was so scared I used to watch your mother going down the sidewalk with other boys carrying her books and I didn't dare speak to her."

Nancy shook her head sadly. "That doesn't sound like you, daddy. You make so much noise all the time."

"You never had to just watch and dream, did you, Nan?"

"A girl has to do it all the time, daddy!"

"Not if she knows the boys are just as scared as she is."

"That's pretty hard to believe, daddy, when you spend your life waiting for a telephone to ring."

"Nan, I went to a dance once. At the same Auditorium you're going to."

"With mother?"

"I didn't even have a girl, Nan. And it was my graduation dance."

"You didn't have anybody?" Nancy was slightly incredulous.

"Nobody."

"Mother always says she met you at a dance and you chased the daylights out of her."

"That was the dance, Nan. And she went with somebody else. I was too scared to ask her."

"And you went alone?"

"It was my graduation, wasn't it?"

"Gee, daddy, it must have been awful to go to your own graduation dance alone!"

"It was wonderful, Nan. After a while, that is."

"Something wonderful must have happened, daddy."

"It did. Your mother was dancing by—I was a stag, you see—and your mother smiled at me."

"It must have been a pretty potent smile, daddy."

"It was."

"I don't think mother would like to hear you say that."

"That was what happened, Nan. I knew that smile, the minute I saw it, was just for me."

"You did?"

"A boy knows. Especially if he's scared."

"And then you chased the daylights out of her?"

"Well, we got married anyway."

Nancy breathed ecstatically. "Gee, daddy, you and mother must have had a wonderful love story!"

"We did, Nan," said Walter Fenton humbly.

Then Nancy's face fell. "But you weren't Henry Williams."

"Do you really want him to ask you again?"

"Oh, daddy," Nancy said scornfully, "any girl would want him to ask her again! He has curly hair and blue eyes and plays on the basketball team and——"

"You give him a smile, Nan. Just for him."

"But, daddy, he didn't really ask me at all. He had his sister ask me on account of Posy White stood him up on account of she has chicken pox."

"Maybe he was too scared to ask you himself. You just give him a smile that's just for him."

"Do you think it would work, daddy?"

"I married your mother, didn't I?" said Walter Fenton.

Suddenly Nancy bounced from her bed. "Oh, mother-r-r-r!" she bawled. "I need you!"

Nancy had gone to the dance and Walter Fenton was sitting in his living room watching television with Emily.

"Walter, dear, what did you say to Nan?"

"None of your business." Walter Fenton grinned.

"Are you going to wait up and see how many times he kisses her?"

"Not me," said Walter Fenton. "I approve of the stuff."

"Since when have you stopped being the outraged father?"

Walter Fenton just grinned.

"Stop grinning like a drunken cat and tell me what happened between you and Nancy!"

"I ain't talking," said Walter Fenton.

"Well, I," said Emily, "am going to stay up and see what comes of all this."

So Walter Fenton stayed up too. And a little after midnight there were shuffling steps on the porch. Presently Nancy came bouncing breathlessly into the house.

"Oh, mother, I had the most wonderful time!"

"You did?" Walter Fenton beamed.

"And he's the most wonderful guy, mother!" Nancy bounced up and down.

"That's nice, dear," said Emily faintly.

"Did you kiss him?" Walter Fenton crowed.

"Oh, no, daddy," Nancy said gravely. "I wouldn't kiss a boy the first time for anything."

"Just a minute!" Walter Fenton cried in alarm. "There's something wrong here!"

Emily smiled at Nancy. "Maybe you'd better tell us what happened, Nan."

Nancy hugged herself. "Mother, I did just what father told me to and——"

"What your father told you to!"

Nancy hugged herself again. "I smiled at Henry just the way father said, just for him—he's an awful jerk, mother—but he had his dance card filled up, so I had to dance with the other boys, and I kept practicing——"

"Practicing!" Walter Fenton cried.

Nancy sighed wondrously. "And it got the most wonderful results! I guess boys really are afraid of girls, and I was dancing with this boy and——"

"Which boy?" Walter Fenton cried, bewildered.

"Why, the boy with the freckles, father! He has freckles as big as pennies and he's awkward and he doesn't know what to do with his hands and his feet, but he's just wonderful, and he got ahead of all the other boys who wanted dates, and I think——" Nancy ran out of breath.

"Emily, have you any idea what's going on here?" Walter Fenton shouted.

Emily grinned slyly. "I think Nan had a good time," she said.

"But, Emily, I sicked her onto this Henry Williams gink!"

"What you know about girls," said Emily, "would fill a very, very small book."

Nancy was pirouetting in ecstasy. "Oh, mother," she breathed, "it's wonderful to be chased!"

"I know," said Emily. "I know."

It was now long past midnight. Nancy was in bed. And Walter Fenton had slipped in comfortably beside Emily. For some reason, Emily had gone to bed with a trace of irritation, so Walter Fenton nuzzled against her shoulder. Emily always liked that.

"Do you think she's all right now, Emily?"

"A girl is always all right when a boy is chasing her," Emily said. "What did you say to her?"

"I just told her about you and me, Emily."

Emily sat straight up in the darkness. "What did you tell her about you and me?"

"I told her about the graduation dance when you smiled at me."

Emily snapped on the light. "Walter Fenton, I did no such thing!"

"You did, Emily."

"Walter Fenton," said Emily sharply, "I always was a sucker for an underdog, and you took advantage of me!"

Walter Fenton didn't even smile. He just reached over and snapped out the light. For now he knew something he had never known before. Something had caused him to chase a girl, and she had kept him chasing her for the rest of his married life. He liked it that way. And he didn't want to disturb the arrangement.

"I know, Emily," he said.

SHARING YOUR IMPRESSIONS

1. Recall some of the social fears you had as a teenager.
2. What are some worries that bother the adolescents of both sexes?

3. What are some worries that are unique to adolescent boys? Adolescent girls?
4. Make some suggestions for parents and teachers about ways to help teenagers who lack self-confidence.
5. Comment on the influence extracurricular activities have on students in the upper elementary and high school grades.
6. In what ways does parental counseling of adolescent boys differ from parental counseling of adolescent girls?

15

A TIME FOR WAITING

Helen Laurie Welch

Jean rested her forehead against the glass in the side door. It felt cool and good against her flushed skin. She wanted to stand there in the darkness for a long, long time but she had to go in.

If only her mother had been in bed . . . but she could hear the murmur of voices from the kitchen. She hated to enter that kitchen. Already some of the precious magic of the evening had ebbed away and she couldn't bear to lose it. Not yet, not for just another moment. Dick, Dick . . .

They had walked very close together through the quiet darkened streets, she and Dick. After the show they had gone to Sam's for sodas and they had been very gay and silly with some of the crowd that was in there; but on the way home, somehow, they hadn't had much to say to each other. It was enough for Dick to take Jean's hand in his and place it, still enclosed by his strong young fingers, in his jacket pocket. It was enough to walk quietly like that through the breathless spring night.

At her house, they turned into the driveway. Jean stopped at the side door and looked up at Dick wordlessly. He pulled her gently away from the door and into the yard. They stood in the black shadow of the lilac bush that smelled achingly of all springtimes. The moon rode high, drenching the yard and the small garage in mysterious shadows and silvery light. It seemed a new place to Jean, a place she had never been before.

Dick put his arms around her and she felt her arms slide around his neck, almost with a will of their own. For an instant they stood so, and then Dick kissed her. Her eyes closed and for a brief moment she hoped he would not notice how hard her heart was beating. But then, against her cheek, she could feel his heart pounding, pounding . . .

She ran her fingers over his face lightly so that her hands too would have their memory of this moment. A faint odor of shaving cream came from his smooth cheeks and she felt a curious tender pity for him. His head bent again and her lips trembled in their waiting.

They turned then from the lilac bush and walked slowly back to the side door. *"This is how it must feel to be drunk,"* Jean thought, *"light-headed and foolish, as though there was nothing in the world at all, but just this moment."*

As they stood at the door she saw the flash of his teeth in the darkness and she knew how his blue eyes must look, with that kind of gentle softness in them she had seen sometimes when he looked at her.

"I'll call you first thing in the morning," he said, quietly, tipping her face upward and kissing her lightly on her forehead.

She stood in the hall with her head against the glass pane thinking, *"How wonderful, how very wonderful . . ."* She sighed deeply and mounted the stairs feeling as though she were in a trance. She opened the kitchen door.

The shock of the electric light's glare startled her and her eyes blinked in protest. Her mother and Mrs. King from next door sat at the kitchen table drinking coffee. Jean wanted to draw back into the protective shadow behind her but she smiled at them both.

"Hello, Mamma; hello, Mrs. King," she said. "What are you two doing up?"

Her mother's thin lips twitched and she said sharply, "I might say the same to you, miss. It just happens Mrs. King and I went to the show ourselves tonight. We got home near an hour ago."

Mrs. King, her heavy legs spread comfortably apart, said with a wink at Jean's mother, "Oh, you know these kids today!" She turned to Jean, "What was it, Jeannie, a little spooning? No—smooching they call it today!"

Jean recoiled involuntarily at the words. They seemed to have no connection to anything she knew. They belonged with fat Mrs. King in this stuffy little kitchen. Her mother and Mrs. King were waiting for her to speak, her mother's mouth pursed, Mrs. King's lips loosely smiling, waiting . . .

"We stopped at Sam's for a soda. Some of the kids were there," she answered vaguely. If she could only turn and run from this room—

"I saw Jean's fellow call for her tonight, you know," Mrs. King was talking to Jean's mother again. "I thought he was a real cute boy. Only thing is, can you trust him? I often say, Mrs. Dennis, when my Tommy was born, I wished he was a girl, but now I thank God I don't have no worries about—well, you know!"

Jean looked at her mother, knowing the expression she would see there. A look of distaste, almost a pained look, accompanied the words, "Well, the way I brought Jean up, I can trust her, never fear. There's not a thing she hasn't been warned against."

Jean walked stiffly across the kitchen to the sink. She turned on the faucet and filled a glass with water. She could feel Mrs. King's eyes on her back. Greedy eyes, wondering eyes . . .

She turned around holding the glass of water and pressed the small of her back into the rim of the sink, pressed hard until it hurt. Now she could think of the pain and escape from them.

Mrs. King chuckled, "Oh, you know, Mrs. Dennis, I didn't mean anything. I know Jean's decent. You can always tell the decent ones."

Jean's eyes traced the worn pattern on the linoleum. She couldn't bear to look at Mrs. King's small pale eyes or see her fat red fingers clutching the coffee cup. She could feel those eyes watching her and her mother's too—darting at her and away, as though afraid to see the bright cheeks, the tender lips.

Mrs. King was talking again. "Just the same, I wouldn't mind being twenty years younger myself. Seems to me they have more fun than we used to. Some of them go too far, of course—"

"Let me tell you, Mrs. King," Mrs. Dennis interrupted, her breathing short and rapid, "I'll have no carrying on around this house. I'm bringing my daughter up clean and decent."

Mrs. King laughed, a little embarrassed, "Oh, I didn't mean your girl, of course, but you know how kids'll do."

Mrs. Dennis' mouth tightened. "I do indeed. I've heard tales. But Jean's a good girl and I mean to see she stays that way." Her eyes swept Jean, hard, possessive.

Something dark and ugly had come into this room. Jean shivered a little, feeling its presence but not knowing where it might strike her. She set her glass down carefully.

"I'm going to bed now. I'm awfully tired. Good night."

Out of the kitchen, she took a deep breath to put down this nauseous feeling that rose in her. She could hear her mother get up to get the coffee pot from the stove.

"Thanks, Mrs. Dennis, just a little," Mrs. King murmured politely. "You know, Jeannie's a real pretty thing. If I was you, I'd be real careful."

The chair creaked as Jean's mother sat down. "Don't you worry. Jean knows all about men and what they're after. I told her straight out often enough."

Mrs. King replied, "It's a good thing. Why, the things I could tell her about men! Let me tell you, Mrs. Dennis—"

Jean fled to her bedroom and closed the door. She leaned back against it, breathing as though she had run a great distance. For a minute she stood, then she crossed to the window that looked out into the yard. It was a dreary sight. The moon was under a cloud and in the half light the yard was a rutted muddy field. The garage loomed, a square grey shape, the paint blistered and peeling. From here she couldn't see the lilac bush at all.

She turned and went the few short steps to her bed. She lay down and stared dry-eyed into the darkness. Her throat held a strange fullness and it was hard to swallow.

Suddenly she rose and returned to the window. The magic belonged to her—she had seen it, she had felt it. She pushed back the curtains and raised the window. The night air felt fresh and cool against her hot face. If she leaned way out, she could see the lilac bush at the corner of the house. The perfume rose, heavy and sweet.

She knelt then at the window and rested her chin on her folded arms. The moon would be out soon again. She could wait.

SHARING YOUR IMPRESSIONS

1. As an adolescent, how were your dating intentions judged by your parents? By other adults?
2. Compare the worries of parents who have adolescent daughters with those of parents who have sons.
3. If you could have children "made to order," what qualities and characteristics would you want your child to possess?
4. What effect has the Pill had on parent fears about adolescent sexual behavior?
5. Comment on the possibility of a collaboration between home and school to provide sex education.
6. Provide some examples for your opinion on whether the level of parental trust has changed in recent years.
7. How can parents demonstrate their trust to teenagers?

16

IN RETIREMENT

Bernard Malamud

He had lately taken to studying his old Greek grammar of fifty years ago. He read in Bulfinch and wanted to reread the *Odyssey* in Greek. His life had changed. He slept less these days and in the morning got up to stare at the sky over Gramercy Park. He watched the clouds until they took on shapes he could reflect on. He liked strange, haunted vessels and he liked to watch mythological birds and animals. He had noticed that if he contemplated these forms in the clouds, kept his mind on them for a while, there might be a diminution of his morning depression. Dr. Morris was sixty-six, a physician, retired for two years. He had shut down his practice in Queens and moved to Manhattan. He had retired himself after a heart attack, not too serious but serious enough. His first heart attack, he had decided, would be his last. His wife was dead and his daughter lived in Scotland. He wrote her twice a month and heard from her twice a month. And though he had a few friends he visited, and kept up with medical journals, and liked museums and theater, generally he contended with loneliness. And he was concerned about the future; the future was old age advancing.

Reprinted with the permission of Farrar, Straus and Giroux, Inc., and Eyre Methuen, Ltd., from *Rembrandt's Hat*, by Bernard Malamud. Copyright © 1968, 1972, 1973 by Bernard Malamud. "In Retirement" appeared originally in *The Atlantic*.

After a light breakfast he would dress warmly and go out for a walk around the Square. That was the easy part of the walk. He took this walk even when it was very cold, or nasty rainy, or had snowed several inches and he had to proceed very slowly. After the Square he crossed the street and went down Irving Place, a tall figure with a cape and cane, and picked up his *Times*. If the weather was not too bad he continued on to Fourteenth Street, around to Park Avenue South, up Park and along East Twentieth back to the narrow, tall, white stone apartment building he lived in. Rarely, lately, had he gone in another direction, though when on the long walk he stopped at least once on the way, perhaps in front of a mid-block store, perhaps at a street corner, and asked himself where else he might go. This was the difficult part of the walk. What was difficult was that it made no difference where he went. He now wished he had not retired. He had become more conscious of his age since his retirement, although sixty-six was not eighty. Still it was old. He experienced moments of anguish.

One morning after his rectangular long walk in the rain, Dr. Morris found a letter on the rubber mat under the line of mailboxes in the lobby. It was a narrow, deep lobby with false green marble columns and several bulky chairs where few people ever sat. Dr. Morris had seen a young woman with long hair, in a white raincoat and maroon shoulder bag, carrying a plastic bubble umbrella, hurry down the vestibule steps and leave the house as he was about to enter. In fact he held the door open for her and got a breath of her bold perfume. He did not remember seeing her before and felt a momentary confusion as to who she might be. He later imagined her taking the letter out of her box, reading it hastily, then stuffing it into the maroon cloth purse she carried over her shoulder; but she had stuffed in the envelope and not the letter. That had fallen to the floor. He imagined this as he bent to retrieve it. It was a folded sheet of heavy white writing paper, written on in black in a masculine hand. The doctor unfolded and glanced at it without making out the salutation or any of its contents. He would have to put on his reading glasses, and he thought Flaherty, the doorman and elevator man, might see him if the elevator should suddenly descend. Of course, Flaherty might think the doctor was reading his own mail, except that he never read it, such as it was, in the lobby. He did not want the man thinking he was reading someone else's letter. He also thought of handing him the letter and describing the young woman who had dropped it. Perhaps he could return it to her? But for some reason not at once clear to him the doctor slipped it into his pocket to take upstairs to read. His arm began to tremble and he felt his heart racing at a rate that bothered him.

After the doctor had got his own mail out of the box— nothing more than the few circulars he held in his hand— Flaherty took him up to the fifteenth floor. Flaherty spelled the night man at 8:00 A.M. and was himself relieved at 4:00 P.M. He was a slender man of sixty with sparse white hair on his half-bald head, who had lost part of his jaw under the left ear after two bone operations. He would be out for a few months; then return, the lower part of the left side of his face caved in, though it was not a bad face to look at. Although the doorman never spoke about his ailment, the doctor knew he was not done with cancer of the jaw, though of course he kept this to himself; and he sensed when the man was concealing pain.

This morning, though preoccupied, he asked, "How is it going, Mr. Flaherty?"

"Not too tough."

"Not a bad day." He said this, thinking not of the rain, but of the letter in his pocket.

"Fine and dandy," Flaherty quipped. On the whole he moved and talked animatedly and was careful to align the elevator with the floor before letting passengers off. Sometimes the doctor wished he could say more to him than he did; but not this morning.

He stood by the large double window of his living room overlooking the Square, in the dull rainy-day February light, in pleasurable excitement reading the letter he had found, the kind he had anticipated it might be. It was a letter written by a father to his daughter, addressed to "Dear Evelyn." What it expressed, after an irresolute start, was the father's dissatisfaction with his daughter's way of life. And it ended with an exhortatory paragraph of advice. "You have slept around long enough. I don't understand what you get out of that type of behavior anymore. I think you have tried everything there is to try. You claim you are a serious person but let men use you for what they can get. There is no true payoff to you unless it is very temporary, and the real payoff to them is that they have got themselves an easy lay. I know how they think about this and how they talk about it in the lavatory the next day. Now I want to urge you once and for all that you ought to be more serious about your life. You have experimented long enough. I honestly and sincerely and urgently advise you to look around for a man of steady habits and good character who will marry you and treat you like the person I believe you want to be. I don't want to think of you anymore as a drifting semi-prostitute. Please follow this advice, the age of twenty-nine is no longer sixteen." The letter was signed, "Your Father," and under his signature, another sentence, in neat small handwriting, was appended: "Your sex life fills me full of fear. Mother."

The doctor put the letter away in a drawer. His excitement had left him and he felt ashamed of having read it. He was sympathetic to the father and at the same time sympathetic to the young woman, though perhaps less so to her. He tried to study his Greek grammar but could not concentrate. The letter remained in his mind like a billboard sign as he was reading the *Times*, and he was conscious of it throughout the day, as though it had aroused in him some sort of expectation he could not define. Sentences from it would replay themselves in his thoughts. He reveried the young woman as he had imagined her after reading what the father had written, and as the woman—was she Evelyn?—he had seen coming out of the house. He could not be certain the letter was hers. Perhaps it was not; still, he thought of the letter as though she was the woman he had held the door for, whose perfume still lingered in his senses.

That night thoughts of her kept him from falling asleep. "I'm too old for this nonsense." He got up to read and was able to concentrate, but when his head lay once more on the pillow, a long freight train of thoughts of her rumbled by, drawn by a huge black locomotive. He pictured Evelyn, the drifting semi-prostitute, in bed with various lovers, engaged in various acts of sex. Once she lay alone, erotically naked in bed, her maroon cloth purse drawn close to her nude body. He also thought of her as an ordinary girl with many fewer lovers than her father seemed to think. This was probably closer to the truth. He wondered if he could be useful to her in some way. He then felt a fright he could not explain but managed to dispel it by promising himself to burn the letter in the morning. The freight train, with its many cars, disappeared in the foggy distance. When the doctor awoke at ten o'clock one sunny winter's morning, there was no sense, light or heavy, of his usual depression.

But he did not burn the letter. He reread it several times during the day, each time returning it to his desk drawer and locking it there. Then he unlocked the drawer to read it again. As the day passed he was aware of an unappeased insistent hunger in himself. He recalled memories, experienced intense longing, desires he had not felt in years. The doctor was worried, alarmed by this change in him, this disturbance. He tried to blot the letter out of his mind but could not. Yet he would still not burn it, as though if he did he would shut the door on certain possibilities in his life, other ways to go, whatever that might mean. He was astonished—even thought of it as affronted—that this should be happening to him at his age. He had seen it in others, in former patients, but had not expected it in himself. The hunger he felt, a hunger for pleasure, disruption of habit, renewal of feeling, yet a fear of it, continued to grow in him like a dead tree come to life and spreading its branches. He felt as though he were hungry for exotic experience, which, if he were to have it, might make him forever ravenously hungry. He did not want that to happen to him. He recalled mythological figures, Sisyphus, Midas, who for one reason or another had been eternally cursed. He thought of Tithonus, become a grasshopper living forever. The doctor felt he was caught in an overwhelming emotion, a furious dark wind.

When Flaherty left for the day at 4:00 P.M. and Silvio, who had tight curly black hair, was on duty, Dr. Morris came down and sat in the lobby, pretending to read his newspaper. As soon as the elevator ascended he approached the letter boxes and quickly scanned the nameplates for an Evelyn, whoever she might be. He found no Evelyns, though there was an E. Gordon and an E. Cummings. He suspected one of them might be she. He knew that single women often preferred not to reveal their first names in order to keep cranks at a distance, conceal themselves from potential annoyers. He casually asked Silvio if Miss

Gordon or Miss Cummings was named Evelyn, but Silvio said he didn't know although probably Mr. Flaherty would because he distributed the mail. "Too many peoples in this house," Silvio shrugged. Embarrassed, the doctor remarked he was just curious, a lame remark, but all he could think of.

He went out for an aimless short walk and when he returned said nothing more to Silvio. They rode silently up in the elevator, the doctor standing tall, almost stiff. That night he again slept badly. When he fell deeply asleep a moment his dreams were erotic. He woke with desire mixed with repulsion and lay quietly mourning himself. He felt powerless to be other than he was.

He was up before five and, though he tried to kill time, was uselessly in the lobby before seven. He felt he must find out, settle in his mind, who she was. In the lobby, Richard, the night man who had brought him down, returned to a pornographic paperback he was reading; the mail, as Dr. Morris knew, hadn't come. He knew it would not arrive until shortly after eight but hadn't the patience to wait in his apartment. So he left the building, bought the *Times* on Irving Place, continued on his walk, and because it was a pleasant morning, not too cold, sat on a bench in Union Square Park. He stared at the paper but could not read it. He watched some sparrows pecking at dead grass. He was an old man, true enough; but he had lived long enough to know that age often meant little in man-woman relationships. He was still vigorous and bodies are bodies. He was back in the lobby at eight-thirty, an act of great restraint. Flaherty had received the mail sack and was alphabetizing the first-class letters on a long large table before distributing them into the boxes. He did not look well today. He moved slowly. His misshapen face was gray; the mouth slack, one heard his breathing; his eyes harbored pain.

"Nothin' for you yet," he said to the doctor without looking up.

"I'll wait this morning," said Dr. Morris. "I ought to be hearing from my daughter."

"Nothin' yet but you might hit the lucky number in this last bundle." He removed the string.

As he was alphabetizing the last bundle of letters the elevator buzzed and Flaherty had to go up for a call.

The doctor pretended to be absorbed in his *Times*. When he heard the elevator door shut he sat momentarily still, then went to the table and rifled through the C pile of letters. E. Cummings was Ernest Cummings. He shuffled through the G's watching the metal arrow as it showed the elevator beginning to descend. In the G pile there were two letters addressed to Evelyn Gordon. One was from her mother. The other, also handwritten, was from a Lee Bradley. Almost against his will the doctor removed this letter and slipped it into his suit pocket. His body was sweaty hot. This is an aberration, he thought. He was sitting in the chair turning the page of his newspaper when the elevator door opened.

"Nothin' at all for you," Flaherty said after a moment.

"Thank you," said Dr. Morris. "I think I'll go up now."

In his apartment the doctor, conscious of his whisperous breathing, placed the letter on the kitchen table and sat looking at it, waiting for a tea kettle of water to boil. The kettle whistled as it boiled but still he sat with the unopened letter before him. For a while he sat there with dulled thoughts. Soon he fantasied what the letter said. He fantasied Lee Bradley describing the sexual pleasure he had had with Evelyn Gordon, and telling her what else they might try. He fantasied the lovers' acts they engaged in. Then though he audibly told himself not to, he steamed open the flap of the envelope. His hands trembled as he held the letter. He had to place it down flat on the table so he could read it. His heart beat heavily in anticipation of what he might read. But to his surprise the letter was a bore, an egoistic account of some stupid business dealings this Bradley was concocting. Only the last sentence came surprisingly to life. "Be in your bed when I get there tonight. Be wearing only your white panties. I don't like to waste time once we are together." The doctor didn't know whom he was more disgusted with, this fool or himself. In truth, himself. Slipping the sheet of paper into the envelope, he resealed it with a thin layer of paste he had rubbed carefully on the flap with his fingertip. He tucked the letter into his inside pocket and pressed the elevator button for Silvio. The doctor left the building and soon returned with a copy of the afternoon *Post* he seemed to be involved with until Silvio had to take up two women who had come into the lobby; then the doctor thrust the letter into Evelyn Gordon's box and went out for a breath of air.

He was sitting near the table in the lobby when the young woman he had held the door open for came in shortly after 6:00 P.M. He was aware of her cool perfume almost at once. Silvio was not around at that moment; he had gone down to the basement to eat a sandwich. She inserted a small key into Evelyn Gordon's mailbox and stood before the open box, smoking, as she read Bradley's letter. She was wearing a light blue pants suit with a brown knit sweater-coat. Her tail of black hair was tied with a brown silk scarf. Her face, though a little heavy, was pretty, her intense eyes blue, the lids lightly eye-shadowed. Her body, he thought, was finely proportioned. She had not noticed him, but he was more than half in love with her.

He observed her many mornings. He would come down later now, at nine, and spend some time going through the medical circulars he had got out of his box, sitting on a throne-like wooden chair near a tall unlit lamp in the rear of the lobby. He would watch people as they left for work or shopping in the morning. Evelyn appeared at about half-past nine and stood smoking in front of her box, absorbed in the morning's mail. When spring came she wore brightly colored skirts with pastel blouses, or light slim pants suits. Sometimes she wore very short minidresses. Her figure was exquisite. She received many letters and read most of them with apparent pleasure, some with what seemed suppressed excitement. A few she gave short shrift to, scanned these quickly and stuffed them into her bag. He imagined they were from her father, or mother. He thought that most of her letters came from lovers, past and present, and he felt a curious anguish that there were none from him in her box. He would write to her.

He thought it through carefully. Some women needed an older man; it stabilized their lives. Sometimes a difference of as many as thirty or even thirty-five years offered no serious disadvantages, granted differences in metabolism, energy. There would of course be less sex, but there would be sex. His would go on for a long time; he knew that from the experience of friends and former patients, not to speak of medical literature. A younger woman inspired an older man to remain virile. And despite the heart incident his health was good, in some ways better than before. A girl like Evelyn, probably at odds with herself, could benefit from a steadying relationship with an older man, someone who would respect and love her and help her to respect and love herself more than she perhaps presently did; who would demand less from her in certain ways than some young men awash in their egoism; who would awake in her a stronger sense of well-being, and if things went quite well, perhaps even love for one particular man.

"I am a retired physician, a widower," he wrote to Evelyn Gordon. "I write to you with some hesitation and circumspection, although needless to say with high regard, because I am old enough to be your father. I have observed you often in this building and sometimes as we passed by each other in nearby streets, and I have grown to admire you deeply. I wonder if you will permit me to make your acquaintance? I wonder if you would care to have dinner with me and perhaps enjoy a film or performance of a play? My intentions, as used to be said when I was a young man, are 'ancient and honorable.' I do not think my company will disappoint you. If you are so inclined—so kind, certainly—to consider this request tolerantly. I will be obliged if you will place a note to that effect in my mailbox. I am respectfully yours, Simon Morris, M.D."

He did not go down to mail his letter at once. He thought he would keep it to the last moment. Then he had a fright about it that woke him out of momentary deep sleep. He dreamed he had written and sealed the letter and then remembered he had appended another sentence: "Be wearing only your white panties." When he woke he wanted to tear open the envelope to see whether he had included Bradley's remark. But when he was thoroughly waked up, in his senses, he knew he had not. He bathed and shaved early and for a while observed the cloud formations out the window. None of them interested him. At close to nine Dr. Morris descended to the lobby. He would wait till Flaherty answered a buzz, and when he was gone, drop his letter into her box; but Flaherty, that morning, seemed to have no calls to answer. The doctor had forgotten it was Saturday. He did not know it was till he got his *Times* and sat with it in the

lobby, pretending to be waiting for the mail delivery. The mail
sack arrived late on Saturdays. At last he heard a prolonged buzz,
and Flaherty, who had been on his knees polishing the brass
doorknob, got up on one foot, then rose on both legs and walked
slowly to the elevator. His asymmetric face was gray. Shortly
before ten o'clock the doctor slipped his letter into Evelyn
Gordon's mailbox. He decided to withdraw to his apartment but
then thought he would rather wait where he usually waited while
she collected her mail. She had never noticed him there.

The mail sack was dropped in the vestibule at ten-after, and
Flaherty alphabetized the first bundle before he had to respond
to another call. The doctor read his paper in the dark rear of the
lobby because he was really not reading it. He was anticipating
Evelyn's coming. He had on a new green suit, blue striped shirt,
and a pink tie. He was wearing a new hat. He waited in anticipation and love.

When the elevator door opened, Evelyn walked out in an
elegant slit black skirt, sandals, her hair tied with a red scarf. A
sharp-featured man with puffed sideburns and carefully combed
medium-long hair, in a turn-of-century haircut, followed her out
of the elevator. He was shorter than she by a half a head. Flaherty
handed her two letters which she dropped into the black patent-
leather pouch she was carrying. The doctor thought—hoped—
she would walk past the mailboxes without stopping; but she
saw the white of his letter through the slot and stopped to remove
it. She tore open the envelope, pulled out the single sheet of
handwritten paper, and read it with immediate intense concen-
tration. The doctor raised his newspaper to his eyes, though he
could still watch over the top of it. He watched in fear.

How mad I was not to anticipate she might come down with
a man.

When she had finished reading the letter, she handed it
to her companion—possibly Bradley—who read it, grinned
broadly, and said something inaudible when he handed it back
to her.

Evelyn Gordon quietly ripped the letter into small bits, and
turning, flung the pieces in the doctor's direction. The fragments
came at him like a blast of wind-driven snow. He thought he
would sit forever on his wooden throne in the swirling snow.

The old doctor sat lifelessly in his chair, the floor around him littered with his torn-up letter.

Flaherty swept it up with his little broom into a metal container. He handed the doctor a thin envelope stamped with foreign stamps.

"Here's a letter from your daughter just came."

The doctor, trying to stand without moving, pressed the bridge of his nose. He wiped his eyes with his fingers.

"There's no setting old age aside," he said after a while.

"Not in some ways," said Flaherty.

"Or death."

"It moves up on you."

The doctor tried to say something kind to him but could not.

Flaherty took him up to the fifteenth floor in his elevator.

SHARING YOUR IMPRESSIONS

1. What are some of the ways your grandparents influenced your life as a child? As an adolescent? How do they influence your life today?
2. Tell about the retirement experience as you know it from personal observation.
3. Look ahead to your own retirement. What are some of the concerns you have about getting old?
4. Comment about the merits and disadvantages of living in a retirement community.
5. What assets can today's grandparents contribute to society, and which roles should we entrust to them?
6. Propose a plan by which the very young and the elderly could be with each other more often than is now the case.
7. What is the likely future of grandparents in our society as it relates to their social significance and self-concept?

5

IDENTITY
AND
SELF-CONCEPT

17

THE CISSY

Frank O'Connor

1

Some kids are cissies by nature but I was a cissy* by conviction. Mother had told me about geniuses, and I wanted to be a genius. It was an important task, and I could see for myself that fighting, as well as being sinful, was dangerous. You could get badly hurt at it. The children in our part of Cork were always fighting. Mother said they were savages, and she wished I was old enough to go to school. She said I needed friends, and I would be sure to meet nice friends when I went to school.

My way, when someone wanted to fight and I couldn't get away, was to climb on the nearest wall and argue like hell in a shrill voice about Our Blessed Lord and good manners. This was a way of attracting attention. It usually worked because the enemy, after staring incredulously up at me for several minutes, wondering if he would have time to hammer my head on the pavement before some old woman came out and chased him, usually yelled something like "blooming cissy" and went away. It was not nice being called a cissy, but it did not interfere with the free flow of my thoughts as a hammering would have done. I was

*Cissy is a British spelling of sissy.—Ed.

very sorry for the poor mongrels who slunk through our neighborhood, and took to their heels when anyone came near them; and I always tried to make friends with them. I felt that they too had no proper chance of going on with their own thoughts.

I toyed with games, and enjoyed kicking a ball gently before me along the pavement, but when I discovered that any boy who joined me grew violent and started to push and kick, I took a dislike to games as well. I preferred little girls because they didn't fight so much, but otherwise I found them insipid and lacking in any solid basis of learning. The only women I cared for were grownups, and my most intimate friend was an old washerwoman called Miss Cooney who had been in the lunatic asylum and was very religious. It was she who had made me feel sorry for dogs. She would run a mile after anyone she saw hurting an animal and even go to the police about them. The police never paid any attention to her because they knew she was mad. She was a sad-looking woman with grey hair, high cheek-bones and toothless gums. While she ironed, I would sit for hours in the hot, damp kitchen, turning over the pages of her religious books. She was very fond of me, too, and told me she was sure I would be a priest when I grew up. I agreed that I might be a bishop but I wasn't sure. I told her there were so many other things that I couldn't tell what I'd be eventually, but I could see she didn't quite know what I meant. Miss Cooney thought there was only one thing a genius could be and that was a priest.

One of the things I thought I might be was an explorer. I became reconciled to exercise in the form of long voyages of discovery which I made alone. Our house was in a square between two roads, one terraced above the other, and I could leave home, follow the upper road for a mile past the barrack, turn left on any of the intersecting roads and lanes, and return home almost without leaving the pavement. Down every laneway and road was a view of the valley of the city framed between the houses, and I stood at each, trying to identify streets and churches. When I came home, I wrote down my adventures in a book called *"The Voyages of Johnson Martin.* With Many Maps and Illustrations. Irishtown University Press. 3s. 6d. Nett." "Johnson Martin" was my pen name. I was also compiling "The Irishtown University Song Book for Use in Schools and Institutions by Johnson Martin" which would have all the words and music of my favourite songs. I could not read music, of course, but I copied it from anything that came handy, and preferred staff to tonic sol-fa because it looked more imposing on the page. I still was not sure what I was going to be, a bishop, an explorer, a musician or a painter. All I knew was that I was going to be famous and have a statue put up to me somewhere close to that of Father Matthew, the Apostle of Temperance, in Patrick Street. So far our town hadn't a genius of the sort that Mother meant, but I intended to fill the gap.

But my work continued to bring home to me the great gaps in my knowledge. Mother understood my difficulty and worried herself endlessly finding answers to my questions, but neither she nor Miss Cooney had a great store of the sort of information I needed, and Father was a hindrance rather than a help. He was talkative enough about subjects that interested himself, but they were very limited. "Ballybeg," he would say. "Market town. Nearest station Rathkeale. Population 648." When I asked him about other things, he was quite forthcoming, but later, Mother would take me aside and explain that he was only joking again. It made me mad, because I never knew when he was joking and when he wasn't.

I can see now, of course, that he didn't really like me. It wasn't the poor man's fault. He had never expected to have a son who was a genius, and it filled him with forebodings. He looked round at all his contemporaries who had normal, bloodthirsty, illiterate children, and shuddered at the thought that I would never be good for anything only being an old genius. It wasn't himself he worried about most, but there had never been anything like it in the family before, and he dreaded the shame of it. He would come in from the front door with his cap over his eyes, and his hands in his trousers pockets and stare at me moodily while I sat at the kitchen table, surrounded by papers, producing fresh maps and illustrations for my great Book of Voyages or copying the music of *The Minstrel Boy*.

"Why don't you go out and play with the Horgans?" he would ask wheedlingly, trying to make it sound attractive.

"I don't like the Horgans, Daddy," I would reply politely.

"What's wrong with the Horgans?" he would ask testily. "They're fine, manly kids, it seems to me."

"They're too fond of fighting, Daddy."

"But what harm is that? Can't you fight them back?"

"I don't like fighting, Daddy, thank you," I would say, still with perfect politeness.

"The dear knows, the child is right," Mother would say, coming to my defence. "The children round here—I don't know what to make of them."

"Ah, you have him as bad as yourself," Father would snort, and stalk to the front door again, to scald his heart with visions of the nice natural son he might have had if only he had married the girl next door as his mother had wished him to do. Grannie had never had the same opinion of Mother from the night she refused to eat with her fingers, and prophesied that Father would "sup sorrow" with her.

So he felt it almost a filial duty to sup sorrow. He was always watching me, expecting the insanity to break out; almost willing it to break out. It was like that the night the Opera House took fire. The Opera House was a cardboard box I had mounted on two chairs in the dark hallway. It had a proscenium cut in it, and I had painted a back-drop with mountains and sea. The characters were pictures cut out, mounted and coloured, which I pushed about on bits of stick. It was lighted with candles for which I had made coloured screens, greased so that they were transparent, and I made up operas from story-books and bits of songs. I was singing a passionate duet for two of the characters while twiddling the screens to produce the effect of moonlight when one of the screens caught fire, and everything went up in a mass of flame. I screamed, and Father came out to stamp out the blaze, and he cursed till even Mother lost her temper with him and told him he was worse than six children, after which he wouldn't speak to her for a week.

Another time when I decided to have a lame leg because it struck me as being so pathetic, there was hell in the home for days, because Mother had no difficulty at all in seeing that my foot was already out of shape. She insisted on Father's looking at it, but he only sniffed contemptuously. I was furious with him, but Mother decided he was a monster. They quarrelled for days over that, and it became quite an embarrassment to me because I felt I should be letting Mother down by getting better. At the same time, I was bored stiff with limping and wanted to play engines, which is impossible with a limp. When I went down the Square, lurching from side to side, Father stood at the gate, looking after me with a malicious, knowing smile, and when I finally walked home one evening, having discarded my limp, he said with a grin that made me writhe, "Well, I see your leg is better."

The way he mocked Mother about that was positively disgusting.

2

As I say, they squabbled endlessly about what I should be told. Father was for telling me nothing.

"But Mick," Mother would say earnestly, "the child must learn."

"He'll learn soon enough when he goes to school," he snarled. "Why do you be always at him, putting things into his head? Isn't he bad enough as he is? I'd sooner the boy would grow up a bit natural."

But either Mother didn't like children to be natural, or she thought I was natural enough as I was. Women, of course, don't mind geniuses half as much as men do. I suppose they find it a relief after ordinary men.

Now, one of the things I wanted to know was where babies came from, but apparently this was something no one would or could tell me. It was all very mysterious. I was sure Mother would know, but, the moment I asked her, she started to get upset and talked about birds and flowers. I came to the conclusion that even if she had known, she must have forgotten and was ashamed to say so. Her memory was very bad. Miss Cooney only smiled wistfully when I asked her and said, "You'll know all about it soon enough, child."

"But, Miss Cooney," I said with great dignity, "I have to know now. It's for my work, you see."

"Keep your innocence while you can, child," she said in the same tone. "Soon enough the world will rob you of it, and once 'tis gone it won't come back."

But whatever it was she was talking about, the world was welcome to it so far as I was concerned, so long as I could get a few facts to work on. How can a fellow be a genius if he can't find things out. I appealed to Father and he told me they dropped babies out of aeroplanes, and if you caught one you could keep it. "By parachute?" I asked, but he only looked pained and said, "Oh, no, you don't want to begin by spoiling them." After that, Mother took me aside again and explained that Father was only joking. I went quite dotty with rage and told her that one of these days Father would go too far with his jokes.

Finally, Mother decided she must tell me herself. It was a heavy responsibility, and she disliked it intensely—a deeply pious woman like her who never talked about it at all if it could be avoided; but I was the only genius she had met, and she wouldn't give it to say that she had frustrated me about anything I wished to know. But first, when she asked Father's advice, the pair of them had a thundering row. He said she was going out of her mind, and trying to drive me out of my mind at the same time. She was very upset, because she had considerable respect for his judgment, but when she discovered something she took to be a duty she could be very obstinate.

She took a long time over it, and blushed and mumbled and went off at tangents—it was a summer day, and we were sitting on the bank of a stream in the Glen—but at last I made out the fact that mummies had an engine in their tummies, and fathers had a starting-handle that made it go, and once it was started it went on till it made a baby. This explained an awful lot of things I hadn't understood up to this; for instance, why fathers were necessary at all, and why Mummy had buffers on her chest while Father had none. It made her almost as interesting as a locomotive, and for days I went round filled with regret that I wasn't a girl and couldn't have an engine and buffers on my own instead of a measly old starting-handle like Father.

I had really no practical use for the information, so it satisfied me completely till I started going to school and met Una Dwyer. I was not very happy in school because I was too small to be moved up to the big boys' and the other "infants" were still at the stage of spelling "cat" and "dog." I tried to tell the old woman who taught us about my work, but she only smiled and said, "Ssh, Larry." I hated being told to hush. Father was always saying it to me.

I was standing at the playground gate one day, feeling very lonely, when a tall girl from the Senior Girls' School came up and spoke to me. She had a round, pale face and jet-black hair.

"What's your name, little boy?" she asked with a smile.

I told her.

"Is this your first time at school?" she asked.

"Yes."

"And do you like it?"

"No," I said gravely. "I hate it. The children can't spell and the old woman talks too much."

Then I talked myself for a change, and she listened attentively while I told her all about myself, my voyages, my books and the time of trains from all the city stations. As she seemed interested, I told her I would meet her after school and tell her some more.

So I did. When I had finished my lunch, instead of going on further voyages, I went back to the Girls' School and waited for her to come out, and we went home together. She lived up Gardiner's Hill, a steep, demure suburban road with trees that overhung the walls of a demesne. She lived in a little house in a square at the top, and was one of a large family. Her little brother, John Joe, had been killed the previous year by a car. I waited while she had her dinner and then she took me across the fields to the top of the hill overlooking the city.

"Thank God!" Mother said when I went home and told her. "I knew you'd make nice friends when you went to school. It's about time for you, the dear knows."

That was what Mother thought. Others, I discovered, took a different view. I was a creature of habit, and every day at three I was waiting for Una outside the school. When it rained and Mother would not let me out, I was miserable. One day, there were two senior girls there and one of them said with a giggle, "Your girl isn't out yet, Larry." The other put on a shocked face and asked in astonishment, "And do you mean to tell me Larry has a girl?" "Oh, yes," replied the first. "Una Dwyer is Larry's girl. He goes with Una. Don't you, Larry?"

I replied politely that I did, but in fact, I was exceedingly alarmed. I had not realized that Una was my girl. It had never happened to me before, and I had not understood that meeting her in this way outside school each day would be regarded in such a serious light. I think now that the girls were probably right anyhow, for that is how it has always happened with me. A woman has only to shut up and let me talk to make me fall head and ears in love with her. But at the time I did not know. I realized that going with somebody meant you intended to marry them. I had always assumed that I should marry Mother, and now it seemed I was to marry someone else, and I wasn't quite sure if I should like it, or if, like football, it would prove to be one of those games that two people could not play without pushing.

A week or two later I was asked to a party at Una's house. All the Dwyer children, their friends and their mother were gathered in the front parlour, and we sang songs. Una had warned me that I should be expected to sing, so I was ready for the occasion. I sang the Gregorian "Credo," which I was very fond of. Some of the children giggled, but Mrs. Dwyer looked at me in a kindly way that I found encouraging.

"I suppose you'll be a priest when you grow up, Larry?" she asked.

"No, Mrs. Dwyer," I replied. "As a matter of fact, I intend to be a composer. I shall compose operas."

That seemed to surprise her. I was quite prepared to continue the discussion, but all the children talked together. I was used to planning discussions so that they went on for a long time, but here I found that whenever I began one, it was immediately interrupted, and it was hard to concentrate. Besides, all the children shouted, and their mother, for all her sweetness, shouted with them and at them. At first I was alarmed, but I soon saw that they meant no particular harm, and the party ended by my jumping up and down on the sofa, shrieking louder than anybody, while Una, in hysterics of giggling, encouraged me. She seemed to think I was the funniest thing ever.

It was a November night, and the moon was up, and lights were burning in the little cottages below us when Una brought me home. On the road outside she stopped uncertainly and said, "This is where little John Joe was killed."

There was nothing remarkable about the spot, and I saw no chance of acquiring any useful information.

"Was it a Ford or a Morris?" I asked, more out of politeness than anything else. I was happier than I had been for years, and I knew now that marriage to Una was the very thing for me.

"I don't know," she replied with smouldering indignation. "It was Donegans' old car. They can never look where they're going, the old shows!"

"Our Lord probably wanted him," I said perfunctorily.

"I dare say," replied Una, though she didn't speak with any particular conviction. "That old fool, Donegan—I could kill him whenever I think of it."

"You should get your mother to make you another," I suggested helpfully.

"What's that?" Una exclaimed in bewilderment.

"Tell her to make another brother for you," I repeated earnestly. "It's quite easy, really. She has an engine in her tummy, and all your daddy has to do is to start it with his starting-handle. That's how all babies are made."

"Oh, cripes!" she said, and clapped her hand over her mouth in an explosion of giggles. "Imagine me telling her!"

"But it's true, Una," I said obstinately. "It only takes nine months. She could make you another little brother by next summer."

"Oh, Jay!" Una exclaimed in another fit of giggling. "Who told you all that?"

"Mummy did. Didn't your mother tell you?"

"Oh, she says you buy them from Nurse Daly," said Una, and began to giggle again.

"I wouldn't really believe that," I said with dignity.

But the truth was, it came as a real shock to me to hear it. I had always known there was some doubt about the matter, and had never got a really straight answer from anybody. Now I realized that I had never been fully convinced by Mother's explanation. If there was anything that woman could get wrong, she unfailingly did so. At the same time, I did not think that this was just one of her usual lapses of memory. I thought she probably had her own reasons for telling me what she did. And it upset me, because for the first time I found myself wanting to make a really good impression on somebody. The party at Una's house had convinced me that this was the sort of life I really wanted to lead.

That night, when I was in bed, I tried to sound Mother about it. I wanted to be tactful because it had always been agreed between us that I should marry her when I was old enough, and I did not wish her to see that I had changed my mind.

"Mummy," I asked, "if a gentleman asks a lady to marry him, what does he say?"

"Oh," she said shortly, "some of them say a lot. They say more than they mean."

She was so irritable that I guessed she had divined my secret and was sore because I wasn't willing to marry her after all. I was genuinely grieved, and I did, in fact, remain awake quite a long time, wondering if it weren't my duty to marry her after all.

"If a gentleman said, 'Excuse me, will you marry me?' would that be all right?" I persisted.

"Ah, well, he'd have to tell her first that he was fond of her," said Mother, who no matter what her feelings might be could never bring herself to do me wrong by misinforming me.

This made it sound rather difficult, so I decided to let it alone for the present. But the more I thought of it, the more attractive it seemed. Una and I would have six children, and I should teach them all reading, drawing and music. The great advantage of children, from my point of view, was that they gave you an opportunity for teaching, and I loved it. When I had no one else, I would take a stick that resembled a pointer and teach myself.

But I still had the major problem on my mind. For days I made the most pertinacious inquiries at school as to how babies came, and received some startling information. One boy had actually come floating down on a snowflake, wearing a bright blue dress, but to his chagrin and mine, the dress had been given away to a poor child in the North Main Street. I grieved long and deeply over this wanton destruction of evidence. The balance of opinion favoured Una's solution, but of the theory of engines and starting-handles, no one in the whole school had ever heard. That story might have been all right when Mummy was a girl, but it was now definitely out of fashion.

The more I thought of it, the more I realized that Mother had not merely been forgetful as usual. She had been ashamed to tell me the truth and admit that she had bought me from the nurse exactly as she would have bought any other commodity. No doubt the truth humiliated her too much. It humiliated me too, but I was too old to have things concealed from me. Now, because of her, I had been exposed to ridicule before the one woman whose good opinion I really valued. It was hard enough keeping up my dignity with a girl who was doing algebra without falling into childish errors that only made her laugh. And she did not allow me to forget it. Once when we were going up Gardiner's Hill together she stopped to look at a baby in a pram. The baby cooed at her and she gave him her finger to suck.

"I suppose that was another engine, Larry?" she said, and went off into giggles again.

Four times at least she mentioned my silliness, twice in front of other girls, and, though I let on not to have noticed, I was pierced to the heart. But I was determined not to be exposed again. Once, Mother asked Una and her sister, Joan, to tea, and all the time I was in an agony of self-consciousness, dreading what she would say next. I felt that a woman who had said such things about babies was capable of anything. The talk turned on the death of little John Joe, and it all flowed back into my mind on a wave of shame and mortification. I made two efforts to change the conversation, but Mother returned to it. She was full of pity for the Dwyers, and had almost reduced herself to tears. Finally, I got up and ordered Una and Joan out to play. Then Mother got angry.

"For goodness' sake, Larry, let the children finish their tea!" she snapped.

"It's all right, Mrs. Delaney," Una said good-naturedly. "I'll go with him."

"Nonsense, Una!" Mother said sharply. "Finish your tea, and finish what you were saying. Your poor mother! How can they let people like that drive cars?"

At this I set up a loud wail. At any moment now I felt she was going to get on to babies.

"Will you behave yourself, Larry!" Mother said in a quivering voice. "Or what's come over you in the past week? You used to have such nice manners, and here you are, behaving like a little corner-boy. I'm ashamed of you."

How could Mother know what ailed me? How could she

realize that I was imagining the family circle in the Dwyers, and Una, between fits of laughter, describing my old-fashioned mother who still talked about babies coming out of people's tummies? It must have been real love, for I have never known a case of true love in which a boy wasn't ashamed of his mother or a girl of her father.

It lasted for weeks. I still enjoyed going home with Una in the afternoons, and, while she ate her dinner in the kitchen, sitting at the piano and pretending to play, but whenever she called at my house for me, I grabbed her by the hand and tried to drag her away so that she shouldn't talk to Mother. Mother noticed it herself and was very upset.

"Ah, don't be talking to me!" she snapped. "One would think you were ashamed of me, in front of that little girl. I'll engage she doesn't treat her own mother like that."

It was almost a relief when it ended. It happened one day when I was waiting for Una in School Lane. There was another boy waiting as well—one of the seniors. When he heard the screams of the school breaking up, he walked away and stationed himself at the foot of the hill, by the crossroad. Then Una herself came rushing out with her wide-brimmed felt hat, swinging her satchel, and approached me with a conspiratorial air.

"Oh, Larry, guess what's happened!" she whispered. "I can't bring you home with me today. I'll come down and see you during the week, though. Will that be all right?"

"Yes, thank you," I said in a dead-cold voice, and I watched her scamper down the hill to where the other boy was waiting. He looked over his shoulder with a grin, and then the two of them went off together. Instead of following them, I went up the hill alone, and then stood leaning over the wall of the quarry, looking at the valley of the city far beneath me. I knew this was the end. I was too young to be a playmate for Una. I didn't know where babies came from and I hadn't done algebra. The fellow she had gone home with probably knew all about both. That was why he had grinned at me in that mocking way. I was full of gloom and revengeful thoughts. I who had considered it sinful and dangerous to fight was now regretting that I hadn't gone after him to batter his teeth in and jump on his face. It didn't matter to me even that I was too young and weak and that he would do all the battering. At least, it would have relieved the feelings which now threatened to burst in me. I saw that the sweetness of love was a mockery, worse than football, and that I had nothing to look forward to but the day when Una would stand in the crowd on Patrick Street and see my statue put up beside Father Matthew's, and realize what she had missed. It seemed for the time being a poor consolation.

I went home, and without saying a word, I took out the work I had been neglecting for so long: my great Book of Voyages and The Irishtown University Song Book. They seemed to have lost their appeal, as though there had never been anything in them but my fancy. All the same, I firmly ruled five lines and began to trace the difficult sign of the treble clef.

"Didn't you meet Una, Larry?" Mother asked in surprise, looking up from her sewing.

"No, Mummy," I replied, too full for speech.

"Wisha, 'twasn't a falling-out ye had?" she asked in dismay, coming towards me.

Then I put my head on my hands and sobbed, and she comforted me, running her hand through my hair.

"Wisha, never mind, childeen!" she murmured: "I always thought Una was a bit old for you. You'll soon make new friends, take my word for it."

I did not believe her. That evening there was no comfort for me, not a scrap. My great work meant nothing to me. I went at dusk to the top of the Square where there was a view of the Glen that Mother and I went walking in, and I saw the dusk settle over it, and realized that there was no happiness in the world; that everything was illusion, even the pretence that babies came out of their mothers' tummies when the truth was that they were bought from the nurse. I thought I knew now why Mother had tried to conceal that sordid fact from me. She did not want me to know. Now, there was nothing that I did not know about life.

SHARING YOUR IMPRESSIONS

1. Describe some of the sexual expectations you have been subject to at home and at school.
2. How have the concepts of "masculine" and "feminine" changed since you were a child?

3. Why do you suppose than "tomboys" (girls) are more socially acceptable than "sissy" boys?
4. Speculate about the influence on the child when his or her parents hold differing expectations.
5. What alternatives can a teacher or parent offer the child whose peers call him a sissy?
6. Suggest some ways for eliminating sex-role stereotypes in our society.
7. Try to remember some misconceptions about sex that you were taught as a child. In each case suggest how your parents could have been helpful.

18

THE HUNT

Susan Kuehn

No matter how hard I try, I don't suppose I will ever forget that day. And the funny thing about it is, it started out so fine. We were going to harvest, and when we went to bed the night before, it looked a little threatening toward south, but in the morning it was bright enough for five summer days all pushed together into one. Even my brother Game, who's nineteen but not quite bright, seemed excited about the weather.

Mother was up first, like she always is, and when she woke me up she was already in her apron and ready to cook dinner for the nine men who came from farms close by to help harvest each summer.

I was fifteen then, just old enough to be noticing boys for the first time, or at least noticing them so that I wanted them to pay some attention to me. So I took one of my school dresses out of the back closet. I wanted to wear it instead of my overalls that day. I went downstairs in my slip and carried the dress so I could press it before breakfast. When I got to the kitchen, Mother was busy putting the bread in the oven and Dad was out in the barn.

"What do you want to go and make extra trouble for, Fay Anne?" Mother asked. "Don't I have my hands full enough?"

I said I would iron the dress myself.

"That doesn't matter," she said. "I was planning on having you help me, starting right now."

"It won't take long," I promised. "Anyhow, I can do it when everyone else is eating breakfast."

"You have to eat, too," Mother told me. Then she wasn't mad any longer. She just sighed and asked me why I wanted to get all dressed up that day in particular.

The question kind of embarrassed me. I couldn't answer right off. I couldn't say that I wanted the Jensen boys and Henry Bushman to notice me and maybe ask me into town for a movie or something. All the other girls in high school talked a lot about going out, and I hadn't even had one date. Of course having Game around the place didn't make things any easier. He scared them off, I guess. So I didn't answer right away.

"Oh, go ahead and get your ironing done now," Mother told me. "I'll fix the table. But don't fool around about it." Mother was all right. It was a shame I couldn't tell her things that I felt. They all were tied up too much with Game, though, and she wouldn't stand for any criticism of him.

After I hauled the heavy ironing board out of the closet and unwound the old sheet that kept the dust covering the board, I got to work. I had taken a pale blue cotton that Mother made for me the spring before. She loved nice clothes herself, and I guess she was a knockout when she was younger—from what people said. Not that she is bad-looking now, just sort of tired.

As I ironed I could see the wheat stretching out for acres beyond the window. It always looked prettiest just before it was ready to come down. It swayed a little, and I remembered a poem we read in school once about how wheat was supposed to look like waves in the ocean. The air was so clear and the sun so warm that it didn't seem quite natural. It was about time that we had one good harvest day, though, I kept thinking. It had rained the year before and soaked half the crop. And Game had tried to help, which made things even worse, because he started messing up what was already shocked.

I finished the dress finally, and while it didn't look like Mother had done it, it wasn't too bad. I'd had enough practice from pressing small things. I put it on and combed out my hair. I had left it in metal curlers until then, and the bumps had hurt my head while I was sleeping. Game came downstairs just then and didn't say anything about how I was dressed. That's one thing I will say for him. He doesn't ever tease me. I suppose it's because he never notices things.

Dad came in from the barn about the same time. All of us except Mother started to eat. She said she wanted to get the bread in the oven first. I was pouring the coffee and when I got to Dad's cup, Game moved his head so quickly that I nearly burned him.

"I'm going hunting today," he said in his low man-voice. He had slicked back his hair like a clown, but still if you looked at him fast you wouldn't suspect at first that Game was different. I saw Mother jerk a little when he said that, and then stiffen. She always seemed to hope that someday Game would improve. Dad just drank his coffee and then told Game that they would talk about hunting later. He didn't act surprised at all.

"You're not serious, Garrett!" Mother said. She came to the table now, but she didn't start eating. She didn't do anything at all except look at Dad, who turned away to light his pipe. The same look passed across her face that I always saw when Game wanted to do something he wasn't able to do. When she had to admit out loud that Game was—well, hopeless—she acted like this. I suppose it bothered Dad too, but he didn't show it.

"I don't know, Mabel," my father said. "It would keep him out of mischief." I couldn't tell by his voice whether he was serious or not.

"It would be terribly dangerous. You know that."

"It's a good day for hunting," Game said. He always spoke his words carefully. He had been to school for a while, Mother says, but it was before I was old enough to remember. He went as far as the second grade, but he couldn't learn to read when the other kids did, and so he didn't go any more.

"Not today," Mother told him.

Game pushed back his chair to get up from the table, but he must have caught his foot against the leg because he stumbled and knocked against the dishes. It pulled off part of the table-cloth, and Dad's plate fell off the table on his lap. Game stood with a dazed look and watched Dad wipe himself with a napkin.

This sort of thing happened every now and then, and I didn't see any reason for it making Dad so angry that day in particular.

"Are we going to go through this again today?" he asked.

"He couldn't help it, Garrett," Mother said, wiping away at the soiled place on Dad's lap. Game wandered out of the room and went up the stairs to his bedroom.

"I know it. He never *can* help it, but it's hard on all of us."

"Hush," Mother said. "Hush."

I had to agree with Dad, but I felt sorry for Game too. He was tall but never seemed to remember that he was, and he still bumped his head no matter how many times he walked through the back porch to get outside. He kept cutting his fingers just by touching things too hard. And he could make such awful noises sometimes. That was the worst of all, and still he seemed to get a look that was almost clever then, and the sounds were like certain animals you could recognize.

"Good heavens, Mabel, don't you suppose he'll do this again today?" Dad asked. "He'll put his finger in the machinery or knock over the wheat as soon as we shock it."

"He's going to stay around today."

"He'd be better off in the woods."

Mother stood up. "He's not going anywhere today, Garrett. I'll keep an eye on him."

"I still don't think it's a good idea," my father said. He lighted his pipe, which had gone out, and left the table. "They'll be coming in half an hour. I can't watch out for him."

That's the way Game always was, in the way for all of us. I started wishing that he could be off just this one day. That way I wouldn't have the feeling that people were looking at me as Game's sister. Once, when I was just starting out at school, a girl in my class named Verna asked me if I was funny in the head like my brother. She used to live down the road from us and moved away about seven years ago, but I remember her because she said that. I really loved Game, but it wasn't like loving a person.

When Dad left for the barn after breakfast, I cleared the dishes so Mother could eat, but she didn't even look at the food. After a while she said we'd better get to work. We were having stewed chicken and biscuits and rhubarb pie. My favorites.

While we were working, Game walked sullen-faced through

the kitchen. He must have known that Dad was kidding him along at breakfast. It wasn't exactly fair, because he wanted to go hunting so bad.

But we couldn't trust him too far from the house. He puttered around in the fields, always digging for things and bringing what he found back to his room. I helped clean that room in the spring, and I found some feathers and stones knotted in a handkerchief in his drawer. It was funny how clean they were, while Game was so messy. Well, no—untidy was a better word for it.

And he always asked to hunt. When Dad left on a hunting trip with the other men in the neighborhood, Game got a queer, bright look and tried to follow. Dad made it plain every time that he wasn't supposed to go along. Then, panting as if he had run a long way, Game would lower his head and go back to the field. He found a little gray bird once, and the discovery tickled him so that we made out we thought it was quite something. Because he forgot things so soon, it wasn't hard to bury the pile of feathers later.

I was just trying to decide if Mother would be mad if I put on some lipstick, when Game came in again. It was a hot June morning, but he wore heavy boots and a red winter cap. He must have kept them hidden somewhere, because I had sorted all the winter things in the attic when I helped with the cleaning.

"I'm going to get some ducks," he announced. When we didn't answer, he stood around and watched us cook for a while. "I'm going," he said in a dreamy voice. "There's a tree out there in the woods. It's fluffy on top like a chicken. That's where I'll find my duck."

Dad brought the milk pails in from the barn and set them by the side of the kitchen door. "I've decided to let him go hunting, Mabel," he said.

Mother looked at him. "Are you joking?"

"There won't be anybody in the woods today, with the harvest going on," he said.

"You don't mean you're going to give him a gun?"

"Only an old one," Dad said. "It won't be loaded." He said the last part in a soft voice, so that Game couldn't hear.

"He might get lost."

"He knows that woods better than he does the house,"

Dad told her. It was true. He used to take both of us there on Saturdays when we were smaller, and Game still went now and then.

"I don't know," Mother said.

"It all depends on you," he told her in a patient voice. "I won't send him if you don't say so. They'll be along now, in about ten minutes. Why don't you pack Game a lunch and have him off by the time they come?"

"Would it be safe?" she wanted to know, beginning to give in.

"Safer than around here. We'll finish the work up quick, and then I'll go out and get him. What do you say?"

"Oh, I don't know." From her voice you could tell she had given in. I, for one, was relieved.

"Then it's settled," Dad said. He told Game to come along with him, and they would get the gun ready. Mother turned away and started packing a lunch, even though she hadn't finished the pies yet. She made peanut butter and jelly sandwiches as a special treat for Game and packed everything in a little paper box.

"Maybe it will be a good thing," she said. "Game's growing up now. He may be able to get around to different places by himself."

"Sure, Mother," I said.

"Why, before long maybe he can do some errands for us," Mother told me. "Wouldn't that be fine?"

I said that it would, because I was happy enough to agree with anything when I thought of having people over for a whole day without Game around to spoil it. I decided I might as well put on that lipstick after all.

Dad and Game came back into the house together to pick up the lunch. Game carried an old gun that was rust-marked in spots. Dad must have given him a worn-out gun that he didn't use any more, I thought, and it made me kind of sad to think that Game always had to have old things. He held the gun as if it might break any moment—his clumsy hands were that gentle with it.

"I'm going hunting now," he said proudly. He sat next to the table while Mother finished wrapping the sandwiches in wax paper. She put them all in the box and tied it with a string.

"There you are," she said. "Fit for any hunter. That's what your father eats when he goes out. Do you want milk?"

Game nodded that he did. He took off his cap and put it back on, and the proud look on his face was something to see.

Mother poured the milk into a half-pint bottle that she asked him to bring back if he remembered.

"Look at my gun," he announced. He aimed the barrel toward me. "See?"

"No!" Dad touched Game's arm with a jerk. "Be careful of that."

His voice took me by surprise. "It's not loaded?" I asked.

"Only with blanks," Dad said. "I thought there might be a day like this. I bought them in town last year."

"Oh, Garrett," my mother said, and for a minute I thought she might cry. But instead she reached up and kissed Game's cheek. "Do be careful," she warned him.

He carried the lunch things in one arm and shouldered the gun, in a graceful way he didn't usually have, with the other.

Dad went back into the barn, and Mother and I stood at the back door and watched while Game crossed the field toward the woods. Inside the forest it was a cool, damp green blanket of quiet. Game would probably forget and wander for the whole afternoon. The sun died down, suddenly, and I saw the sky turn fish-colored. The change seemed threatening, and it looked as though it might rain after all.

Mother called after Game to make him stop, but when he gave no sign he heard, she was quiet. The sun flickered back to its old brightness. Though it wasn't eight yet, the rays spread out, noon bright, on the scanty patch of flowers near the back stoop and the long stretch of field behind them. As I walked out into the yard to shake the kitchen tablecloth, I could see Henry Bushman and his father come down the road in their Chevvy, pulling the binder after the tractor. Duane and Paul Jensen were setting out from their farm, too. I stood in the sun for a minute, because it felt so good. I liked to see it glitter down on Mother's geraniums, and when I drew some water from the pump for the flowers, the sun made the wet petals look like precious stones, when usually they seemed kind of scrawny and pathetic.

Although Game had walked quite a ways by then, I could still see him in the distance, getting close to the woods. I noticed that Dad was still watching him, too. The sun flickered across Game's red cap and shone on the bright places of his rusty gun. From the back, you would have thought he was like anyone else.

The dinner couldn't have gone better. Everything came out of the oven just right, and the men pretended to think I had baked the pies myself. The three boys kidded me about how much I had grown since I saw them last. Then, about an hour after they had finished eating, Henry Bushman came back to the house for a drink of water. When he asked me to a party at the church the following Sunday, I was just about as happy as I could ever be. It was the first time I got something just by wishing hard for it. I told Mother after he had gone outside again, and she said she would see about getting me some material for a new dress.

As we were washing the dishes, I could feel it getting hotter outside, and the air seemed to hang all around us, damper than before. The sun glittered down on the field.

Then it happened, so quick that we never had the chance to get ready for it. The sky darkened all of a sudden, turning the color of mud. Mother ran to the front rooms and slammed down the windows to protect her good lace curtains against the rain. When I was closing the upstairs windows, I could see the men covering the binder with canvas. Then it began, in soft penny-size drops at first and swelling until it nearly burst open the dry ground. I thought of Game, but it just looked like a summer rain. They never lasted long, and besides rain never frightened Game. He loved to hear the thunder.

But this wasn't just any summer rain. Big blasts of water tore at the windows, and it seemed as if they crashed as the rain hit the ground, instead of it being the sky that made the noise. In a couple of seconds, the sky turned pitch black, and there wasn't any chance of reaching Game. The whole outdoors seemed to explode when the lightning began. And it wasn't day any more, but night.

"Game," Mother shouted at me. "We've got to find him."

"We can't," I yelled back, above the noise. "We couldn't get out in that."

But she grabbed a coat from the closet and would have run

out if I hadn't kept her away from the door by standing in front of it.

"I'll go. You just wait here," I said.

I was a little surprised she let me go like that, but I got away so fast she never had a chance to stop me. I wore the coat I had snatched out of her hand and put a dish towel across my head, but the water whipped hard across my face and back. I had to stop before I had gone a quarter of the way to the woods because I knew full well I could never make it. Heading back into the pounding sheet of water, I turned toward the barn, with the wind bursting across the field and tearing at my clothes. It pushed my skirt high above my legs, and as I pulled it back down, the cloth swept right off my head. The wind lunged across the ground, taking me with it, and knocked me against something that rose up from the earth. The rain nearly blinded me, and I couldn't see what it was at first, then it turned out to be the pump. My leg had caught against the handle, and I wrenched it away. It surprised me to hear myself sobbing.

The house came first and then the barn. The men weren't anywhere. I knew they must have gone into the barn, but the wind wouldn't let me reach it. I screamed once, but couldn't even hear my own voice. I saw two windows break as I looked toward the house, and I watched the shades lash out through the broken glass.

The wind sang in the air. It was like the buzzing of a million bees. I pushed open the back door to the kitchen and collapsed, on legs that felt as if they were made of soggy string, against a chair. From a great distance away, I could hear Mother asking me if I had seen Game. Another window broke somewhere, and water poured across the kitchen table and spilled into my lap.

Half hidden by the steaming rain, the barn didn't look real. Lightning hissed across the sky, splitting an apple tree down the center. As the tree broke, a big orange circle of lightning closed in around it, and the sky was a brilliant blue.

"What can we do about Game?" Mother kept saying, but I was too out of breath to answer.

"He'll be killed!" Mother put her hands around my shoulders, and her fingers closed down so tight that it hurt. "I'm going out there."

"You can't make it. The storm keeps pushing you down."

The door smashed open, and Dad stood there. He sat down at the table, dripping but calm enough.

"Where are the others?" I asked him.

"Back in the barn. They're safe enough there. I came in because I thought I saw you in the yard, Fay Anne. You might have been killed."

"What about Game?" Mother asked him. "We've got to get him."

"It's no use," he said. "We couldn't make it."

"We've got to try." Mother went toward the door, but Dad told her not to be foolish, that nothing could be done then. She suddenly turned weak and sat down at the kitchen table. We sat looking at each other dully. Then I saw the men were making a dash for the house, and I ran to let them in. They piled into the kitchen, like so many damp mounds of cloth.

"The barn didn't look safe," Duane Jensen gasped. The men stamped water from their shoes. It gushed out as if there were springs in the leather.

An electric shudder tried to break the world in pieces. Down the field as far as I could see, something caught fire and burned.

"That would be the Hofstroms' place," Dad said. "A man works all his life to build something, and a storm can carry it off without so much as a backward glance."

"This storm is nearly as bad as the one back in '27," Mr. Bushman said. We all looked at him, with a new feeling of hopefulness. It was good to hear that there had been a worse storm and that people talked about it afterward because they came through it all right. Still it didn't do Game any good, I thought. Mother was bearing up pretty well, but she kept working her hands in her lap until it made me nervous.

Once, I remember, Henry Bushman patted my shoulder and told me it would be over soon.

I don't know how much later the storm cleared away, but finally it was gone. Outside we found that the crop was lost, and the wheat lay limp on the ground.

Right away, we all started walking toward the woods. Dad tried to make Mother and me stay in the house, but it wasn't any use. I was afraid, and in a way I didn't want to look for Game. But I couldn't have stood it alone in the house. The ground was wet and uncertain under our feet, and I slipped a couple of times.

Oh, please make Game be all right, I kept saying over and over in my mind. I think I was scared of what I might have to see. I was shaking by the time we reached the edge of the woods. Mother walked ahead. The rain splashed down from the trees in big streams. But we only went a few steps under the wet leaves when we heard something coming.

It was Game, and he wasn't even touched. Instead, he looked very happy, as if he had forgotten about the storm. I was relieved, but I didn't say anything. Mother ran toward Game and hugged him. She just couldn't believe it. It was then I noticed that he held something in his arms. A dead pheasant.

"Look," Paul Jensen said. "A bird got hit in the storm."

"By George, that's what happened," said Mr. Bushman, reaching for the pile of matted feathers.

But Game was stubborn. "No," he said. "It's mine. I shot him."

Everyone knew about the blanks, and I saw them smiling at each other. But Dad was quiet. "Give me your gun," he told Game.

Game handed over the gun with a surprised look on his face, as if he were being punished for something he couldn't understand. "It shot good," he said.

"Yes." Dad started to laugh in a funny way. It wasn't right to make fun of Game like that, but of course I couldn't say anything.

"Now I can hunt with you," Game said. He gave Dad a look, and for a moment it seemed that he was completely bright, even more clever than most men. It seems funny to think that could ever happen, but that's the way it looked to me. Then Game was back to himself again. "My duck. I shot my duck," he crooned happily. He stroked the crumpled feathers, and I saw something that made me jump. Although I hated to touch it, I asked Game for the pheasant.

He had forgotten about his unwillingness and handed it to me, but he kept right on talking.

Then I knew I was right. I covered the bloody place with my hand, because I could see that the feathers had been ripped apart by a real bullet. It hadn't been any storm that killed the bird. And Dad had said he put only blanks in the gun. I could hardly look at him, and it made me feel sick to hold the bird, but I didn't dare let go.

The men wanted to hand it around, and I don't know how I ever kept them from doing it, but they weren't even suspicious. I broke away, still holding the pheasant, and said something about how awful it was to handle a poor, dead thing that got killed by the storm. I sneaked off and buried it hurriedly in the woods before they could stop me. They all thought it was kind of peculiar, I guess, but Dad said he thought I must be upset. He knew darn well what I was doing and why. I just crammed the bird in a hole next to a fallen tree, and I couldn't stop thinking how it might have been Game that was dead instead of just that pheasant.

I was afraid to go back, so scared that the feeling squeezed everything else out of me until I could hardly move my feet. I wiped my hand against the wet leaves to get the blood off, but even after it went away I could still feel it on my skin. Even though it got hot again right after the storm cleared away, I started to shake.

Twice I started back, but I just couldn't quite make it all the way. Somehow I had it in my mind that Dad would try to get me too, because he had seen me discover what happened. But in another way I was just as scared of having Mother catch on to what I was doing, and I went back.

Game was still going on about his duck, and the excitement made him talk even worse than usual. The words rolled around in his mouth like loose marbles before they came out. I caught Henry Bushman looking at Game and I felt ashamed. I remembered then that he hadn't seen Game for years, because he had been in the merchant marine for the last harvests. I went over and stood close to Game. More than anything, I wanted to tell someone.

Then it hit me. I couldn't tell Henry Bushman or anybody else ever. It just came to me for the first time, really, that I would be telling on my own father. Before I was just afraid for myself and for Game, but now it was bigger than that. I was shut up in a trap, and there wasn't any way I could get out without doing something worse than what had happened.

The rest of that day until bedtime just crawled by. I didn't want to go to bed in the dark, but I couldn't stand being in the same room with Dad and feeling him look at me. I knew he was trying to make me look back at him, but I kept my face away. I couldn't pay any attention to the magazine I started, so I asked Mother if she didn't have some mending for me to do. That took me all evening, and I could watch the thread instead of Dad. Game was so good that night, just sitting on a chair and not even talking much. Then we went to bed.

I lay there thinking about the whole thing, and I knew I wouldn't be able to go to sleep at all. I felt sorry for Game, but it was all mixed up now with my own life. I had seen that look Henry Bushman gave Game, and I remembered the whole afternoon so closely that I could still see Henry Bushman walking away afterward. He hadn't said anything at all to me about the church party when he left. I wondered if he would bother to think of any excuse.

Game never meant any harm, but it was just in him to mess things up without knowing it.

After a while, I was so tired I would have given anything to sleep, but I didn't dare close my eyes. I was afraid of what I would see. When the door opened, I didn't even turn over to face it at first. It was as if I had expected him all the time.

My father closed the door behind him and came close to my bed. He stood there, looking down at me, and I couldn't move. When it got so I could see his face in that half dark, I remember thinking how I had never seen him without his glasses before.

"Don't be scared, Fay Anne," he said in a low voice that didn't quite seem to belong to him.

"What is it?" I made my voice sound sleepy on purpose, because it seemed safer like that.

Dad pulled my straight-backed chair away from the window and sat on it, beside my bed. "You know what I did, don't you?"

"What do you mean?" I asked, but I couldn't keep my voice sleepy like before.

"The blood got on your hand. I saw it," he said. It was awful hearing him talk like that. It wasn't like my father at all.

"Sure, there would be a little blood," I made myself say. "That bird was hurt in the storm, and it died."

"You know what I mean." For some reason, his voice took

me back to the times when I was little and made up excuses for why I hadn't learned my Sunday school lesson. Then Dad's voice would be something like this. He always wanted to hear the truth, he would say.

"Yes," I whispered.

"Then say it," he told me. "I want you to tell them what I did." Even in that funny strained moonlight, I could see his face clearly, but he looked different.

"No." They mustn't know. Game wouldn't understand, and it would only make it worse if Mother knew. "You didn't do anything."

"You saw it," he said. "I want you to say it. I can't have it go on being a secret."

"I won't tell them anything," I said.

My father turned his head away, as if I weren't there any more.

"Game won't ever go hunting again. I don't know why I let him go like that today," Dad said. He let out a heavy breath like a shudder.

"I know why you sent him," I said finally.

"Why? Say it."

"Because we all wanted you to. Is that what you want to know? It's my fault, too."

He didn't say anything more. We sat there in the quiet for a very long time, and after a while Dad left.

I hadn't known I was going to talk like that, but it was the truth. Blaming Dad just didn't do any good, and he wasn't anything to be afraid of any more. I had sent Game hunting that day as much as Dad. I hadn't wanted him to be hurt, but I remembered the let-down feeling I had when Game stepped out of the woods that afternoon. I was relieved when I saw him, but I wasn't happy. And Mother had sent him, too. I wondered how long she would go on hoping Game would do something clever—and if she ever thought of him as a burden although she would never say it out loud.

But none of us would ever say it. Dad hadn't put it into words, either. We were all guilty—that was it. Every time we had wished that Game wasn't around—or had thought that he wasn't quite bright—it had been a kind of killing of him. Maybe Dad was the most honest of us all.

SHARING YOUR IMPRESSIONS

1. How do you feel about being around a retarded person? Someone who is emotionally disturbed? The physically handicapped?
2. How do you feel about legislation to prevent retarded adults from having children?
3. Describe the kinds of schooling you believe should be provided for the retarded.
4. How do you suppose the life of mentally retarded children and adults is different from that of persons who are normal?
5. Make some guesses about the self-concept of school children who are retarded.
6. Explain your reasoning on the issue of whether parents with mentally retarded children ought to give up hope for normal behavior.
7. What effect does a retarded person have on the life of other members in the family?
8. In your opinion, is it the school's function to inform parents of a realistic level of expectation for their retarded youngster? What about expectations for the normal children?

19

THE HERO'S SON

Dale Eunson

"Don't let it spoil your trip," Ann said as the *No Smoking* sign blinked off.

"It's your trip too," John said.

"I didn't mean it that way."

"Well, that's the way it sounded."

The bloated 747 leveled off and cruised over floating-island clouds that smeared the Mojave 35,000 feet below. John unsnapped his seat belt and tried to attract the stewardess taking drink orders.

"I could use one too," Ann said. Her tentative smile coaxed no response from him. "Can't we not think about it for awhile?"

"I wasn't thinking about it," John said. "I was wondering if he'd remember to give Scotty his Digitoxin."

"Darling," Ann said, "Little John is nineteen years old. You don't have to remind him of everything."

"That, as my old man used to say, is a moot point." He frowned. "What do you have to do to get that idiot girl to look at you?"

"For openers," Ann said, "you might try pinching her behind as she passes."

John glanced at Ann and readjusted the grim set of his

features into something resembling a smile. "I'm sorry," he said. "It's just that whenever I think about that dumb kid . . . ah, Miss, how about a couple of very dry martinis?"

They ate lunch high above the Wasatch Mountains of Utah. As they passed over Wyoming and the Dakotas, John sat hooked to the sound track of the movie, hoping Woody Allen could divert his mind from the problem that had come to a head yesterday. Come to a head *again*, rather, because it was always there. But this time it had been worse, and Ann finally cried out, "Stop it, both of you!" And then for the first time in her life she had resorted to emotional blackmail. "Do you love me?" she asked her son.

"Why, yeah, sure, Mom," the boy answered. "So what?"

"Then do me a favor. Listen to your father."

"I've been listening."

"Not with your mind. It's clamped shut. Maybe you're right, but it's possible your father's right too. He's lived a lot longer than you have. He might have learned something in all those years."

"But he talks to me like I'm a ten-year-old."

"And by God, that's giving you the benefit of a few years!" John said, whirling on his son.

"John! Please please please!" Ann put her hand on her son's arm. "Nothing can be settled today. I want you to promise me to remain in college till we come home. Stay here and take care of things—the house, Scotty, the plants—and then—"

"But, Mom," the boy said, "they need me now. This is the only meaningful thing I've ever wanted to do."

"Oh, Lord!" John groaned. "Meaningful. Can't you kids think up another word this year? And spare me *relevant*. I'm up to here with relevant too."

"Please, can we skip the lecture on semantics?" Ann turned back to Little John. "Nothing very significant will be lost if you postpone joining the campaign for a month, will it?"

"He needs all the help he can get, man," Little John said.

John winced; then, in the same sarcastic tone, said, "No doubt he does, man. But you may be losing your hold on pure, indigenous wisdom. Nineteen . . . why, you're old enough to vote, God help us every one!"

"I can't talk to him, Mom," Little John said.

The boy stole a furtive glance at his father, who was staring at him with all the puzzled fascination of a scientist attempting to identify a rare specimen under his microscope. The specimen lowered its head, long hair completely concealing the face. "I'll tell ya, man," it mumbled, "it's like, well, he knows where it's at."

"I see," John said slowly. "And you—out of vast experience acquired in the sandbox—are an authority on politics and politicians, is that it?"

"Ya see, Mom?" the boy said shrugging shoulders that seemed already set in a permanent shrug.

"John," Ann said hopelessly. She turned and stared out the library window at Scotty who had treed a cat and was barking for his family to come share his triumph.

"Go on. I'm waiting," she heard John say to their son.

"I mean—well—you wouldn't have to keep on giving me an allowance while I was campaigning for the senator."

Which was not what the boy meant to say at all, Ann suspected, but why did he have to let such a stupid thing come out of his mouth?

"Did you hear that, Ann?" John asked. "We wouldn't need to support the senator's brain trust. I knew if we kept up these round-the-clock bargaining sessions we'd win some valuable concessions." He turned to the boy. "I'll tell you what, Mr. Meany. Your mother and I want very much to go to England for a few weeks. You stay here and take care of the house while we're gone, and I'll pay you a hundred dollars. And when we come home you may pack up your mind-blasting rock records, rip out your stereo, sweep up your beads and hair ribbons, load them all on your horrible Honda and present them—and yourself—as a campaign gift to the senator of your choice!" . . .

"If you look down to your left at ten o'clock," the pilot's voice was saying, "that's Winnipeg coming up on the Red River."

Ann looked out the window of the plane, but she did not see Winnipeg. What she saw was John's dear young face, blurred by the anesthetic they had given her. His eyes were red, and he was telling her that the baby had not lived. A boy, it had been. Perfect in every way. It just had not lived, that was all.

Three years later Little John, as they called him, was born. He was handsome and normal—and he had lived! And few children have known such love.

They would shield him, John swore fervently, from all the things his own tender psyche had been exposed to (and somehow survived). He was to be nourished at prescribed intervals, sleep according to the schedule recommended by Dr. Spock, be spared the unconscious chauvinism of military toys and exposed to the virus of television only enough to immunize him. Any talent that might bubble to the surface would be coddled and fertilized. And when Little John reached the age of six, Big John was already weighing the merits of one college against another.

Yet all this protection and love did not produce the child John had anticipated. Little John's capacity to learn was only average. His lack of physical coordination made him indifferent at competitive sports. As he approached adolescence, he seemed deliberately unresponsive—negativistic was the child psychiatrist's term for it. "Most children," this authority assured the Hastingses, "pass through a similar phase. It is assertion of ego, a perfectly normal rebellion against authority and direction."

"But the boy has nothing to rebel against," John told him. "Nothing but our love for him."

"That may be the trouble," the doctor told them. "He's got to rebel against something. Most of us have palpable grievances as children. Plenty of our parents *are* stupid, unfair, selfish—not at all the omnipotent gods we think they are when we are toddlers. In the case of your boy, I suspect he has translated your love and concern into a fence. Lower the fence. Make it easy for him to climb over—and come back across."

"That is a lot of bull," John said as he and Ann drove home to their puzzling 13-year-old. "He admitted he had no kids of his own. You're damn right he hasn't!"

"Let's just try to ignore what Little John does and says," Ann said. "Try not to keep at him about studying for awhile."

"Then he'll never crack a book."

"Let him. He'll have to take the consequences. Not you."

"But he's my son!" John cried.

And so everything and anything became an issue. There was

the matter of his posture, his long scraggly hair, the shattering rock music and the beat-up motorcycle that he bought with his allowance, took apart and wired together regularly once a week.

Ann tried to act as buffer between father and son, but John interpreted this as defense of the boy's inadequacies: to the boy it was interference in his resistance to what he maddeningly termed his father's square life-style.

"Don't you see, Mom?" he once said in a rare moment of closeness between them. "It's not how you look—or what you say or do—it's what you are inside."

But what was the boy inside? Ann wondered. And why didn't how he looked, or what he said or did, give them a clue? He did not even fall in love at 16 or 17 or if so, he kept it secret.

"What girl would be foolish enough to go for our pride and joy?" John said. "You don't suppose he's working up to being a queer; do you?"

"They all look like that these days," Ann said.

"Mine won't, if he continues to live in my house!" John said darkly.

Ann had hoped that going off to college would not only mature the boy but that the absence of daily friction between father and son would begin to heal scar tissue. But Little John did not go away. His grades were too low for him to be accepted at any of the first-rate universities, and John could see no point in shelling out what it would take to board him at some distant state college when a duplicate local branch lay within five miles of home.

The sight of Little John taking off for a day at State was, Ann had to admit, ludicrous. To his father, it was closer to agony than humor. When he kicked the Honda into life and rocketed off, wearing run-over cowboy boots, skintight jeans, beads, a torn sweat shirt impregnated with a photograph of W. C. Fields, long hair tied at the back with a psychedelic ribbon, Little John was not precisely his father's notion of a clean-cut American boy entering the halls of Academe.

Watching him disappear around the corner, John said, "If he's trying for Mr. Repulsive, he's a smash."

"John, you sound as if you hate him."

John thought this over, then he said, "No. I'm just appalled.

My God, the kid's going out in the world one of these days. It's rough. Who'd give him a job? If his grades don't pick up soon, he'll even get kicked out of State. And that's not easy, man!"

Darkness came swiftly as the 747 droned eastward. Only four hours after sunset the northeast horizon crimsoned, and presently the plane settled into the bumpy veil of clouds below, and then suddenly, there was England with her clean little row houses, the gentle, intimate green landscape dotted with sheep and cattle, a well-behaved river meandering between manicured meadows. "That's the Thames," John said. "Brother! Was that a sight for sore eyes when we finally made it back from the Continent! Look, there's Windsor! Our base was only a few miles to the north."

Peter Proctor was at Heathrow to meet them. It was difficult for Ann to reconcile this middle-aged Londoner—settled, inclining slightly to paunch, hair graying (what was left of it), neat pin-striped suit—with the crazy American youngster John had told her about. They'd been quite a pair, those two, John the P-38 squadron leader and Pete, his buddy and constant concern.

"I daresay Johnny has regaled you with tales of my sticky derelictions," Peter said to Ann as he drove them toward London.

"A few hair-raising highlights," Ann admitted.

"All gross libels," Peter said. "Substitute Johnny's name for mine, and you'll approximate the truth."

John laughed. It was the first time Ann had heard the sound since the crisis. "Listen to Pomona Pete. He's turned into a Limey."

Peter Proctor's love affair with England had begun when he read the legends of King Arthur, and it had been intensified by the romantic notion that he was something of a knight himself, coming to the rescue of prostrate Britannia in 1943. It was inevitable that he should fall in love with an English girl, and he had. She was a fashion model, and her name was Sarah Calvert. After the war Peter married her. He promptly got a job in the London branch of Hamilton Assurance, Ltd., and was now assistant manager.

The Proctors lived in a pleasant, airy flat two blocks off Hyde Park in Kensington. John and Ann were to occupy the room that had been their son's before Gerald married.

Sarah Proctor, while still pretty, no longer possessed the figure of a model. "All that Devonshire cream," Pete said, patting her fanny.

After dinner that evening Gerald, now 24, and Ellen, his very pregnant young wife, came by to pay their respects to their father's old friends. They seemed to be smudgy carbon copies of many American young people—long-haired, healthy, rumpled, relaxed. "Gerald," Sarah explained, "does something tedious about recording the prenatal mewlings of fetuses."

"That's why I got Ellen pregnant," Gerald explained. "It beats getting picked up for approaching strange women in Piccadilly," he said, laughing.

"It's cold—having a microphone strapped to your belly," Ellen said.

"Do you mean to say that you're going to market these —uh—recordings? You are putting us on, aren't you?" John asked.

"Not at all, old man," Peter said. "Gerald's got a firm contract for twenty-five thousand first pressings."

"You see, Mr. Hastings," the young man said, peering at John through his bangs, "we amplify those sounds five thousand times, and it comes out like—like Genesis. And the birth is Exodus."

"Beautiful!" Ellen sighed. "The way God would have wanted you to hear it if he'd thought of four-track stereo."

It had been, both John and Ann agreed when they were finally alone, an unsettling evening, to say the least. Maybe, Ann said, they were merely victims of jet lag, and it had not really happened; it seemed impossible that nice, average parents like Peter and Sarah could casually accept—even seem to love and admire—such a far-out son and daughter-in-law.

During the next few days the Hastingses visited St. Paul's and the Tower and Parliament; they paid their respects to Sherlock Holmes and Dr. Watson in Baker Street, to Leslie Howard in Berkeley Square and to Sir Winston Churchill at 10 Downing Street.

On Sunday morning the *Times* assured them that skies

would clear by noon. Sarah packed a lunch, and the four of them drove to a peaceful meadow that, almost three decades ago, had been home base for Lt. John Hastings' squadron of the P–38 wing of the U. S. Army Air Corps.

The government had chosen, wisely, to reclaim the land for a park, to plant trees and shrubs and create a man-made lake around which flowers and children blossomed, to set up tables and benches and yet leave space for the ubiquitous cricket fields, now dotted with slim figures in white. Nothing remained of the military installation, nothing was there of what had been except two middle-aged men who presently strolled across the field, watched the cricket players and noisy children and peaceful picnickers, and frequently paused and seemed to cock their ears (for the drone of a plane that would never come back?). As they returned to Ann and Sarah, they were speaking softly as one does on the steps of a church after a funeral.

"It was so long, so long ago," John was saying.

"God . . . a lifetime," Peter said, and bent to kiss Sarah.

"If it hadn't been for the war we'd never have had each other," Sarah said, as though John and Ann were not there.

"And Gerald would never have been."

"The *ifs* of life," Sarah mused, and turned to Ann. "Can you imagine your life if you'd never met Lieutenant John Hastings?"

Ann stared at John. "It wouldn't have been life," she said simply, and then tried for a lighter tone. "The uniform—that's what got me."

"So you have the Air Corps uniform to thank for your kid," Peter said. And after a moment, "What's with your boy, Johnny?"

John turned away, focused on a child chasing a purple balloon. "Well—we've had our problems," he finally said.

"We all have," Sarah said.

"As long as you haven't killed each other, there's hope." Peter laughed.

"It's the damnedest thing," John said, and jammed his fist into the spongy English earth. "All these years—not caring a damn for anything but his own selfish comfort. And now—now after he finally gets into the only college that will have him—now he wants to drop out and promote the election of some senator! You'd think if he didn't, the world would come to an end."

"That's a healthy sign," Sarah said quietly.

"Healthy sign of what?" John asked, trying to suppress his anger.

"I don't know anything about your senator," Sarah replied, "but at least your son finally believes in something enough to do something about it."

"But *I* think the senator's an idiot," John exploded.

Sarah and Peter did not comment on what John had just said. No comment was needed. Presently Peter spoke. "When we were having our last hit-and-run rhubarb with Gerald, I felt I had to have help. We went to a shrink—"

John snorted. "Psychiatrists!"

"Yes, I know, I know. Maybe we were just lucky and found a sensible man," Peter continued amiably. "What he said was, playing father isn't always the hero part in the play. We get fouled up in a self-admiration society and—how did he put it, Sarah?"

"He said a father seldom loves his son as a separate entity. He loves his own image in his son. And if the son grows up and doesn't turn out to be you at all, you—I mean the father—either want to chain him to the nest or kick him out. Something like that."

Peter nodded. "When the only thing to do is let him go. And pray a lot."

John got to his feet and brushed the grass off his trousers. "It's not that at all," he said. "It's—I know what the kid's going to be up against. I want what's best for him—that's all."

Peter stood beside his old friend. "Johnny, I wanted what was best for Gerald too, but he didn't give a damn about that, still doesn't . . . How old is—young John?"

John seemed not to hear the question. "Nineteen," Ann finally said.

"Just our age when you were my all-wise squadron leader," Peter observed.

John turned and stared at him, then looked out across the park. In his mind's eye he saw the base as it was 28 years ago—the bleak barracks and hangars, the control tower and, right where the lake was now, the runway. It was cloudy as always—like today—and then breaking through the clouds came the wobbly, stricken wreck of a twin-fuselaged plane, a grinning grasshopper impudently appliquéd on one nose. The pilot was bringing her home, hanging onto the controls with naked nerve endings, letting her down—by some miracle—right on the runway. And then he must have blacked out because the plane suddenly went into a dive and crashed—about *there*—beneath that flaming laburnum tree flaunting its gaudy yellow clusters . . . .

And *there*—right there among the stark-white cricketeers—was young Lt. Hastings, strapped beneath the bubble of his own P–38, waiting to be flagged off once the rubbish of Hoppy's plane and body could be scraped off the runway. What was he thinking? *God, I don't remember! How did I have the guts—or was it plain stupidity!—to gun my plane when I finally got the flag? Didn't I have any imagination at nineteen? Nineteen . . . I was only nineteen. Little John's age!*

"But we were men!" There was anguish in John's voice when he finally spoke.

"We sure as hell were," Peter said. "And if we didn't get into the fight the world would come to an end." He shrugged. "Maybe it has anyhow, but we gave it all we had because we believed. We believed we could do something about it, damn it!"

When they got back to the flat in Kensington there was a cable under the door and the telephone was ringing. Sarah picked up the cablegram and hurried to the phone. It was Gerald. Ellen was in labor and would like Sarah to go to the hospital with her. Gerald had all that sound equipment to lug.

"I'll be right there!" Sarah cried, hung up the phone and reported that she was about to be made a grandmother. She pecked Peter's cheek and rushed out the door only to return a second later and hand John the cablegram. "Silly me," she said. "This is for you."

The cable was from Dr. Patterson. Little John had been in an accident and was in the hospital. The doctor did not want to alarm them unduly, but for the boy's peace of mind he felt they ought to come home at once.

Two hours later they were on a plane headed for Los Angeles.

Dr. Patterson's cable had really told them nothing. Not how the accident had happened or how seriously Little John was injured. Was he maimed? Would he be a cripple? Blinded? His brain damaged? Both of his parents immediately assumed that his head had been injured in a crash of that damned motorcycle. It had to be that, didn't it?

Once John took Ann's hand in his and closed his eyes. She hoped he could doze for a few minutes, but his eyes were closed by acute distress, not sleep. "And I told him to pack his junk and get out," he muttered.

"I know," Ann said. "But he knew you were provoked. People say things they don't mean when they're—"

"I meant it at the time," John said, punishing himself. "I wonder now . . . am I so all-fired anxious to get home and make him well again? Or is it mixed up with my wanting to make sure he's forgiven me—in case—"

"Don't say it!" Ann said sharply.

John seemed not to hear her. "Little John . . . . Who said it first?"

"I don't remember . . . . Does it matter?"

"Me, probably. Right away I tried to make him a pint-size version of the old man."

"Hush," Ann said. She lifted her hand and turned his troubled face to hers. "It'll be all right," she murmured. "Everything will be all right, you'll see," and she knew as she said it that there was no reason in God's world—if indeed it was, or ever had been, God's world—to suppose that anything would be all right again.

They went straight to the hospital from the airport, and it was still only nine that same evening. It was insane. Ellen probably had her baby by now, and no doubt its mother's every moan and its first gasp for breath had been lovingly taped for the record's soaring climax. Exodus indeed!

"What room is John Hastings in?" Ann asked.

"Four-sixty-five," the young woman at the reception desk said. "But visiting hours are over."

Then he's not dead, Ann thought, and leaned against the wall for support. "We're his parents," John was saying.

The door to 465 was ajar. John pushed it open and held it for Ann to enter. A dim night-light burned. A black boy, his leg in a cast, occupied the first bed. A white boy lay in the bed near the window, but he was obviously not Little John. He was asleep, or seemed to be.

"You lookin' for somebody?" the black boy asked.

"Yes, but we must be in the wrong room," Ann said.

The figure in the other bed spoke. "That you, Mom?"

Ann caught her breath, hurried around the black boy's bed and leaned over her son. "Darling, darling," she said, kissing him lightly on the cheek, then drew back and looked at him. His head was bandaged, the long hair gone. Without the wild, scraggly hair, his face looked different. She realized that it had changed. It hadn't really matured, but it was no longer the pimply, baby face of an adolescent.

"Baby, what happened?"

"A car hit me," he said.

"I was sure of that," Ann said. "Knocked you off your motorcycle?"

"No. I knew you'd think that."

"It doesn't matter. I'm sorry I said it."

"It wasn't my fault. Honest. I was just standing there by the curb, waiting for Scotty to lift his leg on the hydrant, and this car comes highballing around the corner and can't quite make the turn. Man, next thing I know I'm on the ground and Scotty's licking my face."

"But what happened? I mean, how were you hurt? How badly?"

"Compound fracture—back here," the boy said, indicating the back of his skull. "I get dizzy. Sometimes I don't see so good either."

"He's gonna be okay," the black boy volunteered. "His doc says he just needs to stay flat on his back for a spell. So don't go showing off trying to scare your folks, whitey."

"My *folks*?" Little John murmured. "You mean Dad came home too?"

"Why, of course," Ann said. "Whatever made you think . . . ?"

"Well, I don't know. I just—"

John came forward and took the boy's hand in his own.

"I'm sorry I fouled up your trip," the boy said.

"Don't—don't," John said. He leaned over, fearful lest the gesture he ached for would be rebuffed. Closer, closer, then he put out his arms, and, after a long moment, the boy's arms reached out and went around the father, and they clung to each other and felt the other's heartbeat and breath and warmth. And finally John drew back and looked down into the face that was undeniably the spit and image of Lt. John Hastings, P–38 squadron leader, age 19.

"Listen, Dad," the boy said.

"I'm listening." *And keep me listening.*

"Well—I'm kinda mixed up. Maybe it's this"—he tapped the bandage at the base of his skull—"but—I don't know. Maybe I shouldn't drop out when I get well and go off campaigning for the senator if you're so dead set against it."

"*But I want you to,*" John cried out, and was shocked to hear his own voice saying it, because he had not consciously thought it before.

"You want me to?"

"I mean—you mustn't let me talk you out of anything you really believe in," John said. "You're a man now—your own man. You do what you've got to do—and I'm with you."

The boy looked from his father to his mother, his brow furrowed. "I don't get it," he said. "You're treating me as if I'm going to die. I'm not."

"I'm treating you as if you're going to live—your own life," John said.

Ann could see their son think this over, weigh it, test the sudden burden of it.

"But maybe I won't want to go—"

"That's up to you," John said. "It'll be your decision."

The man and the young man stared at each other for a long, long moment. Something was happening to them, between them, a current beginning to alternate that had been short-circuited somewhere, somehow, a long while ago. It was coming on too fast, too strong, too sudden to be coped with. John looked away.

"They had to cut my hair," the boy said with a grin. "Close enough for you this time, Dad?"

"Too close," John whispered. "Too close."

SHARING YOUR IMPRESSIONS

1. When you were a teenager, what part did your parents play in affecting your choice of a career?
2. Why do you suppose so many parents expect more from their children than they themselves achieved?
3. Parents' unrealistic expectations may get in the way of a good relationship with their children. Try to remember an unrealistic expectation your parents held for you.
4. Adolescent ideals are sometimes seen as obstacles to personal development when the ideals conflict with their parents' goals. Illustrate this circumstance with an example from your own observation.
5. Give your opinion on whether fathers tend to set higher expectations for sons than mothers do.
6. How realistic are the vocational aspirations expressed by high school students?
7. How do you react to the idea that dropping out of school may sometimes be a sensible move?
8. Think of some ways in which today's adolescents might be given increased adult responsibilities.
9. How do you imagine relationships between teenagers and parents may change over the next 20 years?

20

THE REGULARS

Gilbert Rogin

The Ashers graded the days of their vacation, which they spent at the Sun 'n Sea Motor Inn in Key Biscayne and at the Whispering Sands Resort Motel on Sanibel Island, C+, B, D, A, B−, C+, B, A−, D, F, C. These grades reflected the weather.

During their vacation, the Ashers noted license plates from twenty-eight states and two Canadian provinces.

The bad things that happened on their vacation (and which they wrote down) were:

1. No gas cap.

On the way from the airport to the Sun 'n Sea, a woman in a station wagon, in which a little boy intently turned a toy steering wheel, kept honking her horn and shouting at Asher. Motorists frequently blew their horns at him or shouted unintelligibly as they passed. Asher almost never knew why. Off and on, he appealed to his wife, who didn't drive. She reminded him that he had made her navigator, and that such appeals didn't come under her department. On this occasion, however, Asher finally understood that he was leaking gas. He parked: no gas cap.

On Key Biscayne, Asher drove from one gas station to another, looking for a gas cap.

"Make a note of the mileage," he told his wife.

"What ever for?"

"I'm going to have Hertz deduct it."

"We've only been in Florida forty-five minutes and you're already preparing to create a scene."

"But I'm in the right."

2. No Unit 21.

The Ashers had come to Key Biscayne every year since 1963, when they had honeymooned at the Crandon Park, formerly the Crandon Palm. In 1965, they switched to the Sun 'n Sea. There they had always had Unit 21, which differed from nearly all the other units in that the bathroom was on a breezeway and had a louvered window. Each year, the first thing Asher did after he put down the bags was stand on the toilet seat, unplug the ventilator fan in the ceiling, and crank open the window.

This year, they had Unit 33: not on a breezeway.

"I specifically requested Unit 21," Asher told his wife, trying the bathroom light switch, which also operated the fan.

"You can still unplug it," she said.

"But the point is," Asher said, raising his voice so he could be heard above the great melancholy roar of the fan, "the point is that this unit has adjoining units on both sides, so the possibility of people having their television on too loud at night is twice what it is in Unit 21."

3. Spooky galleys.

In years past, the print above their bed at the Sun 'n Sea had shown a curve of beach, some palm trees, the wrecked hull of a native fishing boat. This year, the print showed several fantastic galleys that seemed to be rotting in a backwater, sails in theatrical tatters, oars drooping in the stagnant, faintly phosphorescent water. Asher's wife maintained that it actually glowed in the dark; Asher said she was overreacting.

Asher peeked into some other units, including 21. The galleys were hanging all over.

"What do you think made them put them up?" Asher's wife asked.

"What do you think they did with fifty-four native fishing boats?" Asher asked.

4. Portuguese men-of-war.

The ocean was choppy, turbid, and dotted with innumerable men-of-war, so Asher was loath to go swimming. He sat on the beach in his collapsible chair, from which an accumulation of baggage tags fluttered; he had bought the chair the day before they got married and took it to Florida each year.

Asher's wife spread her towel beside the chair and sat down.

"I'm waiting for a lull," he told her, "but they keep coming."

5. No binocs, no bird book.

Asher had forgotten his binoculars and his Peterson.

"If you see one you don't know," Asher's wife told him, "ignore it."

6. No mask, no snorkel.

Asher had forgotten to pack his wife's face mask and snorkel. He said he was sorry, adding that there was too much sediment to see anything anyway.

7. No pajama bottoms.

Asher had packed two pajama tops and no bottoms.

8. No pumpernickel raisin, no whole-wheat onion.

Asher's favorite restaurant was Chippy's, in Coral Gables, because pumpernickel raisin bread and whole-wheat onion rolls came in the breadbasket. This year, the nights the Ashers were there they didn't serve any.

9. South Dixie Highway at night.

The traffic had become murderous.

10. Abner's.

This was a restaurant on the South Dixie Highway, where they ate one night. Asher had chosen it on account of the modern architecture: it was walled with dark glass. Inside, large color transparencies portrayed slices of rare roast beef and succulent ribs. Their orders came in woven-plastic baskets and didn't resemble the photographs. Asher sat with his chin in his hand, looking through the dark glass at the murderous traffic and at his reflection.

11. Stephen.

Asher's stepdaughter called from New York to say that Stephen, his stepson, had ridden his ten-speed bike over "Santana," "Let It Bleed," and "Revolver."

12. Andrea.

Stephen called to say that Andrea, Asher's stepdaughter, had spent the food money on Indian jewelry.

13. "Z."

A comic strip.

14. "Bob & Carol & Ted & Alice."

"Why do the protagonists in these movies always wear jockey shorts?" Asher asked his wife. "Nobody I know wears jockey shorts."

15. No upstairs at the Whispering Sands.

This was the third year the Ashers had gone to Sanibel. The first two times, they had a unit on the second and top story near the Gulf; the Whispering Sands was built at right angles to the water. This year, they had a unit on the first floor.

"I can't see the ocean from my bed," Asher's wife said after Asher had put down the bags. "On the second floor, I could see the ocean."

"It's the Gulf," Asher said.

When he returned from the office, where he had gone to complain, Asher said, "I told them I had specifically requested a unit on the second floor as near the Gulf as possible. I told them to refer to my letter, which they did. They agreed that I had specifically requested a unit on the second floor as near the Gulf as possible, but they didn't have any. They said their regulars liked the first floor because they didn't have to lug their bags up the stairs."

The good things that happened on the Ashers' vacation (and which they wrote down) were:

1. 9 A.M. plane.

The Ashers had reservations on a 10 A.M. flight to Miami, but because Asher liked to allow plenty of time for eventualities they got to the airport so early they made the 9 A.M. flight, which gave them an additional hour in Florida, fifteen minutes of which, Asher pointed out, they wasted looking for a gas cap.

2. Brindley s.

Asher had forgotten to take pipe tobacco. Vernon's, in the Key Biscayne Shopping Center, had his brand—Brindley's Mixture.

3. Chinese hairless.

Window-shopping on the Miracle Mile one night, the Ashers saw a strange dog. It was black and hairless, except for a tuft that grew out of its forehead. Asher's wife said that the dog looked as though it was made out of clay. Its owners were a man in plaid shorts and a woman who wore socks and heels. Afterward, Asher's wife said the woman must have been the man's mother; Asher said he had assumed she was his wife. The man told Asher the dog was a Chinese hairless. Asher's wife said she hadn't known Chinese hairlesses existed. Asher said he had heard of them. The man said he had never heard of them until he heard on television that a woman who owned four Chinese hairlesses had died, and they were available on a first-come, first-serve basis. "So we went over and got one," the man said. "One was gone already. We got the second."

4. Maids.

Until this year, the Ashers' chambermaid at the Sun 'n Sea had been Augusta. Each year, Augusta asked them why they didn't bring the children with them, and each year they told her they were going to bring them next year. When they didn't, Augusta would throw up her arms and chide them for breaking their promise. This time, they had another chambermaid. They asked her whether Augusta still worked there; the new maid said she did. The next day, they met Augusta by the linen room.

"I heard someone was asking for me," she said, "and I knew it had to be you. Where are the children?"

Later, Asher said to his wife, "I like the maids at the Sun 'n Sea. They do the dishes. The maids at the Whispering Sands don't do the dishes."

5. Portuguese men-of-war gone away.

For two days, following a shift in the wind.

6. Lifeguard.

At Crandon Park, the Ashers met Wayne, a lifeguard they had got to know the year before. It turned out he had seen "Z" the same night as the Ashers, at Wometco Twin II, opposite the Dadeland Shopping Center; in fact, he and his wife apparently had sat behind them. Asher's wife said she thought she had heard a familiar laugh. Wayne said he thought "Z" was a comic strip, too. He and his wife hadn't seen "Bob & Carol & Ted & Alice."

7. Sandbar.

The sandbar off the beach at Crandon Park had become much bigger since last year, and nearer shore. You weren't allowed to swin to it, but, as he had the year before, Wayne let

Asher swim over with him. While Wayne jogged around the bar, Asher looked for shells. Then Wayne and Asher waded to a farther bar, on the edge of the deep. On the way, Wayne told a story about another lifeguard who had been marooned on the second bar; a hammerhead had entered the channel between it and the first bar. He said the lifeguard had run about on the bar, yelling and waving his arms, but nobody could figure out what he was up to. When Asher told the story to his wife, she said Wayne had told it to them last year. She also said that last year Asher had brought her back a shell.

8. Elderly waitress.

Asher's wife said Asher gave the elderly waitress at Chippy's a hard time. Asher said that he was only kidding around. Asher's wife couldn't finish her turkey sandwich. The elderly waitress put it in a doggy bag for her, but she left it in the booth. Two evenings later, when they next ate at Chippy's, the waitress said she had run outside on the sidewalk with the doggy bag, looking for Asher's wife, but she had disappeared.

9. Unidentified bird.

Asher saw a bird he couldn't identify sitting on the end of one of the groins at the Sun 'n Sea. He waded out with his notebook and pencil to sketch the bird, which must have been fearless or exhausted, since it didn't fly away. Where the bird was, the water was up to Asher's shoulders. His first attempt was ruined when spray wet the page. When Asher came out of the water, a woman said to him, "How could you write out there? I couldn't do it." Asher told his wife what the woman had said, adding, "Why didn't she say, 'Why are you writing out there?' Or, 'What are you writing out there?' " Asher's wife asked to see his drawing. "You made the bird look like me," she told Asher.

10. Swimming backward.

On Sanibel, the littoral current was so strong that no matter how hard Asher swam against it he was swept back along the shore. He told his wife about it and made her watch the phenomenon. Asher roared with laughter as he streamed backward, the scenery slipping by. Asher's wife took his picture with their Instamatic.

11. Laughing fit.

On the F day, Asher and his wife were lying in Asher's bed

at the Whispering Sands, beneath a collage composed of seashells, sand dollars, and starfish, when they started laughing and couldn't stop. Neither remembered what had set them off. Asher thought it might have been because of their plight —meaning the rain. Asher's wife thought it was because Asher had been loath to let her in his bed.

The pictures the Ashers took at Key Biscayne showed: Asher standing by their car, a blue Impala custom coupe, in the Sun 'n Sea parking area, smoking his pipe; Asher's wife standing beneath a palm at Crandon Park in her flowered bathing suit; Asher standing on the beach at Crandon Park in his red bathing suit; Asher's wife standing in the Sun 'n Sea parking area; Asher standing on the pool deck at the Sun 'n Sea in his blue bathing suit, smoking his pipe; Asher's wife lying on her stomach on a chaise on the pool deck; Asher's wife looking up a moment later; Asher swimming ashore at Crandon Park, with just his head visible; Asher stepping ashore a moment later; Asher's wife standing by the shuffleboard court at the Sun 'n Sea; Asher standing by the shuffleboard court. One picture didn't come out.

The pictures the Ashers took on Sanibel showed: Asher standing on the beach in his red bathing suit; Asher's wife standing on the first-floor walkway of the Whispering Sands; Asher making a turn in the Whispering Sands pool; Asher's wife lying on a grassy bank by the pool in her flowered bathing suit; Asher being swept backward, laughing; Asher's wife standing on the terrace of their unit; Asher standing on the first-floor walkway; Asher's wife kneeling in the surf in her orange bathing suit; Asher in his bed in one of his pajama tops; Asher's wife in her bed in a nightie with pink ribbons she had bought to wear on her honeymoon; Asher leaning against the trunk of their car before leaving for the airport, smoking his pipe; Asher's wife holding the car door open on her side a moment later.

When they had looked at the pictures, Asher remarked on how little change there had been. The years were differentiated by the cars, he said. To a lesser extent, by their bathing suits.

"Age," Asher's wife said.

How imperceptible! That is, Asher added, from year to year. One is able to believe that one looked that way last year and will look the same next year.

His wife assured Asher he was the same.

Asher wondered, speaking of bathing suits, what had happened to the bathing suit she was wearing when she thought he had drowned.

It had been the first year they had stayed at the Sun 'n Sea. Asher had told his wife he was taking a dip, but he had struck out alongshore and out of sight. When he finally returned, she was standing in the doorway of Unit 21, in a French bikini, a peach print with ruffles, sobbing.

It was the only time she had cried in Florida, Asher said. A mockingbird had been singing by the shuffleboard court, did she remember?

She said she had cried on their honeymoon, in the public library.

They had gone to the Miami Beach Public Library to read their wedding announcement in the *Times* and *Tribune*. Asher had composed it and given it to one of his wife's friends, who worked on the *Trib* and said he would take care of it. The announcement wasn't in either paper. Asher's wife said they mightn't have had room for it that day. Asher looked in the papers dated two days after their marriage; it wasn't there, either.

Now, once again, Asher dwelt on how her friend had let them down.

Asher's wife said she had cried in the public library because Asher had let her down, because she thought he would be interested in her, that he would want her, that they would go out—

"Chippy's is out," Asher said.

—that she would be able to wear her new dresses, she added.

"You wouldn't even lie on the beach with me," she said. "You brought that chair!"

She said she used to look forward to going to Florida, to having a good time. She said she had always thought he was going to change. It was she who had changed. It used to eat her heart out.

"I remember the first time I saw you," she said. "You looked like a nice person, but you didn't want to talk. I should have remembered that."

"Nonetheless," Asher said, "you cried when you thought I had drowned."

"I cried because I didn't know what I would tell your father," she said, "and I didn't know what to do about the car."

Asher said he often felt like that little boy in the station wagon—that he was wrestling with the wheel, but which way was he going?

When he had swum out of sight, he recalled, gleaming bait fish had leapt out of the sea, over his head, and there was, overwhelmingly, a sense of brightness. Terns dived, disappeared, reappeared. Light transfigured their wings. At some point, he was going to have to turn back.

SHARING YOUR IMPRESSIONS

1. Describe the types of situations that lead you to feel bored.
2. Comment on the extent to which boredom affects the people you know.
3. In what ways might the educational responsibility of parents change in a society with greater access to leisure time?
4. Suggest some ways for helping adults learn to cope with extended leisure and vacations.
5. How do you feel about parents taking a vacation without their children?
6. What advice do you have for families who cannot afford distant vacation travel?
7. Give your impressions about what constitutes a successful vacation.
8. Most grown-ups take at least one vacation each year. Think of three questions that you feel more of us should begin asking ourselves about vacations.

6

BELIEF
AND
MORAL
DEVELOPMENT

21

THE SUNDAY ZEPPELIN

William Saroyan

Luke was holding my hand and I was holding Margaret's.
We had a nickel each for collection, and Luke said to me, Don't
forget, Mark, drop the nickel: don't keep it like last time and buy
ice-cream.

You too, I said.

Last time Luke didn't drop his nickel and I saw him. I
bought an ice-cream cone in the afternoon when it was very hot.
Schultz gave me two scoops. Luke saw me eating the ice-cream
cone under the china-ball trees of Emerson School.

He acted like Hawkshaw the detective.

Ah-ha, he said.

Where'd you get the money, Mark?

You know where, I said.

No, he said. Where? Tell me.

Sunday School, I said. I didn't drop it.

That's a sin, Luke said.

I know it, I said. You didn't either.

I did too, Luke said.

No, you didn't, I said. I saw you pass the basket without dropping the nickel.

I'm saving, Luke said.

Saving for what? I said.

For a zeppelin, he said.

How much is a zeppelin? I said.

There's one in *Boy's World*, he said, that costs a dollar. It comes from Chicago.

A real zeppelin? I said.

Two people can go up in it, he said. Me and Ernest West.

I swallowed the last mouthful of ice-cream.

How about me? I said.

You can't go up, Luke said. You're too small. You're a baby. Ernest West is my age.

I ain't a baby, I said. I'm eight and you're ten. Let me go up in the zeppelin with you, Luke.

No, Luke said.

I didn't cry, but I felt sad. Then Luke got me sore.

You like Alice Small, he said. You're just a baby.

This was true. I *did* like Alice Small, but the way Luke said it made me sore.

I felt sad and alone. I liked Alice Small all right, but did I ever do any of the things I wanted to do? Did I ever walk with her? Did I ever hold her hand and tell her how much I liked her? Did I ever say her name to her the way I wanted to, so she'd know how much she meant to me? No. I was too scared. I wasn't even brave enough to look at her long. She scared me because she was so pretty, and when Luke talked that way I got sore.

You're a son of a bitch, Luke, I said. You're a dirty bastard, I said. I couldn't think of any of the other bad words I had heard big boys saying, so I started to cry.

I felt very bad about calling my own brother these names. In the evening I told him I was sorry.

Don't try to fool me, Luke said. Sticks and stones can break my bones, but names can never hurt me.

I never threw any sticks and stones at you, Luke, I said.

You called me those names, he said.

I didn't mean to, Luke, I said. Honest I didn't. You said I like Alice Small.

Well, you do, Luke said. You know you do. The whole world knows you do.

I don't, I said. I don't like anybody.

You like *Alice Small,* Luke said.

You're a son of a bitch, I said.

Pa heard me.

He was sitting in the parlor reading a book. He jumped up and came into our room, Luke's and mine. I started to cry.

What was that, young man? he said. What was that you just called your brother?

Sticks and stones, Luke started to say.

Never mind that, Pa said. Why are you always teasing Mark?

I wasn't teasing him, Luke said.

He was, I cried. He said I like Alice Small.

Alice Small? Pa said.

He hadn't even heard of Alice Small. He didn't even know she was alive.

Who in the world is Alice Small? he said.

She's in my class at school, I said. Her father's the preacher at our church. She's going to be a missionary when she grows up. She told us in front of the whole class.

Pa said:

Tell Luke you're sorry you called him a bad name.

I'm sorry I called you a bad name, Luke, I said.

Luke, said Pa, tell Mark you're sorry you teased him about Alice Small.

I'm sorry I teased you about Alice Small, Luke said. Only I knew he wasn't sorry. I was sorry when I told him I was sorry, but I knew he wasn't sorry when he told me he was sorry. He was only saying it because Pa told him to.

Pa went back to his chair in the parlor. Just before he sat down he said:

I want you boys to occupy yourselves intelligently and not get on one another's nerves. Do you understand?

Yes, sir, Luke said.

So we got a copy each of *The Saturday Evening Post* and started looking at the pictures. Luke wouldn't talk to me.

Can I go up in the zeppelin? I said.

He just turned the pages of the magazine and wouldn't talk.

Just once? I said.

I woke up in the middle of the night and started thinking about being up in the zeppelin.

Luke, I said.

Finally he woke up.

What do you want? he said.

Luke, I said, let me go up in the zeppelin with you when it comes from Chicago.

No, he said.

That was last week.

Now we were on our way to Sunday School.

Luke said: Don't forget, Mark. Drop the nickel.

You too, I said.

You do what you're told to do, Luke said.

I want a zeppelin too, I said.

Who said anything about a zeppelin? Luke said.

If you don't drop your nickel, I said, neither will I.

It looked like Margaret didn't even hear us. She just walked along while me and Luke argued about the zeppelin.

I'll give half, Luke, I said, if you let me go up.

Ernest West is giving the other half, Luke said. We're partners.

Eight more weeks, Luke said, and the zeppelin will come from Chicago.

All right for you, I said. *Don't* let me go up. I'll get even with you some day. You'll be sorry when you see me going around the world in my own boat.

Go ahead, Luke said.

Please, Luke, I said, let me go up in the zeppelin. I'll let you go around the world with me in my boat.

No, Luke said. You go alone.

Ernest West and his sister Dorothy were standing in front of the church when we got there. Margaret and Ernest's sister went into the churchyard together, and me and Luke and Ernest stayed on the sidewalk.

Palka eskos, Ernest said to Luke.

Immel, said Luke.

What's that mean, Luke? I said.

Can't tell you, Luke said. That's our secret language.

Tell me what it means, Luke, I said. I won't tell anybody.

No, said Ernest.

Effin ontur, he said to Luke.

Garic hopin, Luke said, and then they busted out laughing.

Garic hopin, Ernest laughed.

Tell me, Luke, I said. I promise never to let anybody else know what it means.

No, said Luke. Invent your own secret language, he said. Nobody's stopping you.

I don't know how, I said.

The church bell rang, so we went inside and sat down. Luke and Ernest sat together. Luke told me to go away from them. I sat in the row behind them, the last row. In the first row was Alice Small. Her father, our preacher, walked down the aisle and then went upstairs to his private study. That's where he made up his sermons. He was a tall man who smiled at everybody before and after the sermon. During the sermon he never smiled at all.

We sang some songs, then Ernest West called for *At the Cross*, only he and Luke sang, *At the bar, at the bar, where I smoked my last cigar, and the nickels and the dimes rolled away, rolled away.*

I felt jealous of Luke and Ernest West. They knew how to have fun. Even at church. Once in a while Ernest would look at Luke and say arkel ropper, and Luke would answer haggid ossum, and then both of them would try to keep from laughing. They would hold themselves in with all their might until the loud singing began, then they would bust loose with all the laughter that was part of their secret language. I felt miserable being out of all that fine stuff.

Arkel ropper, I said and tried to feel how funny it was, but it wasn't. It was terrible not knowing what arkel ropper meant. I could imagine it meant something funnier than anything else in the world, but I didn't know what it was. Haggid ossum, I said, only it made me feel sad. Some day I would invent the funniest language in the world and not let Luke or Ernest West know what the words meant. Every word would make me feel happy and I would talk no other language. Only me and one other person in the world would know *my* secret language. Alice Small.

Only Alice and me. Ohber linten, I would say to Alice, and she
would know what a beautiful thing that meant, and she would
look at me and smile and I would hold her hand and maybe kiss
her.

Then Harvey Gillis, our superintendent, got up on the
platform and told us about the Presbyterian missionary work we
were helping to pay for in many foreign and heathen countries of
the world.

In Northern Africa, my dear young people, he said in a
high-pitched voice, our shepherds of the Lord are performing
miracles every day in the name of Jesus. The native savage is
being taught the holy gospel and the pious life, and the light of
our Lord is penetrating the darkest depths of ignorance. We can
well rejoice and pray.

Umper gamper Harvey Gillis, Luke said to Ernest.

Luke could barely keep from laughing.

I felt all alone.

If I only knew what they knew. Umper gamper Harvey
Gillis. That could mean so many things about our superintendent. He was a sissy and he talked in a high-pitched voice. I don't
think anybody, except maybe Alice Small, believed a word of
what he said.

Our noble heroes in the field are healing the sick, he said.
They are sacrificing life and limb to prepare the world for the
Lord's second coming. They are spreading His truth to the far
corners of the earth. Let us pray for them. Will Miss Valentine
pray?

Would she? She'd been waiting all week for a chance to
pray.

Miss Valentine got up from the organ bench and took off her
·glasses and wiped her eyes. She was a skinny woman of forty or so
who played the organ at our church. She played it as if she were
sore at somebody and wanted to get even, pounding the keys and
turning around every once in a while to take a quick look at the
congregation. It seemed as if she hated everybody. I only stayed
for the sermon twice in my life, but both times she did those
things, and once in a while she nodded very wisely at something
our preacher said, as if she was the only person in the whole
church who knew what he meant.

Now she got up to pray for our heroic missionaries in dark Africa and other heathen places of the world.

Exel sorga, Ernest said to Luke.

You said it, Luke answered, and more besides.

Almighty and merciful Father, she prayed. We have erred and strayed from Thy ways like lost sheep.

And a lot of other stuff.

I thought it was supposed to be for our noble workers in the field, but all she talked about was straying away and doing wrong things, instead of right ones. She prayed too long too.

For a while I thought Harvey Gillis was going to touch her arm and make her open her eyes and tell her, That will be enough for this morning, Miss Valentine. But he didn't. I opened my eyes the minute she started to pray. You were supposed to keep your eyes shut, but I always opened mine to see what was going on in the church.

Nothing was going on. All the heads were bowed except Luke's and Ernest's and mine, and Luke and Ernest were still whispering funny things to one another in their secret language. I could see Alice Small with her head bowed lower than anybody else's, and I said, O God, some day let me talk to Alice Small in our own secret language that nobody else in the world will understand.

Amen.

Miss Valentine finally stopped praying and we went to the corner of the church where boys between seven and twelve studied the stories in The Bible and dropped their Sunday offering in the basket.

Luke and Ernest sat together again and told me to get away from them. I sat right behind them to see if Luke would drop his nickel. Every Sunday they gave each of us one copy of a little Sunday School paper called *Boys' World*. It told about little boys doing kind things for old people and the blind and the crippled, and it had advice on how to make things. Me and Luke tried to make a wheel-barrow once, but we didn't have a wheel. After that we didn't try to make anything. On the back page were the advertisements with pictures.

Our teacher was Henry Parker. He was a fellow who wore thick glasses and had some red pimples around his mouth. He

looked sick and nobody liked him. I guess nobody liked going to
Sunday School at all. We had to go because Pa said it would
certainly do less harm than good. Later on, he said, when you get
to be older you can stop going or keep on going, as you choose.
Right now, he said, it's good discipline.

Ma said, that's right.

So we went. Maybe we got used to it because we never
asked not to go. There wasn't much else to do Sunday morning
anyway. Ernest West had to go too, and I guess that's why Luke
never tried to get out of it. He could always talk their secret
language with Ernest West and laugh about everybody.

The story was the story of Joseph and his brothers, Joseph
with the brightly-colored coat, and then all of a sudden the whole
class started talking about the movies.

Ah-ha, Luke said to Ernest West.

Now, said Henry Parker, I want each of you to give me one
good reason why no one should go to the movies.

There were seven of us in the class.

The movies, said Pat Carrico, show us naked women dancing. That's why we shouldn't go.

Well, said Henry Parker, yes, that's a good reason.

They show us robbers killing people, said Tommy Cesar,
and that's a sin.

Very good, said our teacher.

Yes, said Ernest West, but the robbers always get killed by
the police, don't they? The robbers always get theirs in the end,
don't they? That's no reason.

Is too, said Tommy Cesar. It teaches us how to steal.

I would be inclined to agree with Mr. Cesar, said Henry
Parker. Yes, he said, it sets a bad example for us.

Oh, all right, Ernest West said.

He looked at Luke wisely and was about to say something in
the secret language, only this time he didn't need to because
Luke laughed out loud anyway, and then Ernest laughed with
him. It seemed as if Luke knew what Ernest was going to say and
it must have been something very funny because they laughed
like anything.

What's this? said our teacher. Laughing in Sunday School?
What are you two laughing about?

I'll tell on them, I thought. I'll tell him they've got a secret language. Then I decided not to. That would spoil it. It was such a funny language. I didn't want to spoil it, even if I couldn't understand any of the words.

Nothing, Luke said. Can't a fellow laugh?

Then it was Jacob Hyland's turn. Jacob was the dumbest boy in the world. He couldn't think up anything. He couldn't make up *any* kind of an answer. He couldn't even guess.

Now, said Mr. Parker, *you* tell us why we shouldn't go to the movies.

I don't know why, Jacob said.

Come, now, Mr. Parker said, surely you know one good reason why we shouldn't.

Jacob started to think. I mean, he started to look around the room, then down at his feet, then up at the ceiling, while all of us waited to hear what he'd think up.

He thought a long time. Then he said:

I guess I don't know why, Mr. Parker. *Why?* he asked.

I'm asking *you*, our teacher said. *I* know why, but I want you to know why for yourself. Now, come, give me one reason, Mr. Hyland.

So Jacob started thinking all over again, and all of us felt sore at him. Anybody could make up some small reason, anybody but a dumb boy like Jacob. Nobody knew what made him so dumb. He was older than anybody else in our class. He kept squirming around in his chair and then he started picking his nose and scratching his head and looking at Mr. Parker like a dog looks at somebody it wants to be friends with.

Well? said our teacher.

Honest, said Jacob. I don't know why. I don't go to the movies much.

You've been to the movies once, haven't you? said our teacher.

Yes, sir, he said. More than once, but I forget quick. I don't remember.

Surely, said our teacher, you remember one little thing you saw in the movies that was a bad example, and a good reason why we should never go.

All of a sudden Jacob's face lighted up with a big smile.

I know, he said.

Yes? said our teacher.

It teaches us to throw custard pies at our enemies and kick ladies and run.

Is that all you remember? said Mr. Parker.

Yes, sir, Jacob said.

That's no reason, Ernest West said. What's wrong about throwing a custard pie?

It gets all over you, Jacob said, and he busted out laughing. You remember, he said, how it drips down a man's face.

It is certainly wrong to kick a lady, said Mr. Parker. Very fine, Mr. Hyland, he said. I knew you would remember a good reason if you thought carefully enough.

Then it was Nelson Holgum's turn.

It's expensive, he said. It costs too much.

Only a nickel at the Bijou, I said. That's no reason.

You can buy a loaf of bread with a nickel, Nelson said. A nickel is a lot of money these days.

True, said Mr. Parker. A very good reason indeed. There are much nobler ways for us to spend our money. If our young people would stop going to movies and give their money to missionary work, think of the tremendous progress we would make in only one year. Why, we could convert the whole world to Christianity in one year on the money spent annually for frivolous amusements like the movies.

Mr. Parker nodded at Ernest West.

The movies teach us to be dissatisfied with what we've got, Ernest said. We see people riding around in big automobiles and living in big houses and we get jealous.

Envious, said Mr. Parker.

We start wanting all them things, Ernest said, and we know we can't have them because we haven't got the money to buy them with, so we feel bad.

A splendid reason, said Mr. Parker.

It was Luke's turn, and next it would be mine.

The music is bad, Luke said.

Not at the Liberty, Tommy Cesar said. Not even at the Kinema. That's no reason.

It's bad at the Bijou, Luke said. They play one song over and over again on the player-piano, he said. It gets monotonous. *Wedding of the Winds.*

That's not true, Tommy Cesar said. Sometimes they play another song. I don't know the name. Sometimes they play six or seven songs.

They all sound alike, Luke said. It gives you a headache.

Now we're getting somewhere, said our teacher. It gives us headaches. It harms our health. And we shouldn't do anything that is harmful to the health. Health is our most precious possession. We must do those things which improve our health rather than those which harm it.

I said we shouldn't go to the movies because when we got out of the theater we didn't like our town.

Everything seems silly in our town, I said. We want to go away.

Then it was time to pass the basket around. Mr. Parker made a little speech about how urgently money was needed and how much better it was to give than to receive.

Tommy Cesar dropped two pennies, Pat Carrico three, Nelson Holgum one, Jacob Hyland a nickel, and then the basket reached Ernest West. He handed it to Luke and Luke handed it to me and I handed it back to Mr. Parker. We didn't drop anything. Mr. Parker took a purse from his pocket, jingled some coins, picked out a quarter so all of us could see it, and dropped it among the other coins. He looked very noble. Everybody hated him for the way he looked, even a dumb boy like Jacob Hyland. He looked as if he was saving the whole world with that quarter.

Then he gave each of us a copy of *Boys' World,* and class ended.

Everybody jumped up and ran out to the sidewalk.

Well, said Ernest West to Luke, aplica till we meet again.

Aplica, said Luke. Then my little sister Margaret came out of the church and we started walking home.

I turned to the last page of *Boys' World* and saw the advertisement of the zeppelin. The picture showed two boys high in the sky, standing in the basket of the zeppelin. Both of the boys looked sad; they were waving good-bye.

We went home and had Sunday dinner. Pa and Ma were very cheerful at the table and we ate till we couldn't get any more down. Pa said, What was the lesson, Luke?

Evils of the movies, Luke said.

What are they? Pa said.

Naked women dancing, Luke said. Robbers killing police. Expensive. Teaches us to throw custard pies.

I see, said Pa. Very evil.

After dinner I couldn't think of anything to do. If I wasn't so scared I would go to Alice Small's house and tell her I liked her. Alice, I would say, I like you. But I was scared. If I had my boat I would go around the world in it. Then I thought of the zeppelin. Luke was in the yard, nailing two pieces of wood together.

What are you making? I said.

Nothing, Luke said. I'm just nailing.

Luke, I said, here's my nickel. When the zeppelin comes let me go up with you.

I tried to give him the nickel but he wouldn't take it.

No, he said. The zeppelin's for me and Ernest West.

All right for you, I said. I'll get even.

Go ahead, he said.

It was very hot. I sat on the cool grass under our sycamore tree and watched Luke nail the boards together. The way he was hitting the nails you'd think he was making something, and I couldn't believe he wasn't until he was all through. He nailed about ten boards together, and that was all. They were just nailed together. They didn't make anything.

Pa heard all the hammering and came out smoking his pipe.

What do you call that? he said.

That? Luke said.

Yes, said Pa. What is it?

Nothing, Luke said.

Splendid, Pa said, and he turned around and went right back in.

Splendid? Luke said.

It ain't anything, I said. Why don't you *make* something?

I could hear Pa singing inside. I guess he was drying the dishes for Ma. He sang very loud, and after a while Ma started singing with him.

Then Luke stopped nailing and threw the boards over the garage.

He ran around the garage and came back with the boards and threw them over again and went and got them again.

What are you playing? I said.

Nothing, Luke said.

Luke, I said, let's go to the Bijou together.

Me and *you?* Luke said.

Sure, I said. You got your nickel and I got mine. Let's go see Tarzan.

I got to save up for the zeppelin, Luke said. I got a dime now. Eight more weeks and it'll be here, and then good-bye.

Good-bye? I said.

Yes, said Luke, good-bye.

You ain't going away, are you, Luke? I said.

Sure, he said. What did you think I wanted it for?

You mean never to come back again, Luke?

I'll come back all right, he said. I'll go away for a month or two, but I'll come back.

Where will you go, Luke? I said.

Klondike, he said. North.

Up there in that cold country, Luke?

Sure, Luke said. Me and my partner Ernest West. Palka eskos, he said.

What's it mean, Luke? I said. Tell me, please. What's palka eskos mean?

Only me and my partner know, Luke said.

I won't tell anybody, Luke. Honest I won't.

You'll go and tell somebody, Luke said.

Cross my heart, I said. Hope to die.

Needles through your tongue, if you do?

Yes, I said, needles and hot irons too, Luke.

On your word of honor?

Yes, Luke. What does it mean?

Palka eskos? he said.

Yes, Luke. Palka eskos.

Good morning, he said. It means good morning.

I couldn't believe it.

Is that all, Luke?

That's all palka eskos means. We got a whole language, though.

Palka eskos, Luke, I said.

Immel, he said.

What's immel mean, Luke?

Immel?

Yes, Luke.

You won't tell?

Same as before, I said. Hot irons through my tongue.

Hello, said Luke: Immel means hello.

Let's go to the Bijou, Luke, I said. We got a nickel each.

All right, he said. The music doesn't really give you a headache. I just said that.

Tell Ma, I said.

Maybe she won't let us go, Luke said.

Maybe she will. Maybe Pa will tell her to.

Luke and me went inside. Pa was drying the dishes and Ma was washing them.

Can we go to the Bijou, Ma? Luke said.

What's that? Pa said. I thought the lesson was the evils of the movies.

Yes, sir, Luke said.

Well, is your conscience clear? Pa said.

Oh, what's playing? Ma said.

Tarzan, I said. Can we go, Ma? We didn't drop our nickels. Luke is saving up for a zeppelin, but he won't let me go up with him.

Didn't drop your nickels? Pa said. What kind of religion do you call that? First thing you know them Presbyterian missionaries will be packing up and leaving Africa if you boys don't keep them supplied with nickels.

I guess so, Luke said, but me and Ernest West are saving up for a zeppelin. We *had* to do it.

What kind of a zeppelin? Pa said.

A *real* one, Luke said. It travels eighty miles an hour and carries two people, me and Ernest West.

How much does it cost? Pa said.

One dollar, Luke said. It comes from Chicago.

I'll tell you what, Pa said. If you clean out the garage and

keep the yard in order next week, I'll give you a dollar Saturday.
All right?

I'll say, Luke said.

Provided, Pa said, you let Mark go up.

If he'll help me with the work, Luke said.

He'll help, Pa said. Won't you, Mark?

I'll do more than Luke, I said.

Pa gave us ten cents more each and said to go to the movies.
We went to the Bijou and saw Tarzan, chapter eighteen. Two
more chapters and it would be all over. Tommy Cesar was there
with Pat Carrico. They made more noise when Tarzan was
cornered by the tiger than all the rest of us put together.

Me and Luke cleaned out the garage and kept the yard in
order all week, and Saturday night Pa gave Luke a dollar bill.
Luke sat down and wrote a nice letter to the people in Chicago
who sold zeppelins. He put the dollar bill in an envelope and
dropped the letter in the mailbox on the corner. I went to the
mailbox with him.

Now, he said, all we got to do is wait.

We waited ten days. We talked about all the strange and
faraway places we would go to in the zeppelin.

Then it came. It was a small flat package with the same
picture we saw in *Boys' World* stamped on the box. It didn't
weigh a pound, not even half a pound. Luke's hand shook when
he opened the box. I felt sick because I knew something was
wrong. There was a slip of paper with some writing on it in the
box. It said:

*Dear Boys: Here is your zeppelin, with instructions on how
to operate it. If every direction is carefully followed this toy will
ascend and stay aloft for as long as twenty seconds.*

And a lot more like that.

Luke followed every direction carefully, and blew into the
tissue-paper sack until it was almost full and almost the shape of a
zeppelin. Then the paper tore and the whole shape collapsed,
the way a rubber balloon does.

That was all. That was our zeppelin. Luke couldn't figure it
out. He said, The picture shows two boys standing in the basket.
I thought the zeppelin was coming out in a freight train.

Then he started talking in his secret language.

What are you saying, Luke? I said.

Good thing you can't understand, he said.

He smashed what was left of the zeppelin and tore the tissue-paper to pieces, then went out to the barn and got a lot of boards and nails and the hammer and started nailing the boards together. All I could do was say to myself, Them people in Chicago are sons of bitches, that's what they are.

SHARING YOUR IMPRESSIONS

1. Describe an experience in which you had a difference of opinion with someone who was your religious teacher.
2. What do we know about those who teach religion to our children? Those who teach them basic skills at school?
3. Make some guesses about what boys and girls learn at Sunday school and catechism.
4. How would you go about improving the religious education of children?
5. Give some reasons for the recent rise in values instruction as a part of the regular school curriculum.
6. How is education similar and dissimilar from religion in its approach to values instruction?
7. Comment about the influence of television in terms of its effect on children's values.

22

THE CONVERSION
OF THE JEWS

Philip Roth

"You're a real one for opening your mouth in the first place,"
Itzie said. "What do you open your mouth all the time for?"

"I didn't bring it up, Itz, I didn't," Ozzie said.

"What do you care about Jesus Christ for anyway?"

"I didn't bring up Jesus Christ. He did. I didn't even know
what he was talking about. Jesus is historical, he kept saying,
Jesus is historical." Ozzie mimicked the monumental voice of
Rabbi Binder.

"Jesus was a person that lived like you and me," Ozzie
continued. "That's what Binder said—"

"Yeah? . . . So what! What do I give two cents whether he
lived or not. And what do you gotta open your mouth!" Itzie
Lieberman favored closed-mouthedness, especially when it
came to Ozzie Freedman's questions. Mrs. Freedman had to see
Rabbi Binder twice before about Ozzie's questions and this
Wednesday at four-thirty would be the third time. Itzie preferred to keep *his* mother in the kitchen; he settled for behind-

the-back subtleties such as gestures, faces, snarls and other
less delicate barnyard noises.

"He was a real person, Jesus, but he wasn't like God, and we
don't believe he is God." Slowly, Ozzie was explaining Rabbi
Binder's position to Itzie, who had been absent from Hebrew
School the previous afternoon.

"The Catholics," Itzie said helpfully, "they believe in Jesus
Christ, that he's God." Itzie Lieberman used "the Catholics" in
its broadest sense—to include the Protestants.

Ozzie received Itzie's remark with a tiny head bob, as
though it were a footnote, and went on. "His mother was Mary,
and his father probably was Joseph," Ozzie said. "But the New
Testament says his real father was God."

"His *real* father?"

"Yeah," Ozzie said, "that's the big thing, his father's supposed to be God."

"Bull."

"That's what Rabbi Binder says, that it's impossible—"

"Sure it's impossible. That stuff's all bull. To have a baby you
gotta get laid," Itzie theologized. "Mary hadda get laid."

"That's what Binder says: 'The only way a woman can have a
baby is to have intercourse with a man.' "

"He said *that,* Ozz?" For a moment it appeared that Itzie
had put the theological question aside. "He said that, intercourse?" A little curled smile shaped itself in the lower half of
Itzie's face like a pink mustache. "What you guys do, Ozz, you
laugh or something?"

"I raised my hand."

"Yeah? Whatja say?"

"That's when I asked the question."

Itzie's face lit up. "Whatja ask about—intercourse?"

"No, I asked the question about God, how if He could create
the heaven and earth in six days, and make all the animals and the
fish and the light in six days—the light especially, that's what
always gets me, that He could make the light. Making fish and
animals, that's pretty good—"

"That's damn good." Itzie's appreciation was honest but
unimaginative: it was as though God had just pitched a one
hitter.

"But making light . . . I mean when you think about it, it's really something," Ozzie said. "Anyway, I asked Binder if He could make all that in six days, and He could *pick* the six days he wanted right out of nowhere, why couldn't He let a woman have a baby without having intercourse."

"You said intercourse, Ozz, to Binder?"

"Yeah."

"Right in class?"

"Yeah."

Itzie smacked the side of his head.

"I mean, no kidding around," Ozzie said, "that'd really be nothing. After all that other stuff, that'd practically be nothing."

Itzie considered a moment. "What'd Binder say?"

"He started all over again explaining how Jesus was historical and how he lived like you and me but he wasn't God. So I said I under*stood* that. What I wanted to know was different."

What Ozzie wanted to know was always different. The first time he had wanted to know how Rabbi Binder could call the Jews "The Chosen People" if the Declaration of Independence claimed all men to be created equal. Rabbi Binder tried to distinguish for him between political equality and spiritual legitimacy, but what Ozzie wanted to know, he insisted vehemently, was different. That was the first time his mother had to come.

Then there was the plane crash. Fifty-eight people had been killed in a plane crash at La Guardia. In studying a casualty list in the newspaper his mother had discovered among the list of those dead eight Jewish names (his grandmother had nine but she counted Miller as a Jewish name); because of the eight she said the plane crash was "a tragedy." During free-discussion time on Wednesday Ozzie had brought to Rabbi Binder's attention this matter of "some of his relations" always picking out the Jewish names. Rabbi Binder had begun to explain cultural unity and some other things when Ozzie stood up at his seat and said that what he wanted to know was different. Rabbi Binder insisted that he sit down and it was then that Ozzie shouted that he wished all fifty-eight were Jews. That was the second time his mother came.

"And he kept explaining about Jesus being historical, and so I kept asking him. No kidding, Itz, he was trying to make me look stupid."

"So what he finally do?"

"Finally he starts screaming that I was deliberately simple-minded and a wise guy, and that my mother had to come, and this was the last time. And that I'd never get bar-mitzvahed if he could help it. Then, Itz, then he starts talking in that voice like a statue, real slow and deep, and he says that I better think over what I said about the Lord. He told me to go to his office and think it over." Ozzie leaned his body towards Itzie. "Itz, I thought it over for a solid hour, and now I'm convinced God could do it."

Ozzie had planned to confess his latest transgression to his mother as soon as she came home from work. But it was a Friday night in November and already dark, and when Mrs. Freedman came through the door she tossed off her coat, kissed Ozzie quickly on the face, and went to the kitchen table to light the three yellow candles, two for the Sabbath and one for Ozzie's father.

When his mother lit the candles she would move her two arms slowly towards her, dragging them through the air, as though persuading people whose minds were half made up. And her eyes would get glassy with tears. Even when his father was alive Ozzie remembered that her eyes had gotten glassy, so it didn't have anything to do with his dying. It had something to do with lighting the candles.

As she touched the flaming match to the unlit wick of a Sabbath candle, the phone rang, and Ozzie, standing only a foot from it, plucked it off the receiver and held it muffled to his chest. When his mother lit candles Ozzie felt there should be no noise; even breathing, if you could manage it, should be softened. Ozzie pressed the phone to his breast and watched his mother dragging whatever she was dragging, and he felt his own eyes get glassy. His mother was a round, tired, gray-haired penguin of a woman whose gray skin had begun to feel the tug of gravity and the weight of her own history. Even when she was dressed up she didn't look like a chosen person. But when she lit candles she looked like something better; like a woman who knew momentarily that God could do anything.

After a few mysterious minutes she was finished. Ozzie hung up the phone and walked to the kitchen table where she was beginning to lay the two places for the four-course Sabbath meal. He told her that she would have to see Rabbi Binder next Wednesday at four-thirty, and then he told her why. For the first time in their life together she hit Ozzie across the face with her hand.

All through the chopped liver and chicken soup part of the dinner Ozzie cried; he didn't have any appetite for the rest.

On Wednesday, in the largest of the three basement class-rooms of the synagogue, Rabbi Marvin Binder, a tall, hand-some, broad-shouldered man of thirty with thick strong-fibered black hair, removed his watch from his pocket and saw that it was four o'clock. At the rear of the room Yakov Blotnik, the seventy-one-year-old custodian, slowly polished the large window, mumbling to himself, unaware that it was four o'clock or six o'clock, Monday or Wednesday. To most of the students Yakov Blotnik's mumbling, along with his brown curly beard, scythe nose, and two heel-trailing black cats, made of him an object of wonder, a foreigner, a relic, towards whom they were alternately fearful and disrespectful. To Ozzie the mumbling had always seemed a monotonous, curious prayer; what made it curious was that old Blotnik had been mumbling so steadily for so many years, Ozzie suspected he had memorized the prayers and for-gotten all about God.

"It is now free-discussion time," Rabbi Binder said. "Feel free to talk about any Jewish matter at all—religion, family, politics, sports—"

There was silence. It was a gusty, clouded November after-noon and it did not seem as though there ever was or could be a thing called baseball. So nobody this week said a word about that hero from the past, Hank Greenberg—which limited free dis-cussion considerably.

And the soul-battering Ozzie Freedman had just received from Rabbi Binder had imposed its limitation. When it was Ozzie's turn to read aloud from the Hebrew book the rabbi had asked him petulantly why he didn't read more rapidly. He was showing no progress. Ozzie said he could read faster but that if he did he was sure not to understand what he was reading. Nevertheless, at the rabbi's repeated suggestion Ozzie tried, and showed a great talent, but in the midst of a long passage he stopped short and said he didn't understand a word he was reading, and started in again at a drag-footed pace. Then came the soul-battering.

Consequently when free-discussion time rolled around none of the students felt too free. The rabbi's invitation was answered only by the mumbling of feeble old Blotnik.

"Isn't there anything at all you would like to discuss?" Rabbi Binder asked again, looking at his watch. "No questions or comments?"

There was a small grumble from the third row. The rabbi requested that Ozzie rise and give the rest of the class the advantage of his thought.

Ozzie rose. "I forget it now," he said, and sat down in his place.

Rabbi Binder advanced a seat towards Ozzie and poised himself on the edge of the desk. It was Itzie's desk and the rabbi's frame only a dagger's-length away from his face snapped him to sitting attention.

"Stand up again, Oscar," Rabbi Binder said calmly, "and try to assemble your thoughts."

Ozzie stood up. All his classmates turned in their seats and watched as he gave an unconvincing scratch to his forehead.

"I can't assemble any," he announced, and plunked himself down.

"Stand up!" Rabbi Binder advanced from Itzie's desk to the one directly in front of Ozzie; when the rabbinical back was turned Itzie gave it five-fingers off the tip of his nose, causing a small titter in the room. Rabbi Binder was too absorbed in squelching Ozzie's nonsense once and for all to bother with titters. "Stand up, Oscar. What's your question about?"

Ozzie pulled a word out of the air. It was the handiest word. "Religion."

"Oh, now you remember?"

"Yes."

"What is it?"

Trapped, Ozzie blurted the first thing that came to him. "Why can't He make anything He wants to make!"

As Rabbi Binder prepared an answer, a final answer, Itzie, ten feet behind him, raised one finger on his left hand, gestured it meaningfully towards the rabbi's back, and brought the house down.

Binder twisted quickly to see what had happened and in the midst of the commotion Ozzie shouted into the rabbi's back what he couldn't have shouted to his face. It was a loud, toneless sound that had the timbre of something stored inside for about six days.

"You don't know! You don't know anything about God!"

The rabbi spun back towards Ozzie. "What?"

"You don't know—you don't—"

"Apologize, Oscar, apologize!" It was a threat.

"You don't—"

Rabbi Binder's hand flicked out at Ozzie's cheek. Perhaps it had only been meant to clamp the boy's mouth shut, but Ozzie ducked and the palm caught him squarely on the nose.

The blood came in a short, red spurt on to Ozzie's shirt front.

The next moment was all confusion. Ozzie screamed, "You bastard, you bastard!" and broke for the classroom door. Rabbi Binder lurched a step backwards, as though his own blood had started flowing violently in the opposite direction, then gave a clumsy lurch forward and bolted out the door after Ozzie. The class followed after the rabbi's huge blue-suited back, and before old Blotnik could turn from his window, the room was empty and everyone was headed full speed up the three flights leading to the roof.

If one should compare the light of day to the life of man: sunrise to birth; sunset—the dropping down over the edge—to death; then as Ozzie Freedman wiggled through the trapdoor of the synagogue roof, his feet kicking backwards bronco-style at Rabbi Binder's outstretched arms—at that moment the day was fifty years old. As a rule, fifty or fifty-five reflects accurately the age of late afternoons in November, for it is in that month, during those hours, that one's awareness of light seems no longer a matter of seeing, but of hearing: light begins clicking away. In fact, as Ozzie locked shut the trapdoor in the rabbi's face, the sharp click of the bolt into the lock might momentarily have been mistaken for the sound of the heavier gray that had just throbbed through the sky.

With all his weight Ozzie kneeled on the locked door; any instant he was certain that Rabbi Binder's shoulder would fling it open, splintering the wood into shrapnel and catapulting his body into the sky. But the door did not move and below him he heard only the rumble of feet, first loud then dim, like thunder rolling away.

A question shot through his brain. "Can this be *me?*" For a thirteen-year-old who had just labeled his religious leader a bastard, twice, it was not an improper question. Louder and louder the question came to him—"Is it me? It is me?"—until he discovered himself no longer kneeling, but racing crazily towards the edge of the roof, his eyes crying, his throat screaming, and his arms flying everywhichway as though not his own.

"Is it me? Is it me Me ME ME ME! It has to be me—but is it!"

It is the question a thief must ask himself the night he jimmies open his first window, and it is said to be the question with which bridegrooms quiz themselves before the altar.

In the few wild seconds it took Ozzie's body to propel him to the edge of the roof, his self-examination began to grow fuzzy. Gazing down at the street, he became confused as to the problem beneath the question: was it, is-it-me-who-called-Binder-a-bastard? or, is-it-me-prancing-around-on-the-roof? However, the scene below settled all, for there is an instant in any action when whether it is you or somebody else is academic. The thief crams the money in his pockets and scoots out the window. The bridegroom signs the hotel register for two. And the boy on the roof finds a streetful of people gaping at him, necks stretched backwards, faces up, as though he were the ceiling of the Hayden Planetarium. Suddenly you know it's you.

"Oscar! Oscar Freedman!" A voice rose from the center of the crowd, a voice that, could it have been seen, would have looked like the writing on scroll. "Oscar Freedman, get down from there. Immediately!" Rabbi Binder was pointing one arm stiffly up at him; and at the end of that arm, one finger aimed menacingly. It was the attitude of a dictator, but one—the eyes confessed all—whose personal valet had spit neatly in his face.

Ozzie didn't answer. Only for a blink's length did he look towards Rabbi Binder. Instead his eyes began to fit together the world beneath him, to sort out people from places, friends from enemies, participants from spectators. In little jagged starlike clusters his friends stood around Rabbi Binder, who was still pointing. The topmost point on a star compounded not of angels but of five adolescent boys was Itzie. What a world it was, with those stars below, Rabbi Binder below . . . Ozzie, who a moment earlier hadn't been able to control his own body, started to feel the meaning of the word control: he felt Peace and he felt Power.

"Oscar Freedman, I'll give you three to come down."

Few dictators give their subjects three to do anything; but, as always, Rabbi Binder only looked dictatorial.

"Are you ready, Oscar?"

Ozzie nodded his head yes, although he had no intention in the world—the lower one or the celestial one he'd just entered—of coming down even if Rabbi Binder should give him a million.

"All right then," said Rabbi Binder. He ran a hand through his black Samson hair as though it were the gesture prescribed for uttering the first digit. Then, with his other hand cutting a circle out of the small piece of sky around him, he spoke. "One!"

There was no thunder. On the contrary, at that moment, as though "one" was the cue for which he had been waiting, the world's least thunderous person appeared on the synagogue steps. He did not so much come out the synagogue door as lean out, onto the darkening air. He clutched at the doorknob with one hand and looked up at the roof.

"Oy!"

Yakov Blotnik's old mind hobbled slowly, as if on crutches, and though he couldn't decide precisely what the boy was doing on the roof, he knew it wasn't good—that is, it wasn't-good-for-the-Jews. For Yakov Blotnik life had fractionated itself simply: things were either good-for-the-Jews or no-good-for-the-Jews.

He smacked his free hand to his in-sucked cheek, gently. "Oy, Gut!" And then quickly as he was able, he jacked down his head and surveyed the street. There was Rabbi Binder (like a man at an auction with only three dollars in his pocket, he had just delivered a shaky "Two!"); there were the students, and that was all. So far it-wasn't-so-bad-for-the-Jews. But the boy had to come down immediately, before anybody saw. The problem: how to get the boy off the roof?

Anybody who has ever had a cat on the roof knows how to get him down. You call the fire department. Or first you call the operator and you ask her for the fire department. And the next thing there is great jamming of brakes and clanging of bells and shouting of instructions. And then the cat is off the roof. You do the same thing to get a boy off the roof.

That is, you do the same thing if you are Yakov Blotnik and you once had a cat on the roof.

When the engines, all four of them, arrived, Rabbi Binder had four times given Ozzie the count of three. The big hook-and-ladder swung around the corner and one of the firemen leaped from it, plunging headlong towards the yellow fire hydrant in front of the synagogue. With a huge wrench he began to unscrew the top nozzle. Rabbi Binder raced over to him and pulled at his shoulder.

"There's no fire . . ."

The fireman mumbled back over his shoulder and, heatedly, continued working at the nozzle.

"But there's no fire, there's no fire . . ." Binder shouted. When the fireman mumbled again, the rabbi grasped his face with both his hands and pointed it up at the roof.

To Ozzie it looked as though Rabbi Binder was trying to tug the fireman's head out of his body, like a cork from a bottle. He had to giggle at the picture they made: it was a family portrait —rabbi in black skullcap, fireman in red fire hat, and the little yellow hydrant squatting beside like a kid brother, bareheaded. From the edge of the roof Ozzie waved at the portrait, a one-handed, flapping, mocking wave; in doing it his right foot slipped from under him. Rabbi Binder covered his eyes with his hands.

Firemen work fast. Before Ozzie had even regained his balance, a big, round, yellowed net was being held on the synagogue lawn. The firemen who held it looked up at Ozzie with stern, feelingless faces.

One of the firemen turned his head towards Rabbi Binder. "What, is the kid nuts or something?"

Rabbi Binder unpeeled his hands from his eyes, slowly, painfully, as if they were tape. Then he checked: nothing on the sidewalk, no dents in the net.

"Is he gonna jump, or what?" the fireman shouted.

In a voice not at all like a statue, Rabbi Binder finally answered. "Yes, yes, I think so . . . He's been threatening to . . ."

Threatening to? Why, the reason he was on the roof, Ozzie remembered, was to get away; he hadn't even thought about jumping. He had just run to get away, and the truth was that he hadn't really headed for the roof as much as he'd been chased there.

"What's his name, the kid?"

"Freedman," Rabbi Binder answered. "Oscar Freedman."

The fireman looked up at Ozzie. "What is it with you, Oscar? You gonna jump, or what?"

Ozzie did not answer. Frankly, the question had just arisen.

"Look, Oscar, if you're gonna jump, jump—and if you're not gonna jump, don't jump. But don't waste our time, willya?"

Ozzie looked at the fireman and then at Rabbi Binder. He wanted to see Rabbi Binder cover his eyes one more time.

"I'm going to jump."

And then he scampered around the edge of the roof to the corner, where there was no net below, and he flapped his arms at his sides, swishing the air and smacking his palms to his trousers on the downbeat. He began screaming like some kind of engine, "Wheeeee . . . wheeeeee," and leaning way out over the edge with the upper half of his body. The firemen whipped around to cover the ground with the net. Rabbi Binder mumbled a few words to Somebody and covered his eyes. Everything happened quickly, jerkily, as in a silent movie. The crowd, which had arrived with the fire engines, gave out a long, Fourth-of-July fireworks oooh-aahhh. In the excitement no one had paid the crowd much heed, except, of course, Yakov Blotnik, who swung from the doorknob counting heads. "Fier und tsvantsik . . . finf und tsvantsik . . . Oy, Gut!" It wasn't like this with the cat.

Rabbi Binder peeked through his fingers, checked the sidewalk and net. Empty. But there was Ozzie racing to the other corner. The firemen raced with him but were unable to keep up. Whenever Ozzie wanted to he might jump and splatter himself upon the sidewalk, and by the time the firemen scooted to the spot all they could do with their net would be to cover the mess.

"Wheeeee . . . wheeeee . . ."

"Hey, Oscar," the winded fireman yelled, "What the hell is this, a game or something?"

"Wheeeee . . . wheeeee . . ."

"Hey, Oscar—"

But he was off now to the other corner, flapping his wings fiercely. Rabbi Binder couldn't take it any longer—the fire engines from nowhere, the screaming suicidal boy, the net. He fell to his knees, exhausted, and with his hands curled together in front of his chest like a little dome, he pleaded, "Oscar, stop it, Oscar. Don't jump, Oscar. Please come down . . . Please don't jump."

And further back in the crowd a single voice, a single young voice, shouted a lone word to the boy on the roof.

"Jump!"

It was Itzie. Ozzie momentarily stopped flapping.

"Go ahead, Ozz—jump!" Itzie broke off his point of the star and courageously, with the inspiration not of a wise-guy but of a disciple, stood alone. "Jump, Ozz, jump!"

Still on his knees, his hands still curled, Rabbi Binder twisted his body back. He looked at Itzie, then, agonizingly, back to Ozzie.

"OSCAR, DON'T JUMP! PLEASE, DON'T JUMP . . . please please . . ."

"Jump!" This time it wasn't Itzie but another point of the star. By the time Mrs. Freedman arrived to keep her four-thirty appointment with Rabbi Binder, the whole little upside-down heaven was shouting and pleading for Ozzie to jump, and Rabbi Binder no longer was pleading with him not to jump, but was crying into the dome of his hands.

Understandably Mrs. Freedman couldn't figure out what her son was doing on the roof. So she asked.

"Ozzie, my Ozzie, what are you doing? My Ozzie, what is it?"

Ozzie stopped wheeeeeing and slowed his arms down to a cruising flap, the kind birds use in soft winds, but he did not answer. He stood against the low, clouded, darkening sky—light clicked down swiftly now, as on a small gear—flapping softly and gazing down at the small bundle of a woman who was his mother.

"What are you doing, Ozzie?" She turned towards the kneeling Rabbi Binder and rushed so close that only a paper-thickness of dusk lay between her stomach and his shoulders.

"What is my baby doing?"

Rabbi Binder gaped up at her but he too was mute. All that moved was the dome of his hands; it shook back and forth like a weak pulse.

"Rabbi, get him down! He'll kill himself. Get him down, my only baby . . ."

"I can't," Rabbi Binder said, "I can't . . ." and he turned his handsome head towards the crowd of boys behind him. "It's them. Listen to them."

And for the first time Mrs. Freedman saw the crowd of boys, and she heard what they were yelling.

"He's doing it for them. He won't listen to me. It's them." Rabbi Binder spoke like one in a trance.

"For them?"

"Yes."

"Why for them?"

"They want him to . . ."

Mrs. Freedman raised her two arms upward as though she were conducting the sky. "For them he's doing it!" And then in a gesture older than pyramids, older than prophets and floods, her arms came slapping down to her sides. "A martyr I have. Look!" She tilted her head to the roof. Ozzie was still flapping softly. "My martyr."

"Oscar, come down, *please*," Rabbi Binder groaned.

In a startlingly even voice Mrs. Freedman called to the boy on the roof. "Ozzie, come down, Ozzie. Don't be a martyr, my baby."

As though it were a litany, Rabbi Binder repeated her words. "Don't be a martyr, my baby. Don't be a martyr."

"Gawhead, Ozz—be a Martin!" It was Itzie. "Be a Martin, be a Martin," and all the voices joined in singing for Martindom, whatever *it* was. "Be a Martin, be a Martin . . ."

Somehow when you're on a roof the darker it gets the less you can hear. All Ozzie knew was that two groups wanted two new things: his friends were spirited and musical about what they wanted; his mother and the rabbi were even-toned, chanting, about what they didn't want. The rabbi's voice was without tears now and so was his mother's.

The big net stared up at Ozzie like a sightless eye. The big, clouded sky pushed down. From beneath it looked like a gray corrugated board. Suddenly, looking up into that unsympathetic sky, Ozzie realized all the strangeness of what these people, his friends, were asking: they wanted him to jump, to kill himself; they were singing about it now—it made them happy. And there was an even greater strangeness: Rabbi Binder was on his knees, trembling. If there was a question to be asked now it was not "Is it me?" but rather "Is it us?. . . Is it us?"

Being on the roof, it turned out, was a serious thing. If he jumped would the singing become dancing? Would it? What would jumping stop? Yearningly, Ozzie wished he could rip open the sky, plunge his hands through, and pull out the sun; and on the sun, like a coin, would be stamped JUMP or DON'T JUMP.

Ozzie's knees rocked and sagged a little under him as though they were setting him for a dive. His arms tightened, stiffened, froze, from shoulders to fingernails. He felt as if each part of his body were going to vote as to whether he should kill himself or not—and each part as though it were independent of *him*.

The light took an unexpected click down and the new darkness, like a gag, hushed the friends singing for this and the mother and rabbi chanting for that.

Ozzie stopped counting votes, and in a curiously high voice, like one who wasn't prepared for speech, he spoke.

"Mamma?"

"Yes, Oscar."

"Mamma, get down on your knees, like Rabbi Binder."

"Oscar—"

"Get down on your knees," he said, "or I'll jump."

Ozzie heard a whimper, then a quick rustling, and when he looked down where his mother had stood he saw the top of a head

and beneath that a circle of dress. She was kneeling beside Rabbi
Binder.

He spoke again. "Everybody kneel." There was the sound of
everybody kneeling.

Ozzie looked around. With one hand he pointed towards
the synagogue entrance. "Make *him* kneel."

There was a noise, not of kneeling, but of body-and-cloth
stretching. Ozzie could hear Rabbi Binder saying in a gruff
whisper, ". . . or he'll *kill* himself," and when next he looked
there was Yakov Blotnik off the doorknob and for the first time in
his life upon his knees in the Gentile posture of prayer.

As for the firemen—it is not as difficult as one might imagine
to hold a net taut while you are kneeling.

Ozzie looked around again; and then he called to Rabbi
Binder.

"Rabbi?"

"Yes, Oscar."

"Rabbi Binder, do you believe in God?"

"Yes."

"Do you believe God can do Anything?" Ozzie leaned his
head out into the darkness. "Anything?"

"Oscar, I think—"

"Tell me you believe God can do Anything."

There was a second's hesitation. Then: "God can do
Anything."

"Tell me you believe God can make a child without
intercourse."

"He can."

"Tell me!"

"God," Rabbi Binder admitted, "can make a child without
intercourse."

"Mamma, you tell me."

"God can make a child without intercourse," his mother
said.

"Make *him* tell me." There was no doubt who *him* was.

In a few moments Ozzie heard an old comical voice say
something to the increasing darkness about God.

Next, Ozzie made everybody say it. And then he made them

all say they believed in Jesus Christ—first one at a time, then all together.

When the catechizing was through it was the beginning of evening. From the street it sounded as if the boy on the roof might have sighed.

"Ozzie?" A woman's voice dared to speak. "You'll come down now?"

There was no answer, but the woman waited, and when a voice finally did speak it was thin and crying, and exhausted as that of an old man who has just finished pulling the bells.

"Mamma, don't you see—you shouldn't hit me. He shouldn't hit me. You shouldn't hit me about God, Mamma. You should never hit anybody about God—"

"Ozzie, please come down now."

"Promise me, Mamma, promise me you'll never hit anybody about God."

He had asked only his mother, but for some reason everyone kneeling in the street promised he would never hit anybody about God.

Once again there was silence.

"I can come down now, Mamma," the boy on the roof finally said. He turned his head both ways as though checking the traffic lights. "Now I can come down . . ."

And he did, right into the center of the yellow net that glowed in the evening's edge like an overgrown halo.

SHARING YOUR IMPRESSIONS

1. Recall some coercive techniques parents or teachers used when trying to educate you.
2. Discuss the dropout of adolescents from church attendance.
3. Discuss the place of curiosity and doubt in religious and moral education.
4. Propose a way for helping parents and teachers accept children's expression of personal opinion and thought.
5. How should parents attempt to teach religious and moral development?

6. How would you go about the selection and preparation of teachers for religious education?
7. Suggest some ways for helping persons when they find themselves in an emotionally desperate situation.

23

CHARLES

Shirley Jackson

The day my son Laurie started kindergarten he renounced corduroy overalls with bibs and began wearing blue jeans with a belt; I watched him go off the first morning with the older girl next door, seeing clearly that an era of my life was ended, my sweet-voiced nursery-school tot replaced by a long-trousered, swaggering character who forgot to stop at the corner and wave good-bye to me.

He came home the same way, the front door slamming open, his cap on the floor, and the voice suddenly become raucous shouting, "Isn't anybody *here?*"

At lunch he spoke insolently to his father, spilled his baby sister's milk, and remarked that his teacher said we were not to take the name of the Lord in vain.

"How *was* school today?" I asked, elaborately casual.

"All right," he said.

"Did you learn anything?" his father asked.

Laurie regarded his father coldly. "I didn't learn nothing," he said.

"Anything," I said. "Didn't learn anything."

"The teacher spanked a boy, though," Laurie said, addressing his bread and butter. "For being fresh," he added, with his mouth full.

"What did he do?" I asked. "Who was it?"

Laurie thought. "It was Charles," he said. "He was fresh. The teacher spanked him and made him stand in a corner. He was awfully fresh."

"What did he do?" I asked again, but Laurie slid off his chair, took a cookie, and left, while his father was still saying, "See here, young man."

The next day Laurie remarked at lunch, as soon as he sat down, "Well, Charles was bad again today." He grinned enormously and said, "Today Charles hit the teacher."

"Good heavens," I said, mindful of the Lord's name, "I suppose he got spanked again?"

"He sure did," Laurie said. "Look up," he said to his father.

"What?" his father said, looking up.

"Look down," Laurie said. "Look at my thumb. Gee, you're dumb." He began to laugh insanely.

"Why did Charles hit the teacher?" I asked quickly.

"Because she tried to make him color with red crayons," Laurie said. "Charles wanted to color with green crayons so he hit the teacher and she spanked him and said nobody play with Charles but everybody did."

The third day—it was Wednesday of the first week —Charles bounced a see-saw on to the head of a little girl and made her bleed, and the teacher made him stay inside all during recess. Thursday Charles had to stand in a corner during story-time because he kept pounding his feet on the floor. Friday Charles was deprived of blackboard privileges because he threw chalk.

On Saturday I remarked to my husband, "Do you think kindergarten is too unsettling for Laurie? All this toughness, and bad grammar, and this Charles boy sounds like such a bad influence."

"It'll be all right," my husband said reassuringly. "Bound to be people like Charles in the world. Might as well meet them now as later."

On Monday Laurie came home late, full of news. "Charles," he shouted as he came up the hill; I was waiting anxiously on the front steps. "Charles," Laurie yelled all the way up the hill, "Charles was bad again."

"Come right in," I said, as soon as he came close enough. "Lunch is waiting."

"You know what Charles did?" he demanded, following me through the door. "Charles yelled so in school they sent a boy in from first grade to tell the teacher she had to make Charles keep quiet, and so Charles had to stay after school. And so all the children stayed to watch him."

"What did he do?" I asked.

"He just sat there," Laurie said, climbing into his chair at the table. "Hi, Pop, y'old dust mop."

"Charles had to stay after school today," I told my husband. "Everyone stayed with him."

"What does this Charles look like?" my husband asked Laurie. "What's his other name?"

"He's bigger than me," Laurie said. "And he doesn't have any rubbers and he doesn't ever wear a jacket."

Monday night was the first Parent-Teachers meeting, and only the fact that the baby had a cold kept me from going; I wanted passionately to meet Charles's mother. On Tuesday Laurie remarked suddenly, "Our teacher had a friend come to see her in school today."

"Charles's mother?" my husband and I asked simultaneously.

"Naaah," Laurie said scornfully. "It was a man who came and made us do exercises, we had to touch our toes. Look." He climbed down from his chair and squatted down and touched his toes. "Like this," he said. He got solemnly back into his chair and said, picking up his fork, "Charles didn't even *do* exercises."

"That's fine," I said heartily. "Didn't Charles want to do exercises?"

"Naaah," Laurie said. "Charles was so fresh to the teacher's friend he wasn't *let* do exercises."

"Fresh again?" I said.

"He kicked the teacher's friend," Laurie said. "The teacher's friend told Charles to touch his toes like I just did and Charles kicked him."

"What are they going to do about Charles, do you suppose?" Laurie's father asked him.

Laurie shrugged elaborately. "Throw him out of school, I guess," he said.

Wednesday and Thursday were routine; Charles yelled during story hour and hit a boy in the stomach and made him cry. On Friday Charles stayed after school again and so did all the other children.

With the third week of kindergarten Charles was an institution in our family; the baby was being a Charles when she cried all afternoon; Laurie did a Charles when he filled his wagon full of mud and pulled it through the kitchen; even my husband, when he caught his elbow in the telephone cord and pulled telephone, ashtray, and a bowl of flowers off the table, said, after the first minute, "Looks like Charles."

During the third and fourth weeks it looked like a reformation in Charles; Laurie reported grimly at lunch on Thursday of the third week, "Charles was so good today the teacher gave him an apple."

"What?" I said, and my husband added warily, "You mean Charles?"

"Charles," Laurie said. "He gave the crayons around and he picked up the books afterward and the teacher said he was her helper."

"What happened?" I asked incredulously.

"He was her helper, that's all," Laurie said, and shrugged.

"Can this be true, about Charles?" I asked my husband that night. "Can something like this happen?"

"Wait and see," my husband said cynically. "When you've got a Charles to deal with, this may mean he's only plotting."

He seemed to be wrong. For over a week Charles was the teacher's helper; each day he handed things out and he picked things up; no one had to stay after school.

"The P.T.A. meeting's next week again," I told my husband one evening. "I'm going to find Charles's mother there."

"Ask her what happened to Charles," my husband said. "I'd like to know."

"I'd like to know myself," I said.

On Friday of that week things were back to normal. "You know what Charles did today?" Laurie demanded at the lunch table, in a voice slightly awed. "He told a little girl to say a word and she said it and the teacher washed her mouth out with soap and Charles laughed."

"What word?" his father asked unwisely, and Laurie said, "I'll have to whisper it to you, it's so bad." He got down off his chair and went around to his father. His father bent his head down and Laurie whispered joyfully. His father's eyes widened.

"Did Charles tell the little girl to say *that?*" he asked respectfully.

"She said it *twice,*" Laurie said. "Charles told her to say it *twice.*"

"What happened to Charles?" my husband asked.

"Nothing," Laurie said. "He was passing out the crayons."

Monday morning Charles abandoned the little girl and said the evil word himself three or four times, getting his mouth washed out with soap each time. He also threw chalk.

My husband came to the door with me that evening as I set out for the P.T.A. meeting. "Invite her over for a cup of tea after the meeting," he said. "I want to get a look at her."

"If only she's there," I said prayerfully.

"She'll be there," my husband said. "I don't see how they could hold a P.T.A. meeting without Charles's mother."

At the meeting I sat restlessly, scanning each comfortable matronly face, trying to determine which one hid the secret of Charles. None of them looked to me haggard enough. No one stood up in the meeting and apologized for the way her son had been acting. No one mentioned Charles.

After the meeting I identified and sought out Laurie's kindergarten teacher. She had a plate with a cup of tea and a piece of chocolate cake; I had a plate with a cup of tea and a piece of marshmallow cake. We maneuvered up to one another cautiously, and smiled.

"I've been so anxious to meet you," I said. "I'm Laurie's mother."

"We're all so interested in Laurie," she said.

"Well, he certainly likes kindergarten," I said. "He talks about it all the time."

"We had a little trouble adjusting, the first week or so," she said primly, "but now he's a fine little helper. With occasional lapses, of course."

"Laurie usually adjusts very quickly," I said. "I suppose this time it's Charles's influence."

"Charles?"

"Yes," I said, laughing, "you must have your hands full in that kindergarten, with Charles."

"Charles?" she said. "We don't have any Charles in the kindergarten."

SHARING YOUR IMPRESSIONS

1. Describe one of the "tall tales" you made up as a child and the consequences that followed.
2. Try to recall a situation in which you substituted a fictitious person as the one having a problem that was actually your own.
3. During early childhood, how normal are lying and swearing among boys? Among girls?
4. When a child makes up stories, how should the parents respond?
5. Select a grade level and illustrate the kinds of questions you recommend for the focus of parent/teacher conferences.
6. Suggest some ways for parents to become more aware of their child's behavior at school.
7. What should parents and teachers tell a child about peers who have lied?
8. Recommend to parents and teachers some ways of reacting to children that would allow them to accept and value fantasy while still emphasizing the importance of truth.

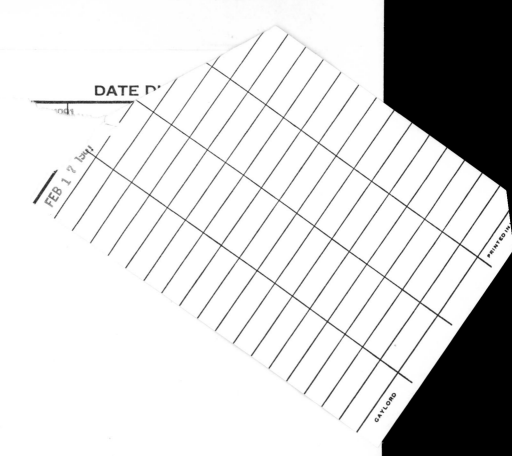